THE
KEY
TO
YOU
AND
ME

Also by Jaye Robin Brown

The Meaning of Birds
Georgia Peaches and Other Forbidden Fruit
No Place to Fall

THE
KEY TO
YOU
AND
ME

Jaye Robin Brown

HARPER TEEN
An Imprint of HarperCollinsPublishers

Library of Congress Cataloging-in-Publication Data
Library of Congress Cataloging-in-Publication Data

Names: Brown, Jaye Robin, author.
Title: The key to you and me / Jaye Robin Brown.
Description: First edition. | New York, NY : HarperTeen, [2021] |
    Audience: Ages 14 up. | Audience: Grades 10-12. | Summary:
    "Two very different girls navigate the bumpy road to love"—
    Provided by publisher.
Identifiers: LCCN 2020023305 | ISBN 978-0-06-282458-5
    (hardcover)
Subjects: CYAC: Dressage—Fiction. | Lesbians—Fiction. | Sexual
    orientation—Fiction. | Coming out (Sexual orientation)—
    Fiction. | Famly life—North Carolina—Fiction. | North
    Carolina—Fiction.
Classification: LCC PZ7.B814197 Key 2021 | DDC [Fic]—dc23
LC record available at https://lccn.loc.gov/2020023305

Typography by Jessie Gang
21 22 23 24 25   PC/LSCH   10 9 8 7 6 5 4 3 2 1

First Edition

For the girls with mud on their boots and
horses in their hearts . . . and the girls who cheer them on.

chapter one

PIPER

I throw my riding clothes into a duffel with one hand and wipe back tears with the other.

"Five pairs of breeches." Sniff. "Six sun shirts." Snuffle. "A helmet visor, boot socks." I grab a Kleenex, blow my nose, and toss the tissue in the garbage, dropping the printed packing list from my grandmother onto the floor. I stoop to grab it but bang my head on the corner of an open drawer instead. "Fuck." I rub at the top of my tender scalp as more tears drop onto the fallen paper, smearing printer ink in the process. This is ridiculous. It's been seven weeks. Why can't I stop crying?

Judith broke up with me at the beginning of April. Her words still sting. *"You care more about any horse than you care about me. I am an afterthought for you."*

Which isn't true at all. She's in every thought. She's there in the stands when I get my future Olympic team medal. She's holding the cut pieces of yarn for me as I braid my future horse's mane. She's behind the wheel as we drive to future horse shows and correcting me as I go through the choreography of my dressage tests out loud. Okay, so maybe it is kind of me-centric, but I love the idea of that kind of partnership. My goals are hers, too. Except they're not. She made that abundantly clear.

Then, as if getting dumped weren't enough, Erik, my trainer, had to have some sort of heart procedure and his training program is on hiatus until he's healed. It's what made me go behind my mom's back and call up my grandmother. I have to get out of here. How can I handle a broken heart without a horse to ride? And even more important, without a stable to show from, how can I chase my competition dreams? My mom may not care about riding anymore, but I definitely do.

My grandmother, Mom's mom, has advocated for years that I come to North Carolina for the summer to ride with this trainer or that trainer and see how serious horse people do it. My mother always rebuts with, "There are plenty of serious horse people here in New England." Which is true, but what is also true is that my mother doesn't care if I show or not. To her, the horse show world is pressure-filled and fraught with danger, both physically and emotionally. For me? It's heaven on earth. I shine on show days. Not to say I don't have a healthy amount of nervous energy, but it's truly what I live for. She may have given it up for good, but that's not my plan. I want more. I want to try for the top.

Which is why I'm packing. My grandmother can teach me things, introduce me to the right people, let my simmering want-to-ride-in-the-Olympics dream have a chance at becoming a waking thought. She's offered every summer since I was ten, but my mother always refused. Too far, too long, too much for your grandmother to spend on you.

Which is stupid. My grandmother has money. She loves me. She loves horses. I'm her skipped generation hope of having another true horsewoman in the family. Until now, I'd never fought my mom about it. But this summer? It's going to be different. She finally agreed to let me go. I'll be there until school starts in the fall. Riding almost every day on top horses with top trainers, and best of all? No chance of bumping into my ex-girlfriend with her new boyfriend.

I grab my bathing suit from the top drawer of my dresser. Judith stares at me from a twig frame. Judith with the twinkling brown eyes. I wonder if she's looking at the boy, Brad, with the same twinkle? I can't bring myself to turn the frame facedown. Even broken, my heart still skips at the sight of her. It also holds on to the slightest hope that this is only a detour and before the summer is over she'll find her way back to me. Which is why my parents have no clue we've broken up. I don't want them to judge her. I haven't even told her I'm leaving, in case that might ruin my chances for a do-over.

A voice rises from downstairs. "Your Uber's here."

My mother's too busy to drive me to the airport. Too pissed off is more like it.

"Mom, I'm sorry. How many times do I have to apologize?" I say it under my breath, pretty sure she won't hear me from where she stands at the bottom of the stairs.

When I'd called and told my grandmother about the temporary closing of Erik's barn and how I couldn't find another show barn in time for the summer season, I knew exactly what I was doing. I knew I'd be invited down. What I hadn't done was think about Mom's reaction. I'd only thought how perfect a chance it was to get away from my failed relationship AND get to ride better horses. My mother did not appreciate being ambushed by the two of us. She only begrudgingly relented when my dad intervened on my behalf, but it'd been the frosty shoulder since then.

"Piper!" My mom's tone gets shrill.

I throw a few more things into my duffel and zip up the bag. I hoist it onto my shoulder and grab my new plaid boot bag in the other.

At the bottom of the stairs are both of my parents. It's unlike my dad to have waited this late to leave for work but I guess in his own way it's a show of solidarity. There's no push/pull of emotions between him and my grandmother—and unlike Mom, Dad thinks my competitive dreams could be laced with a healthy dose of realism given the right circumstances. I'd even go so far as to say he's excited for me to have this opportunity to ride with new trainers at a world-class facility.

"Come here, Mighty." His use of my pet name gets me slightly choked up and I walk into his hug and big cheek kiss. It's awkward with the huge duffel on my shoulder. "Let me have that." He slips it off and takes it in his own hand. He looks as if he might impart a few more words of wisdom but the exasperated sigh from my mother shuts his mouth tight and he heads with my bag toward the car waiting in front of our house.

I turn to face her. "I'm going to miss you," I say tentatively.

"You can still stay. I will be more than happy to help you find a new show barn. There's got to be somewhere, even if we have to drive an hour or so."

"Mom." My voice is a plea.

"Fine." She uncrosses her arms. "But don't let your grandmother push you too far, too fast. You are enough exactly as you are if this doesn't work out the way you expect."

"Mom." This time it comes out exasperated. "I'll be fine. I'm excited. I want this." I put my arms around her and pull her to me in a stiff hug. "I'm going to miss you desperately. I promise." Eventually she caves and hugs me back and it's the good warm Mom hug I need. The horn beeps from the driveway.

"I better go."

"Text us when you land. After you text Judith, of course." Mom winks.

It's all I can do to turn fast enough so she can't see the tears pool in my eyes.

KAT

Betty the Biddy. Giselle the Jilted. Ursula the Unemployed. Putting labels on the three town gossips gathered around the manicure tables makes me feel better about my current label, Kat the Carless. Which I guess is better than my other labels, Kat the Motherless and Kat the Boyfriendless. Neither of which is really true. I have a mother, she's just gone, and I don't want a boyfriend, so that label doesn't matter.

"This sucks." My sister, Emma, isn't talking about the town gossips. She is, however, talking about my minivan, Delilah—as blue as the davenport sofa where we sit at the front of our dad's salon, the Tousled Orchid, and as out of commission as our parents' marriage. Terry, the mechanic, has declared her transmission flawed to the tune of three thousand dollars, which is more than the old girl is worth, in monetary terms anyway. I'm trying to take it with a heaping helping of zen, but my younger sister is not having it.

"I swear, I'm moving in with Mom. With Delilah dead, Harmon, North Carolina, could not get any more boring."

"Like that's an option."

"She said I could come to Dallas."

"To visit. Not to live." Our mother took off a couple of years ago. Motherhood was something her body did just fine, but the walking, talking, sentient part of her? Not so much. It's what the Labeled Ladies of Leisure love to whisper about when they see us. Those Poor Girls. Their Poor Father. Rural Men Don't Own and Operate Hair Salons. Do You Think That's Why the Mother Left? Coming Soon to a Small Town Theater Near You.

I still don't know why my mom married humdrum Texas Stanley instead of staying with our decidedly amazing father, but that's their business not anybody else's. It's cool that Dad started the salon and even though Emma still gripes about Mom, it's not like it really damaged us. Emma's just miffed because she wants to get further with her dance career than she can here in Harmon and Dallas has better programs. But we both know it's a lost cause no matter how much she fantasizes about Mom miraculously inviting her to come live with her.

Emma pokes me with her toe. "Well? What are we going to do all summer? School ends next week. I need a boyfriend. With a car."

Emma and I are exactly twelve months apart. I've heard folks refer to us as Irish twins, apparently some reference to Catholicism and no birth control, even though we are a healthy mix of Irish, English, Lebanese, and Italian—according to 23andMe—and 100 percent practicing agnostics, much to the chagrin of our next-door neighbor, the good pastor Phillips and his wife.

"Remember what happened with your last boyfriend?"

She waves her hand in the air like she's brushing a bad smell away. "Oh, that mess? The one where he told everyone I'd let him feel me up outside the science room lockers. Total lies. He wishes he'd even gotten a chance at my boobs."

At this she lifts her hands to her breasts to showcase them. One of the many ways we are different despite our closeness in age.

She flumps back against the pillows. "People are stupid."

"They said super awful things about you."

"They weren't true. Why do I care? Why do you?"

Emma is so totally herself. It didn't hurt that she got

our mom's olive skin and slight wave to her hair. Or that she's a hell of an amazing dancer with the body to match. Girls are jealous of her because she doesn't conform. She's as beautiful inside as out and makes no apologies.

Me though? I don't think I'm strong enough to withstand people talking about me. I don't have something like dance to throw myself into, or a business like my dad did. I want to be liked, respected, seen as a good girl. Labels and rumors bother me. Which is why I keep so much locked inside. This is a small town. And people talk . . . about everyone and everything.

I nudge her knee with mine. "Don't worry. I'll get Delilah fixed before you know it and be at your beck and call to take you wherever you need to go. You don't need a boyfriend to have a great summer."

Emma picks up a well-thumbed copy of *People* magazine and runs her fingers across the glossy photo of J.Lo and her cohosts on the latest dance competition show. "There's a dance school in Dallas whose students made it to the finals of this show. Pretty sure Delilah won't make it that far."

"No, she won't. But if I get a new transmission, she could make it as far as Greenville. There's got to be a great studio there?" I roll over and lie in her lap with my hands in a prayer position. "Let's get Delilah fixed. Then we'll get you into a better studio." If there are things I can do to make my sister feel happy, I want to do them.

She grins and pokes my nose with her fingertip. "You better get busy. My star's going to fade if I'm stuck at Ms. Kelly's for two more years." She slides out from under me and stands up. "Otherwise, I'm going to need to find a fast boy with an even faster car."

"Oh my god, Emma." She didn't even whisper.

I wish I was as bold.

The door to the salon flings open. Elliot, our cousin, fills the frame and every woman in the room looks up and sighs.

"Delivery complete." He lifts his arms and our younger brothers, the twins, dash beneath them and head straight to the bowl of mints on the reception desk.

Picking Corbin and Cole up from baseball practice is typically my job, but I've managed to rope Elliot into my vehicular tragedy.

"Big thanks, seriously. Dad said he'd trim your hair in exchange."

"Nope, what I want is your sober driving on the night of the bonfire so I don't have to be."

The bonfire is a nonschool-sanctioned event that happens every year the night before graduation. Classes are over and the seniors are amped up and the juniors are pretty amped about becoming seniors. The local police are chill about it, not shutting it down because they'd been seniors once at Harmon High School, too, but we all sign pledges to not drink and drive and, unbelievably, everyone takes it kind of serious and it keeps going.

"My minivan . . ."

He dangles the keys to his SUV. "We'll go in mine."

Emma's attention snaps back from our brothers. "I call shotgun."

In unison, Elliot and I say, "You're not going."

She pouts, even though she knows as a rising junior she isn't invited. She turns to follow the twins back to the stockroom. Over her shoulder she loud-whispers, "I bet in Dallas, I'd get to go wherever I wanted."

Elliot shakes his head. "That again?"

"Yeah," I say.

"You think it will ever happen?"

Out of the corner of my eye I see the Labeled Ladies hanging on my words. I shrug. "You never know. My mother is a wonderful woman."

Three pairs of eyes turn away from me at once.

Some labels are true.

Some rumors are too.

chapter two

PIPER

The drive down the Mass Turnpike to Logan Airport is uneventful. My driver's quiet, but the stereo's French Afro Pop keeps me entertained. As we pass the Boston University high-rise dorm that borders the highway, I look at the windows—at night I always hope for a peek of my two-exes-ago, Sasha, or really anything going on inside those college windows—but it's daytime and summer classes haven't even started yet.

I text her.

Headed away.

She responds in her usual irritating way.

Sorry, kid.

That was her reasoning for breaking up with me a year

and a half ago. She was a senior, I was a sophomore. I obviously didn't know what I wanted yet and she obviously was on her way away from Lincoln-Sudbury Regional. She was wrong on the me not knowing what I wanted part. I knew I only wanted to date girls. Unlike Judith.

I hate when you call me that.

There's a laughing emoji, then, Why do you think I do it? Then a heart. Then, But seriously, have a great summer. Ride your butt off. Come back even more badass and shove it in Judith's face.

I don't want to shove it in her face. I want to kiss her face.

Whatever.

Unlike Sasha, I firmly believed that Judith really did love me. It didn't matter that she chose a guy after me. What mattered was she broke my heart. In a weird way, it felt better to know she was dating a guy because I couldn't do the whole comparison thing.

But I could second-guess everything I'd ever done. Every conversation we'd ever had. Every moment I might have done something better, different, more.

When my driver hits the tunnel, traffic slows to a crawl.

I numbly thumb through my phone, looking at posts from my horse show friends. Everyone's prepping for Summer Lights Classic in Springfield. A tiny bit of guilt squeaks in. Maybe my mom was right, maybe I should be staying and finding an interim program until Erik is back in business. Compete in a familiar pond. Get prepared for an equine program like the one at UConn or UVM. Instead, I'm heading off for a bigger pond with more experienced fish. Girls who homeschool in order to ride the show circuit and have hundred thousand dollar horses. Trainers who've been on Olympic teams and even have medals to show for it. A grandmother who's been painted as too concerned about competitive outcomes my entire life.

A text beeps in. Speak of the devil. My grandmother. The Unsinkable Molly Malone. That's what my dad calls her anyway, even though the real Unsinkable Molly's last name was Brown.

I'LL BE WAITING IN THE CELL LOT. TEXT WHEN YOU GET TO BAGGAGE CLAIM. LOOKING FORWARD TO SEEING YOU. MM—THESE TEXTS MAY BE PENNED BY VOICE SO MAY CONTAIN ERRORS

The all caps is something none of us can stop her from doing, no matter how many times we try to explain she's shouting. The MM voice text bit is a preprogrammed signature she has in her phone to keep from admitting that she might write the occasional curse word. At least that's what I like to believe, that autocorrect is not the thing making my grandmother cooler than the rest of us.

OKAY, I shout back.

Then I add another. Looking forward to seeing you, too. Thank goodness my mom's bad feelings about showing horses hadn't included cutting MaMolly out of our lives completely. My grandmother *is* pretty cool.

The driver pulls up at Terminal B and I take my bags and weave my way inside. To the outside world, I probably look like one of the zillions of Boston-based college students leaving to head home for the summer. Not a girl with a broken heart, leaving to spend the summer with a seventy-something-year-old so I don't have to run into my ex and her boyfriend over the summer.

I get through security, grab a tall iced unsweetened green tea from Starbucks and a bag of protein mix nuts, and head to my gate. I'm in my window seat before the business bro lands in the center seat. I pull out the latest copy of *Dressage Today* and make myself small and invisible and radiate do-not-talk-to-me vibes. Fortunately, center seat business bro pulls out a laptop and gets himself right to work. My phone beeps as the flight attendants walk by snapping shut the overhead compartments.

I take a quick glance.

I have something to tell you. Can you call me?

My heart drops to my toes. It's been weeks since Judith and I talked. I'd texted her to tell her about Erik's illness, and we'd had a little back-and-forth exchange—strictly horse related—until I'd made the mistake of asking if she was still with Brad and there'd been this long lag between texts. When she'd finally come back she'd said that if I was going to keep getting all weird about things, she'd have to rethink us being friends. I couldn't lose her completely.

I rotate the phone inward and start to type.

"Young lady. You'll need to put that on airplane mode now."

The flight attendant has a butter thick Southern accent and is smiling at me, but it's not a friendly smile. It's a don't-make-my-job-harder-you-stupid-teenager smile.

"Can I . . ." My fingers itch to talk to Judith.

She loses the charm. "Now."

Business bro turns and gives me a seasoned traveler scowl, so I don't text Judith back. I put my phone in airplane mode and zip it into my computer bag.

Maybe it won't hurt to make her wait.

KAT

Elliot's SUV smells like the inside of my brothers' shoes, which is perhaps the only bright side of not being the one to drive them around this week.

"Can you please put those back on?" Corbin and Cole are rapidly changing out of their sneakers into their cleats for baseball. One week left of school and they're already practicing for summer league. My dad needs a chauffeur at his beck and call and he, with the help of Elliot's dad, convinced Elliot to keep helping out, since Delilah is kaput for the foreseeable future.

"What's the matter?" Corbin, the three-minute elder of the two black-headed twins, waves his socked right foot in my face. I slap it away.

Cole laughs and begins to make his own feet dance

around in an olfactory choreography of disgusting proportions.

"Y'all stink." But I'm laughing along with them because it's hard not to like my brothers. Even for me.

"What's the matter, cuz. You don't like the powerful smell of testosterone in the afternoon?" Elliot winks at me. Just because he notices guys and I don't doesn't necessarily mean I'm queer. It could be purely coincidental.

My brothers tumble out of the van when we pull up to the curb at the park.

"Be ready when we get back to pick you up!" But I doubt they hear me because they're already slapping high fives and shoulder slamming with their teammates. They're like Emma, all confidence and athleticism.

When we pull up to Elliot's house, he brakes hard. There's a Pool Pardners truck blocking the drive. Elliot leans his head back against the seat and blows out a massive breath. "He's here."

"Who's here?"

"The pool guy."

"Your dad?" I'm confused. Elliot's father, my dad's first cousin, owns the only pool installation and supply company in the area, and since little Harmon, North Carolina, has become a haven for retirees from colder places and the horse show elite, there are a lot of pools. Which means Elliot's dad and mom are loaded, and by proxy, so is Elliot.

"No, not my dad." He whimpers. "His new hire. The one with the massive bulge in his pants."

I put my hand over my ear. "La, la, la, I can't hear you. No bulge talk." Elliot had come out to me and Emma when he was in eighth grade and we were in seventh and sixth. I'd been hearing about his clandestine exploits for longer than he'd lied about dating Penelope Cesar.

"But it's just so . . . bulgy . . . and he's got these tattoos . . . and I swear he winked at me the last time he was here."

"So why are we still in your car when you could be flirting by the pool?"

"The tattoos are of naked women and NASCAR flags."

I shake my head. Elliot at least has a sense of self-preservation if not immaculately bad taste in potential boyfriends.

"What? Don't judge, Miss Never-Met-Anyone-Worthy-Of-Her-Time."

"I'm not judging. Well, okay, maybe I'm judging. But why do you find straight guys so attractive?"

Elliot shrugs. "They're only straight until they're not. Besides, all boys like a good blow job now and then."

"Gross."

"Don't knock it till you've tried it." He sighs once more, but then puts his SUV in reverse. "Want to go to the Bean?"

"Sure. And hard pass on the other. You can keep the bubbas of our fair town all to yourself."

As we drive, my mind drifts. Why can't I just open my mouth and say "Elliot, you're right, I'm not into guys, so maybe I *should* see if I'm actually into girls." But something always stops me. The part of me that's scared to be outside the Harmon status quo.

When we get to the coffee shop, Emma's friend Delaney is working the counter.

"Is it true?" Her eyes widen as we walk in.

For a second I think she's talking about me, but there's no way she could hear what I've been thinking about. "What?" I put my hands on the counter and lean in. Delaney knows all the gossip.

"That you're going to help Emma find a new studio?"

"Wow. Word travels fast."

"She texted." Delaney laughs. "It is Harmon, you know. Anyway, that is supersweet of you and she's really excited."

"She said that?" My sister tends to act like she doesn't care, so it makes me feel good that she's excited enough to have shared with Delaney. And that she doesn't *really* think she'll get to move to Dallas.

"Yep, she did." Delaney puts her hand on the order pad. "What can I get you?"

"Can we get two loaded caramel frappés and a slice of

chocolate cake." Dad harps on me all the time about sugar being bad for people's skin and joints, but a girl can only be so perfect.

Delaney rings it up and puts in her discount for us. I pull out my cash before Elliot can offer to pay. Like my dad, I have a little pride, but maybe I'll have to step back on that hard-and-fast rule if I'm going to earn the money I need to fix Delilah and keep Emma from finding the wrong boy with a car.

"Come sit with us. Take a break. We need to hear all about what's new with you and Antonio . . ." Elliot sings out Delaney's new boyfriend's name with a perfect rounding of the vowels.

She turns beet red—sophomores are so cute—until the door chimes behind us and she regains her composure. "Can't." She tilts her head toward whoever is incoming. I glance behind me.

"Ugh," I say to her. Horse show girls already in town for the spring and summer show season pile through the door of the Bean. They wear tight little breeches and perfect little polos and designer belts and printed socks that come up to their knees stuffed into some kind of identical brand loafer, which nobody outside of a barn would ever wear. "Good luck," I whisper to Delaney and take the plate with our cake before the first girl gets too close.

"I'll need it," she whispers back.

Elliot on the other hand doesn't move at all. He plops his chin down on his elbow and gives all the girls a good looking over before pointing at the clueless fifth girl in line. "What about that one?" he says to me, loud enough for the horse girls and me and Delaney and the whole damn coffee shop to hear.

Now I'm the one who's gone beet red.

I grab him by the arm. "Come on."

But as I walk toward a table, I make the mistake of glancing back. She smiles.

And there it is. The tiniest flutter. The feeling that's been pestering me since puberty.

I push it away.

This town is too damn small to color outside the lines.

chapter three

PIPER

My grandmother sits idling by the curb in her big silver Range Rover and waves through the window when she sees me approach. The passenger window glides down but only a crack.

"Throw your things in the way back, but don't let Jacque and Jill out."

My grandmother's Jack Russell terriers bound over the passenger seat, to the back seat, to the cargo area as I walk alongside the car. It's a real juggling act to push in my suitcase, duffel, and boot bag while holding two hyped-up terriers away from airport arrivals traffic. But my grandmother goes nowhere without them.

Once I'm finally in the car and no dogs have been hurt

in the act, I lean over to kiss her on the cheek, and the scent of her—Guerlain's Shalimar, high-quality timothy hay, and a slight undertone of horse—is warm and familiar. "Hi, MaMolly." My older cousin had started calling her this when he was little, a bastardization of My Molly, and it stuck.

"Hello, love." She pats my knee. "You look good. Fit." She pulls out into traffic, the layers of gold bracelets that she wears everywhere except while riding dangling on her arm.

Jacque jumps from the back into my lap and covers my face with kisses. Jill's right behind him. This is one of the many ways in which my mom differs from her mom. What my mom let go as a competitive rider, she made up for in the way of interior design perfection and cleanliness. My father's English Labrador, Sir Thomaston, would never be allowed anywhere but behind his puppy gate in the way back of Mom's car. I'm promptly covered in fine white hairs. "Are you hungry? Thirsty? Would you like me to stop somewhere for you before we get on the interstate?"

Really what I want to do is pull out my phone and stare at the text from Judith again. I'd started to text her from the tarmac, but business bro had gotten inexplicably chatty and wanted to know about the nature of my business in town and having seen my horse magazine wanted to inform me all about the big Equestrian Center out west of Charlotte. Had I heard of it? Would I be visiting it?

Any horse girl when point-blank asked about horses and riding is bound to spill a little. Especially since I hope I'll be showing at that very center before the summer is over. So, I let Judith wait.

Now I won't text in front of my grandmother because I've learned her generation finds it incredibly rude when my generation pulls out their phones. Plus, maybe, I like making Judith wait. Let her wonder where I am, who I'm with for a change, instead of the other way around.

"No, thank you."

"Are you sure? Last chance for a drive-through Starbucks." My grandmother winks at me.

"I thought you said you'd gotten one in Harmon?" In fact, I know she did, because she sent one of those all cap texts and a picture of the cup with her name scrawled on it in black marker to mark the occasion. Judith thought it was weird that my grandmother is my texting buddy, but not many people have a grandmother as amazing as mine.

"A Starbucks? Oh yes. Big news in town when it happened. Much excitement, let me tell you. However, it's not drive-through. It's in the grocery store. You have to park and go in and inevitably you end up seeing six of your neighbors and have to make godforsaken small talk."

MaMolly acts like this is a big deal, which is a farce, because my grandmother is a social butterfly. She's a member of two different horseback hunts (which she assures me only chase scent not actual foxes), is on the board of a horse rescue league, paints at the local Arts League, and still plays tennis to boot. And those are just the activities I remember.

She doesn't wait for me to agree with her, because obviously she's jonesing for her own jolt of caffeine, which is what I think keeps her seventy-three-year-old self running at high gear. The dogs each get a Puppuccino, so soon I'm covered in not only white fur but dollops of whipped cream.

"Throw them in the back before we get on the highway."

I do—well, I don't actually throw the dogs—and MaMolly whips out a lint roller from her console.

"Thanks," I say, and laugh. If it weren't for my broken heart, this summer would be perfectly set up for nothing but fun. I hope I spend every day covered in horse hair and sweat and have zero minutes in the day to think about Judith and her "I just don't have those kinds of feelings for you anymore" talk.

How can a girl give you the sweetest kisses imaginable on a Friday afternoon, then break your heart on Sunday night? I have a strong feeling I know what happened on the Saturday in between, but I don't want to think about Judith cheating, even emotionally. Leave it the way it is in my mind.

My phone buzzes and despite the risk of disappointing MaMolly, I look at the screen.

Did you get my last text? I really need to talk to you. It's important.

The text dots come up like she's typing more.

Then,

I miss you.

My palms itch with the need to type, but I count backward from ten instead.

It feels good to be the one in charge of the narrative.

KAT

Early morning sunlight streams into my tiny disaster of a room. The twins got the big attic room with the dormer eaves and Emma has the sunny first floor bedroom that used to be a guest room when Mom was still here. After Mom left, Dad tried to give me their room, but the man has more products and a bigger wardrobe than me and Emma combined. Plus, Emma got all pushy that she should have gotten the master bedroom if Dad was giving it up, so I said I'd stay where I was. The man is a saint and needs a little something in his life for all he does for us.

I push old homework papers and dirty clothes off the end of my bed and open my laptop. I'm curious about the dance school in Texas that Emma showed me in the salon's magazine. There's no way our selfish mother would actually let Emma move in with her, but I like seeing what my sister dreams about.

The dance company is incredible. They have a hip-hop team, an intermediate team, even a preprofessional team. Out of curiosity, I search nearby Greenville and find the website for Dazzle Dance Pros. It's for sure better than the local studio, Ms. Kelly's, but not as cutting edge as the place in Texas. They have a page with prices, though, and information about auditions for their professional competition company. For the low, low price of about two thousand dollars, my sister could do a summer intensive and be a member of the group next school year. That doesn't factor in the gas, time, and wear and tear on Delilah to get her there every day, though. But I'd drive her if she wanted. I hate when she gets sad about the mom situation and the local dance situation, and maybe something like this would be what she needed to go next level. She could, for sure, nail the audition.

Which brings it down to money. How can I find five thousand dollars to fix my car and pay for more sophisticated dance lessons to follow through on my promise to help her?

We really need my van.

Dad would say follow your dreams and the money will

follow. That's why he'd gone back to school to learn to do hair and facials. He'd opened the Tousled Orchid to popular—if not entirely financial—success, despite what his male friends and relatives muttered under their breath. When Mom left him not long after he enrolled in classes, the rumors swirled thicker, but Dad doesn't care. He'd gone after his dream, even if it isn't what people expected after his first unhappy career in construction management. Now he's not only an entrepreneur, but a denizen of good skin and healthy hair. But, even though we all love the salon, it's not a place that gives five-thousand-dollar handouts easily. I can ask, but I'm pretty sure I know the answer already.

What does Harmon, North Carolina, need? What is the thing that a teenage girl can do that an adult hasn't already thought of and tried and failed?

Uncle Randall would offer me a job with the pool company for the summer, but at eight bucks an hour and days filled with NASCAR tattoo guys ogling me in a bathing suit and shorts, it doesn't add up. Even if I did it full-time for the whole summer I'd be shy of what I need and that doesn't even factor in having taxes taken out. I need a shot of entrepreneurial genius. But my brain isn't working, I'm coming up with nada, zero, zilch, the big goose egg.

Maybe it's time for a shot of something more potent.

I wander downstairs to the kitchen. It sparkles and smells like natural lavender cleaner. Dad, the only other early riser in the family, looks awfully cute in his "Metrosexual" apron and dish gloves. "Good morning." He opens his arms and I go in for a warm hug. When he releases me he points to the fridge. "There are carrot cinnamon muffins. Gluten-free."

"Espresso?" I ask.

He sighs. "A green smoothie would be better."

"Dad. I'm eighteen. My skin is flawless. I don't drink. I don't smoke. I'm still a virgin. Please. Let me have my caffeine."

He relents—the uncomfortableness of the virgin comment gets him every time—and scoops espresso into the portafilter of the fancy Breville machine Mom sent us last Christmas. I take out two muffins and put them in the toaster oven. The bros will sleep till early afternoon on this rare non-baseball Saturday and Emma spent the night at Delaney's, so it's just me and the pops.

"What do you have planned today?" he asks.

I sip my espresso and hope it will provide the jolt of inspiration I need. "I have to feed Mrs. Phillips' cats."

Our next-door neighbors took an impromptu weekend trip to Atlanta and left me in charge of their two rescue cats. I've already thought of the pet-sitting thing, but at five dollars per visit, it isn't much of anything to add to my kitty. Pun intended. Plus, most people around here need farm sitters and without a car, I'm out of luck.

But then, I have a bit of an epiphany. "Maybe I could come to the salon with you and see if any of your clients have errands they need me to run, or small jobs around their houses. I really want to get Delilah fixed."

"Sweetheart, I'm going to figure something out about the van."

He'll eventually make it happen, I know he will, but it sucks being without wheels even for a couple of weeks.

"But would it be okay for me to try? It'd be cool to figure it out on my own."

I see the flicker of a smile. He likes that I share his entrepreneurial spirit.

"What kind of errands?"

"I don't know." I shrug. "Maybe walk to the Bean and get coffee orders for people. Wash windows? Weed people's gardens?" I have enough babysitting for a lifetime with my own brothers.

"I suppose you could try." He pulls out his phone and scans the salon's scheduling app. "It's a busy day. Sadie's got that new woman from Canterhills. There's the usual Saturday wash and set crew." He looks some more. "Mrs. Malone is my one o'clock."

Perfect. Molly Malone is a genius businesswoman. Dad read us an article in the paper about her when he was restarting his own career. In her sixties, Mrs. Malone developed a line of horse care products and business boomed for her. I remember how excited Dad had been when she'd become a client and, eventually, a friend.

She's the perfect person to consult about potential entrepreneurial opportunities.

But there's one more thing I want to ask Dad about.

"Has Emma mentioned the dance school?" I pause, knowing the impact of my next words. "In Dallas?"

Dad's hands go still under the faucet. He sighs. "Yes."

My mouth goes dry. I know it makes Dad feel crappy when he can't do stuff for us. I mean, here he is, the guy taking care of us, paying the bills, running the business . . . staying. Neither me or my brothers are delusional about what we can expect. But Emma? Helping her out with the dance thing would make him a hero.

"I was thinking . . ."

"Never a good start when it comes to you, my scheming oldest child."

"No, hear me out. Dallas is out of the question, obviously, but what if she could dance better semi-locally? If Emma auditioned for the good company in Greenville and danced with them for the next couple of years, it might give her a way to earn some kind of scholarship for college." Emma's grades on their own were never going to make that happen. Another way she and I are different.

He turns and wipes his hands on a dish towel. "Sounds like time, transportation, and money."

"But if she got in, and you could afford it, I could help get her there for rehearsals."

"That's a big commitment on your part, Kat. It's your senior year next year. You'll be busy with your own activities."

"She'd be so into it. You know she would. And she can use Delilah on the days I'm busy. She'll have her full license by then, so it won't matter what time dance is done."

"Kat. Things are too tight right now. I'm already bartering with Ms. Kelly to help pay for Emma's classes. I don't think anyone's going to drive up from Greenville to get haircuts from me or my staff."

"Oh." The air goes out of my hope balloon. "I didn't know that."

"It's not up to you to know that." He motions for me to settle into a side hug.

"What if I can come up with the money?"

Dad laughs into my hair. "You may be the quiet one, but I swear you're more dogged than your sister. One day she's going to realize what she has in you." He pushes me out so he's looking at me. "It's fine if you want to try and do that for her, but what about you? What are you going to do for yourself this summer?"

"Me?" I step out of his hug.

"Yes, you. Besides earning money. What are you going to do for fun?"

The heat rises into my neck and I'm sure I'm turning nervous, blotchy red because my mind immediately drifts to the horse girl Elliot had pointed at in the coffee shop. What if instead of finding a boy with a car, I found a girl . . . with the same questions as me.

Dad stares like he's looking into my soul. "You know you can tell me anything, right?"

I avert my eyes. "I know, Dad. I know."

And one day, when I have something to tell, I'll go straight to him. But in the meantime, I have to figure out exactly who I am. For me.

chapter four
PIPER

MaMolly puts me in the big guest room with the picture window that looks out over her pastures. It's unbelievably beautiful here—rolling meadows of lush green grass, lines of three-board fencing separating each of the paddocks, even a flock of wild turkeys scratching under the trees. There are five retired show horses that live in a stone and wood barn that people, even in tony Lincoln, Mass, would die for.

I unpack my bag and fold my breeches and polos and place them on the shelves in the closet. My show boots stay in their boot bag, but I put the paddock boots by the door to take down to the tack room later. I brought a few non-horse wear items that I hang up on cedar hangers. When my bag is empty and tucked into the corner of the closet, I sit with my phone on the four-poster bed.

First, I text my mom and dad that I've arrived alive and am at my grandmother's.

Then I stare at the messages from Judith again. Text or call?

I start with the easier.

Hey, what's up?

The answer is almost immediate.

Do you have time to talk?

I text back with a simple, Y

The picture of us, arms linked, taking bites from each other's ice cream cones, pops up as Hayley Kiyoko starts singing "He'll never love you like me." Okay, so maybe it was kind of a tragic choice, but it's how I still feel. How could she just give us away?

"Hey." I run a finger under the edge of my sock, tugging at the elastic as I go. Outside the window, one of MaMolly's horses lifts its head to watch as the turkeys strut toward the tree line.

"Hey." Judith's voice has always been one of the sexiest things about her. Soft with a touch of gravel. I can't decide if I want to quick hit the off button or jump through the phone.

She clears her throat. "How are you?"

Okay, so we're taking the small talk route.

"Fine."

"Have you found a new barn?"

I figured word might have filtered back to her about my decision to come south for the summer, but apparently it hadn't.

"No. I decided to do something different."

"Really?"

I know I'm drawing out the biggest news in the room, but the longer I can draw things out, the longer I can keep her talking.

"Really."

"Wow, I never thought you would give up your riding for anything." And there's the dig. Even though she was a rider, too, her interest was more subdued. Where I rode five days a week, without fail, Judith paid for a weekly lesson to round out her extracurriculars. She liked horses, but she didn't *live* horses. And sometimes I did have to say no to hanging out with her because of my training schedule. But in my mind, that never interfered with the depth of my feelings for and attraction to her. I was okay with somebody having different interests as long as I was on the list.

Might as well tell her the whole story.

"I decided to come to North Carolina for the summer. And stay with my grandmother." I wait for her disappointment. The sadness that's going to follow her I miss you text when she realizes she's going to have to keep on missing me.

"That's great, Piper! I know your mom wasn't ever excited about that idea. But you talked about it and about how it would be good for your goals."

I scrunch my sock tighter. Her support is nice, but also confusing. I thought maybe she'd sound a tiny bit less enthusiastic when she realized I was practically one thousand miles away from her.

"Yeah, she's still not. But I needed to get away. What did you want to talk to me about?"

"Um, yeah, well . . ."

She's hedging and I have no idea why.

"It's just that, well, Brad's friends went to your account the other day and saw that you still have a picture with me as your profile, and Piper, that's kind of weird."

Now I'm mad. "What does that have to do with your missing me?"

There's a pause and I can picture her face in the silence. Eyes darting, hands flexing, as she sorts through a minute of anger and finds the strength to clap back at me. Confrontation was never her strong suit.

"I do miss you. You're my friend. We had a wonderful relationship and I don't want to let that *friendship* go. But I'm with Brad now."

"You're embarrassed that his friends know you're bisexual?"

Now I hear an outward sigh that sounds a tiny bit like a growl. "That's something I'd expect Sasha to say, not you. Of course I'm not. You, of all people, know better than that. Don't be a bitch."

"Fine. I'm sorry. But it hurts, Jude. It still fucking hurts."

There's silence. Then, "Just change the picture, please. It comes across stalkerish." Pause. A couple of sighs. "I'm not your girlfriend anymore."

My heart, which had a few staples starting to join the gaps, falls completely apart again.

MaMolly, in her infinite—albeit clueless to the current situation—wisdom, calls from the hallway. "Piper. Come on down. I want to discuss schedules and agendas with you."

I put my hand to the phone. "Be right there." Then I return to Judith. "Fine," I say. "I'll change the picture. Enjoy your life. I've got to go. My grandmother needs me."

Before she can cajole and flirt with me to reassure herself that our "friendship" is intact, I hit the off button. Fuck her. I hate her.

I open my account profile page and hover over the photo, then I close it out. I said I'd change it. I just didn't say when. Or with what photo. I'll deal with it later.

I shove the phone in my pocket and head downstairs.

My grandmother stands at the bottom with her own plan to mess with my emotions.

She's holding up a set of car keys. My feet start to turn me around to retreat back upstairs.

"Piper Kitts."

My heartbeat quickens. "I can't, MaMolly."

"You can and you will. This nonsense is ridiculous and your parents have let you avoid it for far too long. If I'm to entertain you for the summer, you're going to have to learn to drive."

Stomach acid swirls inside me and my breakfast threatens to revisit the outside world. Driving and me, not going to happen. That's what Lyft and Ubers are for. I've tried driving. I suck.

"Piper," she says. "You rode a 17.2 hand Westphalian at almost Prix St. George levels. I've seen you fearlessly climb on Erik's stallions. Driving is far simpler than riding. How are you going to get your horses to the shows when you become a professional if you can't drive a truck and pull a trailer?"

Now she wants me to pull a trailer, too? "Grooms," I blurt out. "A husband."

My grandmother rolls her eyes. "Unless something has changed since we last talked, the latter is an unlikely prospect. And I'm happy to read you a litany on how difficult it is to find a good groom in this day and age, much less one who you trust with your vehicle. Now, my truck is ten years old and indestructible. You can learn with it."

I'm shaking my head back and forth, but my grand-mother stands firm.

"This"—she dangles her keys again—"is happening."

"My permit is from Massachusetts."

"The lovely state of North Carolina will allow you to learn with an out-of-state learner's permit. Nice try." Jill barks to emphasize MaMolly's point.

I know my reluctance to drive is ridiculous. Yes, I'd seen a bad accident as a kid, but that was years ago. I'd agreed to get my learner's permit to shut my dad up, but that was a written test, not actually operating a motor vehicle. Mostly I just hated the thought of other drivers. I figured I could control me, but how could I control them? And rideshares were just so easy.

I whine. "MaMolly."

"End of discussion. Your coddled days are over."

When I insisted to Mom that I wanted to be pushed, I hadn't meant this. I'd meant horses. But I guess Mom knew a thing or two about her own mother. The really irritating thing, though? I think Mom is going to be in alignment with MaMolly on this one.

KAT

I head to the Bean after taking orders at the salon. Delaney is at the counter again.

"Do you ever get a day off?" I laugh, then look around. "Where's Emma?"

"Still sleeping when I left. My mom's going to get her up and drop her off before she leaves for Saturday errands." Delaney glances back over her shoulder to the kitchen window where her boss is up to his elbows in flour for their amazing pastries. "He needs to hire like three more people, but he's too cheap."

My ears perk up. I could apply here. Maybe if her boss had a solid applicant, he'd consider a new hire. But then I tuck the thought away because Delaney doesn't make much bank at the Bean. Even though working with her would be fun, I have to stick to my plan for finding an entrepreneurial idea. It's the only way to make enough to help fix the van and help Emma.

I read off the morning orders for Dad's stylists and add a handful of pastries that I can resell to hangry clients who forget that a cut and foil will last through lunchtime. Delaney runs my debit card and turns the screen around so I can sign and add a tip. I hover between the amounts and even though I feel pretty shitty doing it, I hit the 10 percent option. Hopefully she won't notice, not that she'd say anything, but still, it is cheap.

"Don't work too hard," I say as she hands me the bag of pastries and a drink tray.

"You either." Then her eyes light up as Antonio appears next to me at the counter.

Perfect timing, she'll be too focused on her hot boyfriend to notice I've suddenly become a chintzy tipper.

"Hey," I say. "Will I see you at the bonfire?" I'm trying to get to know Antonio now that he and Delaney are a couple. We've been in some classes together but never really talked.

"Yeah," he says. "We'll be there. Emma's coming with us, too."

"What?" My sister might be my best friend, but there

are rules and she knows them. She may have already dated, already kissed, already had way more experience in the romance department than me, but I get to keep certain nonnegotiable firsts that come from being older. Like driving and getting a car. Like graduating before her. Like the freaking end-of-school bonfire. I thought I'd made that extra clear with Elliot and now she's getting around it on the technicality that her other best friend is dating a guy in my grade.

Delaney leans forward. "Emma said you'd be pissed but I said you wouldn't. You're not, right?"

What can I say and not look like a douche. "No, of course not." But inside . . . totally pissed.

At the salon, Natascha's working the front counter. She graduated a few years before me and went to the local community college for beauty school, but for the life of me I can't figure out why Dad hired her. She's a hot mess.

"Oh, bless you." She grabs the blended pumpkin spice frappé from the drink tray. I put down my bag and hold out my hand for her cash. She reluctantly hands me her five dollars. "They're only four dollars at the Bean."

"This is a business operation."

Once I distribute all the preordered goods and set up my pastry tray with prices—the profit will keep me in gas money till I figure out where the real cash is coming from—I look around the room at the chairs.

Vlada, Elliot's mom, is at Tanya's station getting her nails done.

"Hey, Aunt Vlada." I lean down to kiss her cheek. We're technically cousins, but we've always called Vlada and Randall our aunt and uncle. They're good to us, always inviting me and my sibs to hang out and graze on the delicacies in their massive subzero refrigerator. "Anything you need me to do for you today? I've decided to start an errand business."

She laughs. "Can you find my son a girlfriend? I don't understand how he doesn't have ten of them. My boy is so handsome."

"How much is it worth to you?" I'm kidding, of course, but she laughs again. Poor Elliot. I never understand why his parents don't get that he's gay. Sure, he's gone to dances with lots of different girls, but isn't it obvious? He never looks at girls' bulges and he's pretty damn obvious about looking at dudes. Somehow though, they remain clueless and I feel bad for him. He dreads coming out to them. Though we're all sad he's leaving for Chapel Hill in the fall, he'll finally get to start living life on his own terms.

"Don't worry, the right person will sweep along into his life any moment now." I hold one finger into the air and give her my best used-car sales pitch. "But for the low, low price of twenty dollars per date, I'm happy to set him up."

"Oh, if only. If you're doing favors, maybe you'd reach down into my pocketbook and pop a piece of that chewing gum into my mouth for me?"

Tanya mutters in agreement. "Do not let her mess up these nails. They are nearing perfection."

I give her the gum and keep moving, talking to people, telling them I'm available to run errands or pet-sit or any little thing they might need. But the morning is slow. People are busy gossiping or texting their families and when my dad waves at me with a flat iron, indicating I'm being more of a nuisance than a tycoon, I plop into the chair behind Natascha.

"Quit looking at my butt." Natascha wiggles it where she stands in front of me.

"I'm not looking at your butt."

"Why not?"

"Because that would be weird."

She glances over her shoulder at me. "Would it?"

Loaded question. I guess, no, it's not weird to look at other girls' butts. Girls do it all the time. Grown women do it all the time. They flip through fashion magazines and talk about wanting a butt like this or a butt like that. But I've always been super shy about looking at other girls' body parts. The locker room before PE class always felt a tiny bit like torture, because here's the thing. I want to look. Like, *want* to look.

"Well?" Natascha wiggles again.

I take a deep breath.

I look at Natascha's butt. It's a nice one, but I have zero physical sensation in my body as a result of staring at her bum.

"Okay, not weird. You have a nice butt."

"That's what Cassidy Phillips says." Natascha loves to talk about her recent hookup with our school's former volleyball captain. Up until it happened, she'd been hooking up with some guy named Otis. But now she's my one living breathing friend who could perhaps provide guidance on the weird flutter I get in the presence of girls my age smiling at me. She nudges my shoe with hers. "You got a girlfriend yet? I think you like looking at my butt."

This could be my opportunity to ask how she ended up with Cassidy. Was it a certain feeling? Did a lightning bolt strike? How did she go from thinking about it to actually doing it? But she asks really loud and now all I can do is look around the salon, relieved that at least four hair dryers are on and nobody is at the front desk to have heard her question.

My response is curt. "Quit trying to make me gay."

Perhaps my biggest regret, to date, was not kissing Alicia Smith when we'd gone to the freshman Sadie Hawkins dance as friends. There'd been a moment. We'd been just inside the alcove created by the closed cafeteria doors. I'd told her how pretty she looked in her yellow dress. She'd buried her smile behind her hand and lowered her eyelids, but then she'd dropped her hand to her side and looked up at me. A full five to ten seconds hung between us, both of us frozen, neither of us moving, then a crush of sophomores turned the corner and the moment disappeared. She'd moved away at the Christmas break and I'd never had another opportunity, with her or anyone else. Maybe a thunderclap would have happened, or the swarm of honeybees that Emma always talks about when she has a crush.

She waves her ringed hand. "Fine, suit yourself. Got a boyfriend yet?"

I shake my head. "No. I have bigger things to deal with."

Natascha smirks. "Oh right, like selling overpriced coffee."

I sigh. "No, like my busted transmission."

Molly Malone saves me from Natascha's interrogation by walking through the door. She slides her big sunglasses up onto her caramel-colored Jackie O cut and her pile of gold bracelets jangle hello. "Girls. How lovely you both look. Straight out of *Steel Magnolias . . .*" She tilts her chin toward Natascha and then to me. "Audrey Hepburn with a side of *Black Swan*." God, I love Mrs. Malone.

"Conrad is still finishing up with his noon appointment, Mrs. Malone. May I get you some coffee or tea while you wait?" Natascha does have a very polite way about her when it comes to the over-seventy crowd, which I guess is why my dad hired her.

"No, dear, I'm fine." She sits down and straightens her slacks as she crosses her ankles.

"Could I talk to you for a moment, Mrs. Malone?" I step out from the counter and toward the blue davenport.

"Certainly." She pats the sofa cushion next to her and I settle on the edge.

"I was wondering if you might have any advice."

"Advice?"

"Well, I know you're a businesswoman and an entrepreneur, like my dad. And, well, I'm trying to get something started."

"And you need seed money?"

"What?"

She adjusts her gold bangles and crosses her manicured nails across her lap. "I'm sorry. An assumption. It seems that's how I'm often seen around this town. Just an old cash cow to be milked dry."

I hope people aren't actually like that to her.

"Oh. No. Not at all. I only want advice."

She pats my hand. Her nails are my favorite shade, Big Apple Red. "Go on."

"I'm starting an errand business to try and get my van fixed. I thought you might have some ideas for me."

"An errand business, you say?"

I nod. "Yes ma'am."

"Without your van?"

I realize how stupid it must sound. "Well, yes. My cousin, Elliot, can help me some if I need to get somewhere. But for now, it needs to be stuff I can do close to the salon."

She sits very still and tilts her head as if she's thinking. Her lips purse, then relax, then purse again until finally she responds. "I may have a business proposition for you."

"Oh?" I cross my legs at my ankles and sit up straighter, mimicking the way she has her hands lightly crossed in her lap.

"It's about my granddaughter."

When she finishes filling me in, things are suddenly looking a whole lot brighter.

chapter five

PIPER

I'm in the barn grooming Fonty when MaMolly returns from her outing.

"I thought I'd find you down here. I have a surprise for you."

I put the curry comb down. My grandmother's surprises are turning out not to be the joyous kind.

"There's a young woman, local, her father is my stylist. Anyway, she has a spark about her and I think it would do her good to meet you and do you good to meet someone your own age around here. She was telling me about this big party the local teens attend and I've arranged for her to take you."

If it were anyone but my grandmother, I'd flat-out

refuse. Instead I can only try to talk my way out of it. "Honestly, I'm super fine staying here. I love your horses. I can even ride Fonty around in the pasture until I meet the woman you've arranged for me to be a working student for, right?" I had a few more days until I started my job— free labor in exchange for lessons with a former Olympic dressage rider who lived in the area—so it *would* be boring until then but connecting with some random local high school girl? Save me now. I try again. "Jacque and Jill need someone to play ball with them when you're off at your board meetings and I can always clean."

My grandmother purses her lips and looks exactly like my mother. "You may be in self-imposed exile, which we'll talk about later, but I will not keep you locked in my castle. This is not up for negotiation. You are going and you will have fun. Also, she's going to help me teach you to drive. We have a business arrangement."

I step away from the horse as I feel my voice rise an octave. "You're getting a teenager to teach me to drive?"

"She's very responsible and more patient than I am."

"Pretty sure it's not legal."

"She's not old enough to be a driving teacher for public hire, but this is a private arrangement, therefore legal enough for me. She's had her eighteenth birthday and has her full license. As long as you stay in the county and don't speed, you should be fine." MaMolly steps forward and puts a hand on each of my shoulders. "You're going to be okay. And you're going to enjoy Katherine and her friends. I know it."

I'd like to think this is an encouraging squeeze, but mentally it feels a bit more like the grip of doom. MaMolly tends not to hear the word *no* unless it's absolutely warranted.

There's no getting out of it. "When is this party?"

MaMolly smiles and releases me. "Thursday night. She'll pick you up here at eight."

The thing about being obsessed with horses is that it's not only about my obsession with horses. It's about being an introvert and incredibly awkward around new people. I'm pretty certain I'm going to have zero in common with a bunch of high school students from Harmon, North Carolina. Unless, of course, someone is willing to talk about horses. But my past observations when visiting my grandmother have been that the horse set is mostly older or weekending here for horse shows, and the local crowd simply tolerates us. This is going to be a disaster.

"When you're done, come on up to the house and we can decide on what to eat for supper."

"Yep," I say. The moment my grandmother leaves the barn I feel the vibration of my phone in my pocket. I grab it, my stomach lurching as I look to see if it's Judith.

It's Erik.

Spoke to your new boss today. She asked me to send some video of you riding Patron and Drambuie. Seems like you're going to have quite an education this summer. Be sure and send a text now and again letting me know how it's going. I'm proud of where you've gotten in your riding. Remember that as you start this new chapter.

He talked to the woman I'm going to be working for? I respond with a thanks, then scroll through my phone. I still hadn't changed the picture Judith was upset about.

I pull it up full-size on the screen. Why was it stalkerish? We're smiling cheek to cheek, a little rainbow flag on my cheek, a bi-proud sticker on hers. We'd taken the selfie at last summer's Pride in Boston. Sure, later that night had been *the* night, but nobody knew that looking at our smiles. Except for me. And her. And now, quote, "I'm not your girlfriend anymore."

I take a quick selfie with Fonty and stick it up in place of the egregious one. Maybe my best strategy is a social media blitz to end all social media blitzes. If I have to hang out with some weirdo kids from Harmon, I might as well act like I'm having the time of my life. Fewer horses, more cute girls. Or something like that.

I make the mistake of checking Judith's feed. She has

her own blitz going on. A Brad blitz. Brad with his perfectly chiseled biceps and full, raspberry-hued lips. Tiny dreadlocks, perfect skin in toasted bronze that more closely matches her own, and a skateboard kicked up against his hand. The guy even wears tortoiseshell glasses that make him look like he walked out of a Warby Parker ad. His smile is nice. Genuinely kind. I can't compete with that kind of perfection.

I bury my face in Fonty's mane and wrap my hand over her wither as I mumble. "Girls. How the hell does anyone do this and succeed?"

The horse bends her head around and pokes me with her nose. I dig into my jeans pocket and pull out the treat I'd stashed there. Horses are simple in comparison. Best I stick to my training program and forget all the rest. Judith is in Massachusetts. I'm here living with MaMolly. I have horses to ride and no one that I know. Focusing on my future will be my new mantra. I give the horse a quick scratch on her neck before putting my phone away.

Easy peasy, lemon squeezie, as Dad likes to say. I hope he's right.

KAT

The turquoise blue of the water shimmers against the black concrete liner, giving Elliot's pool a lake vibe. My brothers are cannonballing off the diving board, then racing each other out of the pool and up to the top of the faux rock water slide before doing it all over again. Emma is laid out on a towel, letting her perfect skin turn no-burn tan.

"So, who is this girl?" Elliot thumbs through the latest issue of *Entertainment Weekly* I brought him from the salon.

"Molly Malone's granddaughter. She's here for the summer and I guess Mrs. Malone wants to give her a taste of the rest-of-us reality."

"And she's paying you how much to do this?"

"She freaking paid to have my transmission fixed."

"Awesome. What's the catch?"

"I have to give this girl driving lessons and hang out with her. For the next eight weeks."

Emma interjects from her beach towel. "I would be so weirded out if someone did that to me. She must be a total freakazoid if her grandmother's paying you to be her friend."

"Hey now, I'm providing a service. And I think Mrs. Malone wanted to help my entrepreneurial vision without it seeming like she was giving me something for nothing. She said she liked my spirit."

"I'm telling you. Freakazoid." Emma rolls over onto her stomach. "Unless of course she's a total bitch."

"Who cares if she is. Delilah is getting fixed as we speak. If she's too heinous, I'll take her to the IGA parking lot on Senior Citizens Day for her first lesson and see how she does with bumper cars."

Elliot laughs. "Sadistic. I like it."

"There is a catch though."

He waits.

"I promised I'd bring her with us tonight."

This gets Emma's attention. She sits up. "Tonight? The bonfire? You're bringing some random but you said I can't go?"

"Don't act all innocent. I talked to Delaney and Antonio. Heard all about your third-wheel invitation. Nice worming your way into our party."

Elliot groans. "Did you think she wouldn't? This is Emma we're talking about."

"I'm right here. I can hear you."

"Well, if you're going, you don't have to be a third wheel. You can be my date." Elliot wiggles his fingers in Emma's direction.

Emma sticks her tongue out at me. "Ooooh, cousin action. More fun. And I'll get to check out the freakazoid."

There's no point in arguing.

The brothers yell from the pool. "Are y'all getting in or what? We need someone to play basketball against." They look like baby seals or Labrador puppies with their hair slicked back and their faces all eager for almost-the-end-of-school fun.

"Fine." I ditch my mirrored Ray-Bans, another expensive present from Mom, and automatically pick up the SPF 90 to spray down Elliot. It's ironic that the son of the pool king is so sensitive to sunlight. I'm rubbing spray on his shoulders when Uncle Randall makes his appearance.

"Are y'all pre-partying for the big party?" He's all cheesy grin and over-tanned face as he waggles his eyebrows at us.

"Dad." Elliot growls.

"What? Did I say something wrong?" He winks at me and Emma.

I don't pay any attention to Elliot. Uncle Randall is, well, Uncle Randall. "Once we take the twins home, we're all about the bonfire. Don't you worry."

He gets all misty-eyed. "Ah, the bonfire night. I remember the first part of it so well, but then after that . . ." He laughs. "Times sure have changed what with all of these sobriety pledges. Back in my day bonfire night was about getting wasted and hooking up. Those were the good times."

Elliot groans out loud. His dad's inappropriateness is legendary. What I think neither of them realizes is just how much alike, save for sexual preferences, they actually are. I have no doubt Elliot will be shit-faced by the time we leave and I also feel pretty sure he'll have found at least one closeted baseball player more than willing to meet him in the woods for . . . whatever.

Bonfire night hasn't changed as much as Uncle Randall thinks.

Too bad there'll be no one there for me to hook up with. Unless, of course, I'm willing to risk the whole town talking about it by sunup.

Nope. I'll stay my course. Unencumbered. Free from experience.

Waiting.

chapter six

PIPER

I'm waiting inside my grandmother's foyer trying to stave off nerves when a silver SUV pulls into the circular drive. A guy is driving and it looks like two other people are in the car with him.

"I thought you said some girl was coming to pick me up?"

MaMolly peers out her living room window. "Oh, she's there. That's her cousin. His father's my pool man. How fun, you'll get to meet the whole family."

"Oh." Part of me hoped MaMolly was going to put her foot down and absolutely not allow me to drive off with some total stranger, but instead she's practically pushing me toward the front door.

I step outside and the girl in the back seat gets out. She's wearing high-waisted black jeans and a red crop top that match her red high-topped sneakers. She has kind of a Snow White vibe with her dark, swingy hair and red lipstick. Cute enough for me to remember my plan. I don't care how dorky my next move seems. "Hey. I'm Piper." I whip my phone out. "Do you mind?" I step next to her and snap a selfie before she even knows what's happening.

The girl in the front seat, who's now looking at me out an opened window, snorts and whispers something to the guy. I don't care what they think. This alliance is temporary and that photo is posted and cross-posted before the girl can even say, "Hi, I'm Kat."

In the car, the other two introduce themselves. Elliot is the guy. Emma is the girl. They're all cousins and the girls are sisters.

"You're from up north?" The sister, Emma, turns to talk to me from the front seat. She's got the same dark hair but is nowhere near as pale as Snow White. I can tell from where I'm sitting that she's athlete fit. But the way she fusses with her miniskirt and keeps tucking her hair behind her ear does not set off my gaydar. Too bad. Not that my heart could even handle a meaningless fling. But maybe my body could. I am a thousand miles away from the scene of my broken heart.

"Yes, outside of Boston."

"What grade are you in?"

"I'll be a senior."

"Oh, same as Kat. Gosh, I imagine the two of you are going to be just the best besties before the summer is over. Aren't you, Kat?" She grins at her sister and I notice the twitch at the corner of the guy's mouth. Rude, but, whatever. I am the one whose been set up with *friends* by her grandmother.

"Maybe." Kat smiles at me and it's warm and genuine. What is it about a genuine smile that melts me every time? People talk about somebody needing to have certain attributes like body size or hair color or eye color or whatever their particular thing is. For me, it's that warm smile and the ability to laugh at yourself. Everything else simply adds up to the person who has that. Which is why I'm having a hard time letting go of Judith.

"What's your story?" Elliot looks at me in the rearview mirror. Gorgeous gray-blue eyes and a sweep of chestnut-colored hair over a chiseled face. Maybe photos with Elliot will make Judith worry I've gone out and found a Brad of my own. Probably not, she knows me better, but at least he's got good angles.

"What do you mean?"

"Why are you here when you could be somewhere?"

I give them the abbreviated, not-too-ambitious account of my training goals and my grandmother's offer. I leave off Judith.

Emma groans. "Oh god, a horse show girl."

Kat thumps the back of her sister's seat with her sneaker.

"What's the problem with that?" My stomach tenses and I want to introvert myself away from this vehicle.

This time Kat speaks up. "Absolutely nothing. We're glad you're here and I do hope we're going to be friends."

Emma snorts again from the front. I wonder how she'd react if I reached across Kat and flicked her on the skull.

The guy, Elliot, jumps in. "Do you drink?"

"Um."

Kat puts her left hand out between us. Her fingers are long, and her nails are manicured, but short. I notice her pointer finger is a different length than her ring finger and I think about that BBC study analyzing this exact feature as a link to sexuality. In a study of sets of female twins, where one was gay and the other straight, the gay twin's pointer and index fingers were different lengths, unlike the straight twin's, whose fingers were the same length. Judith and I had spent the whole day at Pride checking out women's hands as a result of that study. Kat would have fallen in the definitely gay category based solely on this characteristic. Interesting. I cut a quick glance in her direction.

"It's okay if you don't drink," she says, flashing that soft smile again. "I don't. And Emma won't be."

"Says you." Emma snorts for a third time.

"And Ms. Kelly." Snow White thumps the back of her sister's seat again.

"Who's Ms. Kelly?" I ask.

Emma huffs. "My dance instructor."

"She's super serious about shaking her booty." Elliot laughs and turns his car onto a dark gravel road.

I stare at the paved road behind us before looking back where we're headed. "Where are we going?" This is how so many scary movies start.

"To the top of Harmon Mountain." Emma pulls herself out the open window so her butt is sitting on the frame and she's hanging the top part of her body out into the night air. She throws her arms up in the air and howls. Isn't this the way people get tossed from car windows and the zombies appear to drag them into the night and hack them apart with their blunted teeth?

But nobody else seems worried and Elliot does slow the car down a little.

Kat laughs and rolls down her window, but only sticks her head out of the car, howling from the safety of her seat. I take a video for my story and add a few stickers describing the situation. I hit send and hope Judith is still looking at my feed.

"There's no reception here, city girl," Emma yells from outside the window. "Come howl with us."

So much for my plan to livestream my excellent new Judith-free life. But also, so much for any of my plans as I'd seen them earlier in the year. I wasn't driving. And maybe a little liquid courage could help me actually talk to people that weren't horse people.

"Um, Elliot?"

"Yeah?" He turns around to look at me.

"Tonight, I drink."

"Thatta girl." He hands back a flask and I take a swig of some sort of lemony burn before rolling down my own window. I stick my head into the night air, letting the wind blow my hair around, but I can't bring myself to howl. That's a step further down this Harmon path than I'm willing to take just yet.

But I am going to push Judith as far from my mind as possible tonight and try to roll with the flow. Maybe Harmon will surprise me.

Maybe, in this car, with these people, it already has.

KAT

The new girl, Piper, seems like she's down to party and between her, Elliot, and Emma cocking her hip at Jordan McMasters, my night is going to be busy keeping everyone from doing anything stupid. There may be no reception on the drive to the top but we all have five bars now and any blackmail-worthy crap will be public knowledge before dawn.

"Hey, Kat."

I turn. "Oh, hey, Delaney." She's holding hands with Antonio and looks adorable.

"Who's that girl with Elliot? Is she his girlfriend?"

Before I can answer, the pair in question, followed by Emma and Jordan, walk over.

"Selfie." Piper jumps in front and sticks her phone out. Her arms have incredible reach but only half of us show up on her screen. "Gather in." She reaches out her other arm and pulls me close to her side while the rest of the group crowd in. It's a bizarre thing but where her hand brushes the little bit of skin between the top of my jeans and my crop top, my skin glows hot. I try to pull away. I try to breathe through whatever this is.

"No, stay." She smiles at me and presses her fingers against my flesh.

I don't understand exactly what is happening but my knees threaten to buckle.

She snaps the picture and lets go and I practically fall over.

"Whoa." Elliot grabs me. "You're supposed to drive us."

"I'm fine." I shake off the wooziness. I hope I'm not getting sick.

"We're waiting for you to introduce us to your girl-friend." Delaney is all smiles as she stares at Elliot.

"What?" Elliot's face is a ball of confusion.

"Hi." Delaney holds out her hand to Piper. "I'm Del-aney."

Piper snaps her attention back to us. "Wait, what? Did you say boyfriend?"

Delaney nods. Antonio smiles.

Piper takes a fast step away from Elliot. "Whoa. Not sure where you got that. He's not my boyfriend. I'm queer. Not into dudes."

The whole group takes their own step back, kind of like they've been slapped.

"What?" Emma's mouth drops open. She looks at me, looks at Piper, looks back at me, like she's waiting for me to react.

But I'm having a hard time looking at anyone, because my heart ratchets up a notch and my body goes sort of weird and weak and my mouth goes super, super, super dry. The flu. I must be getting the flu.

Jordan McMasters breaks the spell. "Ah snap, dude. You got played." He pushes Elliot's shoulder, then flings his arm over my sister's shoulder. She doesn't move away.

Piper glares at Emma and her friends. "It is the twenty-first century you know." She raises her hands up from her hips.

Elliot throws back his head and laughs really loud before he reaches over and pulls Piper into a huge hug. "Oh my god, I love you. Please, if you're not going to be Kat's best, bestest friend for the summer, be mine."

She stands kind of straight-armed in his hug, her face caught between anger and panic.

I need to say something, do something, but I am frozen

in place. If I move, my knees might wobble out from under me. What in the actual hell is happening? An interior voice laughs inside my head. *Guess what? This horse girl likes girls. What exactly are you going to do for yourself this summer?*

Elliot walks Piper away from me, toward a group of seniors. He passes her his flask and Piper tilts it up. I count five full seconds that it stays at her lips. My stupor lifts. My rational brain clicks back into place. The girl is going to get hammered and her grandmother is my boss. My legs need to move, my breath needs to chill, and whatever this squirmy feeling I have when I look at her needs to calm the hell down. This is business.

Elliot turns back. "Are you coming with us, or what?"

I look in the direction Emma disappeared. Jordan already has a possessive hand on the small of her back and is passing her a red Solo cup.

I shake my head and point toward the group of juniors they've landed with. My sister does not need to end up a bonfire night story and it seems like Piper can handle herself. And if she can't, Elliot will take care of her.

Be honest, girlfriend. Aren't you worried about ending up your own bonfire night story if you follow Piper around? Maybe brain, maybe. But for now, I'm going to focus on Emma.

* * *

Hours later, after I've found my missing sister—somehow, she snuck off for a full fifteen minutes before I located her sprawled with Jordan in the back of Waverley Bach's pickup truck—driven everyone home, and parked Elliot's SUV safely in our driveway, I open up my laptop and google Piper Kitts. Of course, there's tons of horse stuff. Apparently, she's the shit up in New England and has image after image holding trophies and ribbons and looking elegantly badass in her white breeches and dark jacket and helmet. Her social is private though. My finger hovers over the follow button. What the hell. I push it and wait a few minutes to see if she follows me back.

"Are you awake?" Emma stands in my doorway.

"Obviously."

She flops herself next to me on the bed and looks at my phone. "Ah. Friending the new girl, huh?"

"It's no big deal. I'm her driving instructor, and her grandmother did pay to fix our van."

"It was pretty cool how she owned up to being queer like that. Way different than Elliot."

And me, I think. But how can you own up to something you have no physical evidence of? My brain voice chuckles from the rear of my head. *Girl, think about those wobbly legs when Piper made that pronouncement.*

Emma reaches out to scroll through Piper's pics but I

pull my phone away and switch over to my web browser before turning it toward her again. "Look. I found the website for that dance place in Greenville you talked about once."

"Dazzle Dance Pros? What about it?"

"Well, their formal auditions are over but the studio will arrange a private one for you."

"And?"

"I could drive you."

"Dad won't go for it."

"He might. We talked." I don't mention that he said he didn't have the money. "Just go try out. Please? For me? I'll take you. A fun sister outing. We can go get pho after at the noodle place. Maybe when you get in, meet the girls, see how cool it is, you'll find out it's the very best fit for you. You know . . ." My brain kicks in. "Mom will never let you move to Texas, but she might pay for fancy dance lessons if you get in. We just have to find the right moment to ask."

Emma considers. "Charnese from Ms. Kelly's got in there last year. It's a long drive."

I push her with my toe. "I don't care about that. I just want you to be happy."

Emma nods.

"And not have Jordan McMasters's baby while still in high school."

She flips me the bird before leaving to go back to her room. "He's hot. I like him." She pauses. "And he has a truck."

I flip her the bird back.

When she closes my door, I reach for my phone one last time.

No new followers.

chapter seven

PIPER

Sunlight streams in through the large plate glass windows, burning the sockets of my eyes. Last night comes back to me in flashes and blurs and I want to pummel myself for my stupidity. Drinking and my body, not such a great combination.

I roll over and stare into two sets of beady brown eyes, then two ridiculous pink tongues.

"Jacque, Jill, get off." But I don't really mean it and pull the dogs in close for a snuggle. I don't remember bringing them in here when I went to bed, which means MaMolly has probably already checked on me. I hope she didn't figure out I'd been drinking. She wouldn't be a fan.

I grab my phone from the bedside table and see a text

from Sasha with burning questions about the red-lipped hottie in my photos and one from my dad asking me to call home to say hi.

Hottie, huh?

I open up my phone and look at the ridiculous pictures I'd taken last night. It looked like I was having an absolute blast. Stupid cheesy grins. Cheek kissing. Cup raising. There's even a video of me and that Elliot guy doing some sort of dance with fiery sticks. Good. Let Judith think I have an actual life.

There are friend requests, too. Apparently, I made an impression on the locals and now everybody wants to be up in my DMs. The one I'm curious about is Kat. I click on her profile, not private, and scroll through. Mostly photos of her and her siblings. Her sister, Emma, at dance things. Some of her and Elliot by an awesome-looking pool. I zoom in. She's wearing a red bikini, and though she's not muscular like her sister, she's made up of long, clean lines. Kind of like a young Thoroughbred off the track. I like her haircut and how her face is angular and kind of androgynous. She doesn't seem to have much of a social life, at least not one she posts, and no clue to any sort of gayness besides her hands, but I follow her back anyway. At least her photos are good.

Then I follow Elliot and a couple of his friends.

When I'm done, I decide to call my parents.

"Hello." My mom picks up on the first ring, which has to count for something since I know she can see it's me who's calling. Maybe she's resigned herself to Piper Kitts— Professional Equestrian.

"Hey, Mom."

"Hello, Piper."

"Mom." Might as well try again. "I know you wish I had stayed home for the summer, but I swear it's going to be awesome."

She sighs. "There was really no stopping you. Thank your father, he's the one who strong-armed me into the yes. And there's no doubt your grandmother is thrilled to get her calf-leather competition gloves on you for a couple of months."

I half laugh. "It's going to be good. You'll be happy to know that MaMolly is insistent I learn how to drive."

A sliver of sunlight peeks through my mom's voice. "Your father told me after she conferred with him on the subject. Your grandmother certainly likes to keep things interesting." She pauses. "You'll do fine." Then she delivers a bit of sports psychology. "Picture yourself driving well. Imagine yourself smoothly navigating in and out of traffic like you navigate a perfect trot to canter transition. You'll be happy to have the freedom."

"Right." The problem is my mind often goes to fiery wrecks and tangled iron. I'd been ten years old when a car in front of us had crashed into an eighteen-wheeler creating a chain reaction on the turnpike. We'd been lucky. Only a messed-up car and bruised chests. But then? Stuck on the freeway for hours. I'd watched as emergency crews untangled the mess of cars and people in front of us. I'd watched as ambulances arrived and departed. Eventually the tow truck came for us. I'd been terrified to ride in cars for at least six months after, and even though that fear disappeared, the idea that somebody else could randomly hit you had gotten stuck in my of-legal-age-to-drive brain and messed with my driving mojo.

"Here, say hi to your father."

Dad gets on the line. "Hi, Mighty. Your mother's right, you know. Driving is a mental game. You drive a car, I'll bet your Olympic dreams will come true."

"Thanks, Dad." I know he's right, about the getting past it part, maybe not the Olympics, but it's been so easy not driving. The dogs jump off the bed and trot toward my closed door. "I love you, but I need to get up. Jacque and Jill need to go out."

"Give those naughty rascals a squeeze from me. And a hug to my mother-in-law."

"You got it." I push the off button and roll from the

bed, stuffing my feet into slippers before heading to the kitchen to find my grandmother.

"Ah, look who's up." The dogs beeline past where MaMolly sits reading the news on her iPad at the kitchen island to the doggy door in the pantry. The sound of their barks follows. She glances at the window. "Beatriz is here. She's the one who made the connection for you to train this summer." I follow my grandmother's glance and see a young woman climbing out of a truck and greeting the dogs. She's in breeches and her own dog, some sort of hound cross, clambers out to join the terriers in a game of chase and tumble. She disappears into the barn.

"Who's she?"

"My barn manager. She's from near Charlotte, but spent time riding in Germany as a teenager. Very disciplined and excellent horsewoman. I'm lucky to have her take care of my crew on a part-time basis. She works for Schober full-time."

Dilara Schober is the retired Olympic dressage rider who'd moved to this area to raise, import, and train Hanoverians for other people. She's agreed to take me on as a working student for the summer. In exchange for mucking stalls, cleaning tack, and general grunt work, I get to exercise her horses, and hopefully get a word of instruction from her now and then.

"How was your night?" MaMolly holds out her coffee cup for me to refill.

I leave out my debauchery. "It was pretty fun, I guess."

"Isn't Kat a lovely young woman?"

Something about her voice makes me glance sideways at my grandmother. The way she said it almost sounded as if she was trying to hook me up. But she's not looking at me, just sips the coffee I hand back to her and scrolls through the news.

"Yeah, I guess. I hung out more with her cousin, Elliot."

She nods. "Son of the pool impresario. Nice family. A little gauche, but they're honest."

This makes me laugh because *gauche* is a perfect word to describe Sir Elliot, as I'd taken to calling him as the night had progressed. Though he's ridiculously in the closet—he'd made that clear when he started interrogating me about how I'd come out and how he wasn't sure he could ever just blurt it out like I had—hanging out with him might make my summer a tiny bit more interesting. And he looks good in photos for my plan to make-Judith-hopefully-jealous-that-I'm-not-still-pining-for-her.

I grab a protein bar and trade in my slippers for the muck boots by the back door. One of the best things about being at MaMolly's is being able to go out to the barn in my pajamas. "I'll be back, going to see about my training schedule."

She waves me out the door.

Beatriz is already knee deep in shavings. She's young, but not high school young, with a classic equestrian vibe. She also has a tiny stud in her nose and a Pegasus tattoo behind her ear, which makes me think she might be more interesting than your average horse girl. Maybe she'll turn out to be my Southern Sasha. The dogs bark my arrival.

"Hello there," I say.

She looks up from where she's shoveling into the big wheelbarrow. "Ah. Hello. Molly's granddaughter?"

"Piper."

"Beatriz."

Jester sticks his nose out over the yoke of his stall door and bumps my arm for attention. I absently reach out to stroke the side of his big jowl.

She moves the wheelbarrow into the hall.

"I can help," I say.

"Great. Start by turning Jester and Colonel out into the smaller field. I already gave them their supplements. Turn the other three out into the big front field for today."

I do as she says and halter each horse, leading them to their daytime accommodations. It's a good life they have here with big green fields and sunshine.

Back in the barn, I grab a second rake and get to work.

"I need this job, you know." Beatriz arches a skinny dark brow at me.

"I, um, I'm not trying to take your job." Might as well spit it out. "I'm trying to suck up to you in hopes you can tell me all the secrets of working with Dilara Schober."

She relaxes. "Ah. I see. Basically, all you need to know is show up on time, even a few minutes early, work until you're sore, then stay a few minutes late. And do everything she says. If you can manage that, you'll be fine."

Sounds like a typical trainer. "Do you think maybe I could catch a ride to the farm with you sometimes?"

"Why? Your grandmother has that truck. It's out of my way to bring you back here."

I gulp. "Yeah, of course. The truck." MaMolly's Ford F-250 looms large from its parking spot, mocking me. "But I don't have my license yet."

"Really? I thought you were seventeen or eighteen. I made sure I had license in hand on my sixteenth birthday."

Back home, none of my friends gave me grief about not driving. In fact, I had other friends who'd put it off also. Obviously, things were different here. I lean against the stall wall. "I'm seventeen. Still, no license. But soon."

"I'll see how I can help till you get yours. But it's not a given, okay? Dilara keeps me late some nights. You're going to have to tackle that beasty." She points the pitch-fork at the truck.

I look at the giant slab of steel. One good thing about my grandmother's busy schedule.

She'll never know if I spend my summer hailing Ubers instead of driving that monster.

KAT

In the morning, I drive Elliot's car over to his house. Uncle Randall opens the door. "Kitty Kat! How was your first bonfire?"

"Good." I don't want to tell him how out of place I'd felt as one of the few sober people. Or how awkward it was to not be hooking up or doing any of the things that seemed to come so naturally to other people, including my little sister.

"Elliot's still asleep. But if you take him one of those sausage biscuits and a cup of coffee, I bet he'll be glad to see you."

I take a detour into the kitchen, then head up the stairs.

"What's up, Sir Elliot?" Piper had pretty much nailed it with that nickname.

He groans and cracks one eye open. His sparkling blue eyes look like dirty pool water.

"Jesus. H. Christ. On. A. Waffle. How hungover are you?"

"Too much."

He'd been drunk when I dropped him off, but not enough to justify the droop sitting in front of me now.

"I invited all those football jocks and their dates over to swim. We kept going."

"And . . ." These were the moments when my Elliot had game.

He grins, then grimaces and grabs at the sides of his head. "Zander Elloway felt sorry for me."

"You did not."

"I did. Thank God school is over and we're graduating. I'm sure he'd kick my ass in retaliation even though he was the one unzipping his own damn pants."

"Elliot . . ." But there's nothing really to say. He is who he is and so far, he'd managed to stay alive.

"Sorry I deserted you last night. Piper's cool though."

I plop next to him on the bed and take a bite of biscuit. "I guess."

"Aren't you the slightest bit curious?" He rolls over and grabs his phone.

I'd already looked, of course, after she'd accepted my friend request earlier this morning.

"Who do you think this girl is?" He points to a picture of the girl @judith_judith that's tagged in like all of Piper's pictures for the past year and a half.

"I don't know." But of course, I'd made an assumption after I'd spent an hour following every mention until I'd patched together my own version of Piper's story. The Judith girl was her girlfriend, but now it looks like she's with this guy, @bradladmad. Maybe this has something to do with why Piper is here for the summer. She obviously has plenty of horses to ride back in New England based on my internet stalking.

"They're kind of hot together." He scrolls up on the feed again. "But then you look hot with her, too. Hotter." It's the selfie she took when we pulled up in front of Molly Malone's house. There's another one from later in the night when she slung her arm over my shoulder and pressed her cheek against mine. I don't think I look hot. I look like a deer caught in the headlights. Which is how I'd felt in that moment because of the whole buckling-knees-when-she-was-near thing.

I grunt in response

He throws his leg across my leg. "Too bad she didn't go along with Delaney's assumption. Would have made Vlada happy."

I don't say anything for a minute. "Elliot, your parents love you."

"Piper. I'm not their kid. Not by blood. For now, they love me because they think I'm popular and straight and might one day take over the pool business. I'm an adoption success. But once they find out I'm gay, all bets are off. Dad makes jokes all the damn time about people he finds 'light in the loafers.' When I come out, I guarantee our relationship is toast."

Though I don't think Uncle Randall is as black-and-white as Elliot believes, I do get the whole thing about relationships changing when new truths are revealed. It's maybe why I haven't been in a hurry to answer questions about my own sexuality. The reality is, even if there's no one for me in Harmon, there are other towns around, there are internet relationships. I could find someone to explore with even if they weren't *the* one. But I'm happy. Me, Dad, the twins, even Emma, have settled into a Mom-free routine that works and I don't want to rock the boat. Not even with Elliot, who would be the logical one to tell, but he'd want to make a huge deal about it.

"I guess," I say. Then I probe a little about Piper. "So, did she come to your after-party?" I'd dropped her off at her grandmother's but it doesn't mean she didn't find a way back over.

"Nah. But I invited her to come swimming next time I have people over."

I wonder what she'd look like in a bathing suit.

He stares at me. "Should I invite her today?"

"What?! No."

A smug smile plays around the corners of his mouth. "You like her."

"I do not. God, why do you always want me to be a lesbian?"

His smile disappears. "Forget it. I was only trying to help."

"Help yourself."

The room grows silent and I want to say something to lighten the mood but I've ruined it. Which isn't fair. People should be able to come out when they're good and ready. I've never pushed him to tell anybody else and he'd chosen to tell me and Emma on his terms.

"I need to get up and take a shower. Dad's taking me fishing later today before the big ceremony."

It's my cue. "Yeah, sure. No problem." I hesitate. "I didn't mean anything . . ."

"I got it. You don't have to explain."

My phone buzzes. Dad's outside ready to take me to pick up Delilah from the mechanic's. "Are you sure?"

"We're fine, Kat. I'm just trying to help."

Maybe it's time to find out if Elliot knows more about my needs than I do. Maybe it's time to take a leap. Because, there's a girl. A not-from-here girl. A girl who is legitimately out of the closet. A girl who is leaving in a couple of months. My knees get a little wobbly again.

The brain voice speaks up. *Just do it. Send her a message. You're supposed to teach her to drive. Maybe she'll teach you a few things. Make a move, chickenshit.*

My brain voice takes no prisoners in its motivational style.

But I'm able to type a DM as I walk down the stairs and out the front door.

Hope you're not as hungover as Elliot. Also, those pics were cute. Ready for me to come get you for that driving lesson?

It takes a couple of seconds but she responds pretty quickly. No and no.

Whoa. How am I supposed to take that? Disappointment hurtles down through my stomach into my legs and the wobble disappears.

Another message comes through. Sorry. What I should have said was I can't drive today, but tomorrow will work. And yeah, already got a text from a friend about those pics wanting to know who you are. Winky face emoji. She said you were cute.

And . . . the wobble is back.

I trip going down the front steps and manage to grab the railing before I face plant in front of my dad and the twins. But my phone goes flying.

My inner voice laughs. *If the screen's not broken,*

you are ready for this.

I shut the voice up. Bargains don't work that way. I reach for my phone.

Why not? Let's see. Broken or not broken.

The last thing I actually want is a broken phone screen but maybe I'm praying for it a little.

Not broken. My brain voice is triumphant.

But I'm still not sure I'm ready. And tomorrow? That's fast.

chapter eight
PIPER

The following morning, MaMolly invites me to go with her to Spartanburg for a gourmet grocery run and shopping excursion.

"I can't. That girl, Kat, is coming to pick me up for a driving lesson."

A waft of Shalimar settles around me as I get a huge hug. "You're going to be fine. Tell her I said thank you."

"Will do." I look at Kat's picture again. She's totally freaked out in the one when I was squeezing her by the bonfire. Probably panicked that the queer girl was touching her. But maybe I'm wrong. Maybe there's a part of me that hopes I'm wrong.

I text Sasha.

How's it going?

She texts back within a few seconds.

At the barn. Looks like you're having fun down there.

Please, it's just for Judith's benefit. These people are kind of behind the times. You would have thought I was toxic when I told them I was queer. I didn't realize that could even happen anymore.

You're not in Massachusetts anymore, butterfly.

Have you seen Judith?

Funny you should ask. I ran into her last night at Bedford Farms.

With Brad, of course.

Actually not. She was with some friends from school. I asked about her booooooyfriend and she shrugged. She looked kind of sad.

Really!? Do you think they broke up?

My heart, which had been relatively calm for the last twenty-four hours, and maybe starting to think about the possibility of moving on to no-relationship, serious equestrian mode, starts a little tap dance.

What I know is that girl broke your heart bad and you need to take this breather. There's always another girl.

Easy for you to say. But speaking of, Snow White chick in the pictures is coming over this afternoon.

Get it, P. Later daze.

It had been a good thing for me when Sasha let me go.

She'd turned into a player at college and who needs that? I click over to Judith's account and see the pic she'd put up from getting ice cream with her friends from her school. It's a group shot with perfectly lined up ice cream cones. The girl, on the end, Tara, or something, I remember meeting her once, has ice cream on her nose and is falling off the end of the bench and everyone else is laughing. It's cute. But my lock screen photo is cuter. I message her. **Did you get cinnamon again?**

She messages me right back. You know that's my favorite flavor.

I can't help it. **Seems like your favorite flavor changed.** But I don't send it. Bitter snark will not get her back. Instead I go for friendly and available to listen. **Sasha said she saw you and you seemed kind of down. I'm here if you ever want to talk about anything. I am your friend.**

Yeah, okay. Maybe. Thanks. And a heart emoji. It's been at least two months since she sent me a heart emoji. Another message comes through. So. You're having fun?

Breathe, Piper. **Yeah. Total blast. Met these awesome sisters and they took me to this party on top of a mountain. This summer is shaping up to be incredible.** Maybe it's a bit of overkill, but I can't let her see I'm still clinging.

I'm really happy for you.

No. I don't want her to be happy. I want her to be

miserable that I'm having fun without her. But, at least we're talking. Kind of.

Thanks. FaceTime me sometime if you're bored.

She sends back a smiley face and I know our conversation is over. But still, my heart feels kind of hopeful.

The doorbell rings later that day. MaMolly is out for her errands and I've been lying in my bed reading the latest Shanna Beasley novel, the dogs curled at my feet. They tear off the bed and madly scramble down the stairs toward the front door, barking the whole way. My insides freeze up. I'm so not ready for this driving thing.

Snow White Kat stands at the front door in a pair of short jean shorts, a white tank top, and aqua blue flip-flops that match her nail polish. I make a mental note to snap a selfie before we leave. Kat looks supercute and now that Judith is sending me heart emojis again, a few photos might be excellent low-level revenge for my broken heart.

"You ready?" Kat smiles like this is the most exciting thing to happen all year. The genuine quality of her smile makes a second, equally positive, impression on me.

But driving? I don't care how cute my driver is. "I'm not ready. Can we do it tomorrow?"

Kat's expression changes from perky to worried. "I can't. I clean the salon on Sundays and my brothers have a game and it's Elliot's graduation party in the afternoon."

"We'll need to wait until next week then." I'm serious, not serious. Besides, she gets cuter when her eyes go wide, like she needs to solve the problem of me.

"That won't work." She fidgets with her keys. "Your grandmother said she wanted me to start teaching you as soon as possible. She's counting on me. I'm to report back."

I shrug, enjoying the way my reaction is affecting her. "Report it went fine and that I'm a natural. We don't really have to do this. We can pretend and blow it off."

"I can't lie to Mrs. Malone. She's employed me to do this." Then Kat stares at me in a new way, like she's reading me. "You're scared."

I jam my hands into my back pockets and stand up straighter. "I'm not scared."

She doesn't break her look, so I look back harder and she looks away. Victory.

Or so I think.

Snow White Kat smiles as she stares at the pastures. The corners of her light brown eyes crinkle, solidifying the kindness living there, and she re-faces me, her expression determined. "I promise we won't go on the roads today. We'll start at the abandoned textile factory, in the parking lot. It's always empty except for a few carpool cars parked there. No way for you to get hurt or screw up."

"You really are going to make me do this?"

She nods.

"You're starting to annoy me."

Kat looks down at her neatly manicured nails for several long seconds, long enough I think I've offended her and she'll let me out of this, but then she looks me dead in the eyes again.

"I'm not leaving this house without you. Might as well grab whatever you need and come on. If you're good . . ." She rubs her sneaker against the concrete and tilts her head in a way that seems almost like flirting, "I'll take you for ice cream after."

It's the perfect sabotage for Judith. An ice cream photo for an ice cream photo. As much as I don't want to drive, the temptation for a misleading visual opportunity breaks my stalemate.

"Okay. The ice cream is a plus." Then I get real. "But I am seriously scared. You promise there won't be other cars where we're going?"

Kat fidgets with her keys and lifts a shoulder in a shy way. "I promise. Besides, you don't need to worry. I'll go easy on you." Then her cheeks flush red. Like she's the one who's freaking out.

KAT

"What do you do to get around in Massachusetts if you can't drive?" I glance sideways as I ask the question. The little muscle where Piper's jaws connect flinch.

"Would you watch the road, please?"

Wow. Not only is she a nondriver but she's a nervous passenger, too. "I'm a good driver. You don't have to worry."

"I'm not used to being in the front seat."

I know Mrs. Malone is wealthy, but chauffeur wealthy? "Do your parents have, like, a limo or something?"

Piper makes a sound that's almost a laugh. I get that good joke feeling. The one where I make the twins howl over something I've said and there's nothing I want more than to find the next hilarious thing to say.

"There are these things near big cities called Ubers and Lyfts. I open the app and like magic, my driver appears. You don't ride in the front seat with them. Or I don't, anyway."

I've read a lot about both Uber and Lyft in my quest for entrepreneurial knowledge but our area of the world is sorely lacking them. We have maybe two taxis and the county transportation van and that's it. "Yeah, your app's going to come up with a big empty if you open it here."

"Seriously?" Her voice quavers.

"Seriously. I mean, maybe you'll find an occasional driver who's had to drop someone off here from the airport or something, but it's definitely not a thing like it is in bigger places." I put on my blinker and turn onto the factory road. I glance over again and this time I notice she's biting at her cuticles and her hand has a slight shake.

"Are you shaking?"

"No, I'm not shaking." She practically yells it at me.

"You're totally shaking." This time I stop the van in the empty road to the abandoned factory lot. I pivot to look at her. "Piper. I've been driving since I was a freshman in high school. I'm good at it and I'm a good teacher. I helped Elliot. I'm helping Emma. You ride horses, right?"

"Yes." She has her chin on her hand and is pointedly staring out the window away from me.

I want to make her laugh again. I want her to look at me. My brain voice starts to say something but we made a deal before we left home. It's not permitted to talk while I give driving lessons.

"Driving a car is much easier. They're not sentient beings."

"You sound like my dad."

"You're not the first person to tell me that. I mean, not like your dad, of course. But I am good at dad jokes." I grin.

She laughs. Success. My belly gets swooshy and warm thinking I lightened the mood, made her happy, caused that smile that shows her deep dimples and makes her shoulders loosen.

She takes a deep breath. "It's not the same. Besides, even if you teach me how to drive a little, I'm never going to feel comfortable zipping around on these curvy roads as fast as people drive here. Why does it matter if I drive or not?"

To me it doesn't really matter if she does or not. But I do know that I need to get this girl behind the wheel of my van so I can mentally deduct my first week's two hundred and eighty-four dollars from the mechanic's bill her grandmother has paid. Driving does matter in my life.

I reach over and put my hand on her arm. Which turns

out to be a huge mistake because the words of wisdom disappear from where they'd been hovering on the tip of my tongue. It was a move I would have done with Emma, my brothers, Elliot, nothing I gave a second thought to. Except for the minute my fingers touched her arm—her slightly tan, muscled, obviously-lifting-bales-of-hay-strong arm—my skin sizzled and I lost my train of thought.

I squeak, "You got this," but I can't even look at her as I drive the rest of the way to the lot. How the hell am I going to teach her to drive now if I can't even control the thoughts inside my own head?

"Oh, this might be okay."

I snap out of my head chatter to see what she's referring to. The parking lot is empty as I'd promised. Deep breaths, Kat, work mode, Kat, you have a job to do and a sister to save from boredom, Kat.

"There's no guardrail." Piper's voice wavers.

"What?"

She points to the very far side of the lot. Two football fields, maybe two and a half away from where I've parked, the lot falls off and there's a steep bank.

"Delilah has just been revived from the dead. I will not let you re-kill her."

"Delilah?"

I wave my hand around the interior. "My lovely

minivan. Your horse has a name, doesn't it?"

This earns me dimples. And bumblebees. The ones Emma says mean you have a crush. There are bumblebees inside me fanning their wings. This means . . .

Piper interrupts my mental beekeeping. "All horses have names."

I manage a comeback. "So do cars. Well, the ones with good owners anyway."

Piper looks at the bank again. The bees stop fanning as my clever comeback doesn't elicit a smile.

It's obvious Piper feels no burn on her own skin. I've smiled so big and looked so straight into her eyes and there's been nothing even remotely flirtatious in return. I think about the girl I've seen in her photos. Maybe they're still dating and the timeline I've pieced together is wrong. Maybe I'm just not doing it right? I clear my throat.

"No time like the present to work on this driving thing." I point to the gearshift. "P is for Park, R is for Reverse, N is for Neutral . . ."

She cuts me off. "I might not be able to drive yet, but I'm not clueless. I did have to get my permit."

Ouch. The bees leave the hive.

Business. This is strictly business.

chapter nine
PIPER

Kat walks me through the finer points of her van and I'm a bitch. I know it doesn't line up with the cute, friendly photos I plan on taking later, but my fear is getting the best of me. Somehow, being awful keeps the mental disasters flashing in my head on mute. Unfortunately, it doesn't stop her from insisting I try to drive.

"Switch places with me."

My body freezes and I swear every muscle in my hand goes limp and I cannot even begin to open the door. Even I realize it's overkill. I do actually want to be able to drive one day.

"You're going to be fine. I promise." Her accent is not super Southern, like some of the kids I met the other night, but when she's trying to be soothing, it deepens. And kind of works on my nerves in a good way. I open the passenger door.

We pass each other at the rear of the van and she jumps sideways so we don't bump into each other. Note to self, be nicer.

I buckle myself into the driver's seat and wipe my hands on my jeans. I can do this. I think about my dad's words, my mom's words, MaMolly's words. It's just a car. Millions of people do this every single day. I can do this, too.

Kat closes her door and turns in my direction. "Okay, before we do anything, tell me, if I were taking a riding lesson from you and I was as nervous as you are right now, what would you say?"

She's got the Southern soothe voice going and my throat muscles relax enough to form words. "I'd tell you to breathe and that we could go as slow as you needed."

"Okay," she says. "Breathe."

I do.

"Now hands on the steering wheel."

I do that, too.

"Okay. I want you to practice touching the brake and the gas pedals. Brake is on the left, gas is on the right. Press the gas."

I do.

"Press the brake."

I move my foot and press the brake pedal.

"Great," she says. "Still breathing?"

I exaggerate my breath in answer. I might even smile.

"Look at your hands on the steering wheel. Some people say at ten and two as if it were a clock. But that's wrong. Keep your hands at nine and three because of airbags."

I shift my hands.

"Perfect. Okay. I'm going to have you start the van now."

I feel nauseous. "Can't do it. Nope."

"Breathe. You've got this. Delilah is practically indestructible. We are in a big, flat, open parking lot with nothing to hit."

"But a ginormous mountain to hurtle down."

"No wonder you and Elliot hit it off. You're both drama queens. That side of the lot is so far away I have to squint to see it. All you're going to do is turn on the engine. Is your foot still on the brake?"

I whimper and nod and give in to her bold and bossy teacher side.

"Turn the key."

My hand physically trembles as I grip the hard plastic, sending the charms on her key ring into a spasm. The muscle in my jaw flinches.

"Turn the key."

"I heard you the first time." Shit. Bitchy again. "Sorry. Okay." I take a gulp of air and turn the key. The engine thrums to life and we don't move. I take another deep breath.

"See," she says. "Easy peasy. Now turn it off."

"What?"

"Yep. We're going to do that a few more times until you're comfortable turning it on. Then maybe we'll see about rolling."

I glance at Kat. She's smiling to herself in a self-satisfied kind of way. She'd make a good horse trainer. All calm and pragmatic when faced with a basket case of self-doubt and fear. I like this side of her. MaMolly may have been right to think that we'd hit it off. As friends.

After about the sixth time of turning Delilah on, then off, I groan. "Okay, this is boring. Is it time for ice cream yet?"

"I think you're ready to put it into drive. We're going to roll. Just a little way."

I knew she wouldn't let me off so easy. But I realize something. I actually trust her not to push me too far.

"Okay." My knuckles turn white where they wrap the steering wheel. I make myself ease up. Being tense won't help.

"Turn her on."

I release one hand and start the van. Then back to the steering wheel.

"Keep your foot on the brake. Shift down to Drive." I do. But I also hold my breath. Nothing happens. I let it out.

"Nine and three," Kat says. "Now, very slowly, move your foot from the brake to the gas and give it a slow, easy push."

It's like my foot is traveling through the La Brea Tar Pits, but then I land hard on the gas pedal. The van lurches forward. The girliest of all squeals that a girl ever did squeal comes out of my mouth.

Kat snorts from the passenger seat but immediately clamps it down.

Fair enough, I deserved that.

"A little easier this time." She's all soft syllables and elongated vowels. "You startled yourself, that's all. It takes practice. Like going over jumps or whatever."

"I ride dressage."

"Well, dressage this van halfway across the lot, then ease off the gas and onto the brake pedal."

"That makes zero sense." But after my involuntary squeal I'm determined to succeed. I ease carefully onto the gas this time and we roll. Super slow. But I am rolling.

When I get to the next row of parking lines, I ease back onto the brake and stop without giving Kat whiplash.

"You drove." She smiles.

"I drove." I hold up my hand for a high five. She quickly sticks her hand under her leg like she's afraid to touch me. Wow. Okay. Nice but weird. I decide to ignore it. The girl did just get me to roll like a toddler across this parking lot. "Again?"

She nods with way more vigor than necessary. Maybe my driving is scaring her?

"We don't have to, if you've changed your mind about teaching me."

She's as forceful in her reply as her nodding. "No! Keep driving."

I roll some more and manage a few endless circles to the right and then a circle to the left. I pretend I'm doing a training level USDF test. Lots of twenty meter circles with a few halts at X. Or, you know, trying to get as straight as I can in between parking lines. Before I realize it, forty minutes has gone by.

"You did great today. Still want some ice cream?"

I put the van in park. "That'd be great. Hey, would you take my photo? I want to send it to my parents."

"Sure." She pulls out her phone and I flash my biggest cheesiest grin. I give her my number and she texts it to me.

When we cross behind the van, I stop her. "Let's take another with my phone."

"Oh." She hesitates.

"Do I smell bad or something?"

Her cheeks fill with color. Even her neck has turned red and kind of splotchy. "No, it's not that. It's . . ."

"The gay thing? Please, I'm not going to bite you. It doesn't work like that." I guess I was wrong about her flirting.

I throw my arm over her shoulder and snap a fast selfie. A quick glance tells me it's not the most convincing photo ever. But it will have to do for now.

KAT

How *does* it work? That's what I want to ask her. But she's moving her fingers fast on her phone and I have to pay attention to the road in front of me. Now that I've had this golden epiphany about actually maybe moving forward in my quest to determine if these feelings about girls add up to me being legitimately queer, I want to figure out my next moves. But I don't want to ask Elliot and I don't want to mention it to Natascha at the salon because they'd be way too excited about it and I'd never have the time and space to breathe into it.

I go for small talk instead of actually asking.

"Is your horse here for the summer, too?"

She holds up a finger. "Hang on." She finishes whatever she's doing on her phone (I'd look later, of course) and answers me. "No. I always leased horses because my parents knew I was going to outgrow them as I grew in skill and size. My last lease ran out, we couldn't find another horse for me, then my trainer had a health issue come up, and my grandmother gave me a wicked opportunity. I'm going to ride horses for Dilara Schober while I'm here."

"Who?" Piper is obviously excited, but I've never heard that name before. I thought I knew everyone in Harmon, between its tiny size and the Tousled Orchid.

"Former Olympian? Horse trainer?"

I shake my head in the negative and turn into the Hey Y'all Creamery. It's packed with people from school. Including my sister, Delaney, Antonio, and Jordan. My insides go hot. Now that I have a bona fide crush—at least I think that's what my inner voice and trembling legs and bumblebee belly are telling me—how am I going to face my sister without her being able to tell something is up? Almost as though she hears me thinking, Emma looks up and waves.

"Is that your sister?"

"Yeah." I turn off the van and we get out.

"That guy's a couple of years older, huh?"

Jordan has his forearm plopped possessively on Emma's shoulder and is trying to grab her ice cream cone with his other hand. He totally grazes her boob in the process. Emma would kill me if I make a public scene about it—I'd heard, in no uncertain terms, if I ever pulled the same crap as I did the night of the bonfire when I'd split them up, she'd cancel me—so I have to grin and bear the moment until I can reason with her in private. But then again, a Jordan in her summer, if she's not stupid, would probably be fun for her.

"Hey y'all." Delaney smiles big at me, then does a funny nervous twitch in Piper's direction.

I'm too quick to explain. "Mrs. Malone asked me to give Piper driving lessons." Then I take a step away from Piper, my body instinctively wanting to show we're not together, but instantly hating myself for being so basic.

Antonio intervenes. "You can't drive?"

Jordan chuckles. "Whoa, that would suck. Nothing I love more than hauling ass down some gravel roads." He nudges my sister. "We should go drive around."

I put on my best mom voice. I have to at least try for protective. "She can't go drive around. She has dance rehearsal."

Emma swings her leg and connects with my shin.

"How about that ice cream?" Piper breaks the tension.

I rub my leg. "Yeah, okay." We skirt the picnic table and get in line behind some kids in T-ball uniforms. "Crap," I say.

"Your shin?" Piper laughs. "She had feelings for sure."

"Emma's old enough to make her own mistakes, but Jordan is so . . ."

"Dude bro?"

I grimace. "Exactly. But I totally forgot I have to go get my brothers from the ballpark in like twenty minutes. We're going to have to get our cones and go."

"Don't worry about it," Piper says. "You can go and I'll just call an Uber to get back to MaMolly's. You don't have to take me if you're in a rush."

"Go ahead, check your phone, and good luck with that."

"Right, habit, sorry. But seriously, I don't believe you." She opens the app as we get to the window.

The girl behind the counter interrupts. "Hey, y'all. What can I get you?"

"Moose Tracks on a sugar cone." Piper gives her order while frowning at her phone.

"Cinnamon in a cup, please."

"Did you say cinnamon?" Piper's staring at me now, not her phone.

"Yeah? It's my favorite."

She keeps staring, but her face changes to an expression I can't quite qualify and it's making me feel a bit squirmy.

"Is that bad?" I ask.

My question shakes her out of whatever momentary blip she'd been in. Then she laughs. "No, actually it's fantastic."

The girl hands us our ice cream and Piper lifts her

phone again for yet another photo of the two of us. "Make sure your ice cream is in the picture." I tilt my cup forward and smile. I look into her camera lens for all it's worth and try to look natural. Like I'm taking a photo with Emma.

"Perfect." She flashes her phone at me and I nod. It's a good picture. A best friends' kind of picture. Or a sisters' kind of picture. Or maybe, the start of something kind of picture.

She goes back to her rideshare app. "This, though, is not perfect. No Ubers, No Lyfts. Just like you said. I really am going to be screwed." She looks up. "But you."

"Me?"

"Yes. I can pay you. As my unofficial Uber driver. Don't you drive Elliot and his drunk friends around?"

"Well, yeah, sometimes." My brain clicks on. I can't charge her more when her grandmother is already paying me. But then running her to her horsey stuff was never part of the equation with her grandmother. And it's kind of a win-win situation. In more ways than cash. Because even if there are no mutual feelings, she's someone neutral I could talk to about my life and how exactly to get it started.

"So, we go then. Pick up your brothers. You take me home and I'll text you my schedule for the barn." She glances away. "Uh-oh. Or maybe I can help with the Emma situation."

I follow her gaze. My sister's following Jordan to his truck. Piper reaches out for my arm like I'd reached out for hers in the car, and when she touches me it's firm, authoritative. My knees threaten to give. My inner voice swoons.

"Go pick up your brothers without me." She runs toward Emma. "Hey, wait up. I need a favor. Can I get a ride? Kat has to go pick up your brothers."

I stand, my hand touching the spot where hers was. The electric current is back.

A voice behind me whispers, "Who's she?"

I turn.

Natascha must have stopped for ice cream on her way from the salon. And she's watching Piper with interest.

Little claws unspring from my skin. "She's nobody."

"Well, nobody is hot. And my guess is that she plays for team WLW."

"She's a horse girl. Mrs. Malone's granddaughter. They all seem a little gay."

"True, I guess." She purses her lips around the straw in her milkshake, then nudges me. "Maybe you can introduce me to Nobody? Since you're not interested, right?"

Then she winks and blows me a kiss before walking back to where Cassidy Phillips waits at a nearby picnic table.

chapter ten
PIPER

Genius that I am, I manage to get the bag of testosterone to drop Kat's little sister off first. But now I'm stuck in this monster truck, alone, with a cretin. A Southern one at that, which is fueling my stereotyped nightmares. Why did I have to go and get all "let me handle this" when Kat seemed nervous about Emma riding around with this guy. It's obvious they're already thinking about hooking up. I could be in Kat's van, meeting her brothers, laughing at dad jokes, and okay, maybe melting a bit at her pretty smile.

With that thought, I realize this is probably better. I don't need another relationship. I need to concentrate on my sport. I'm here for horses, not for a hookup. Assuming she'd even be into it, which I absolutely can't at this point.

"Do you know where to go?" I'd already given Jordan the address but he has us on some road I've never seen.

"Yeah. Don't worry. I mowed for your grandmother last summer."

"Oh." Everybody absolutely knows everybody in this town. It's so weird. My phone buzzes and I look, thinking it's going to be my mom, or Sasha, or maybe, Judith, but it's not.

Hey, having a graduation pool party tomorrow. You should totes come.

Totes? Who says totes anymore? And though it might be fun to go to Elliot's, I, unbelievably, already have plans. Yesterday afternoon, Beatriz had invited me to go with her to a friend's house and meet some of the other working students in the area and I'd said yes.

Can't. Plans. Then I add, Maybe we can hang out some other time. He is, at least, another fairy soul in the land of mortals.

I get a thumbs-up in response. Jordan takes a curve fast and I grab my armrest. I'm going to have to make small talk and keep his attention on me if I don't want him to give me a panic attack.

"So, you going to Elliot's party tomorrow?" I ask.

"Yeah. You?"

"Can't. Is it nice?" I gasp as he revs the car faster in the straight part of the road.

"What?"

I'm not sure if he's asking about my gasp or my question, so I try to play it fearless. "His pool?"

Jordan lays on the horn when we pass some dude on a tractor in a field. The dude throws up a hand as we blast past. I second-guess my decision to come hang out with MaMolly for the summer.

"Never paid much attention. I go for the bikinis." He screeches to a stop at the stop sign and I count to ten in my head to calm down but he interrupts me before I get to six. "You like girls, right? That's what you said."

Should I educate him on how women are not their bikinis? Probably wouldn't make a difference. "I like girls."

"Yeah, yeah. So, Emma. She's hot, right? Like tits up to here." He lifts a hand practically to his chin.

There's no way I'm analyzing a girl's body with dude bro here. Doesn't matter, he keeps talking like we're locker room buds.

"I'm going to hit that before the summer is over. I'm thinking she's probably not a virgin. Yeah, she's only a sophomore, but nobody's a virgin past freshman year."

So, yes, that was true for me, but I seriously doubt it's true for everyone. I want to call Kat and put this guy on speakerphone so she can crucify him. He keeps blabbering.

"She dances. Bet she's really flexible." Then he reaches over and slugs me in the shoulder. "Flexible girls, ami-right?"

I resist the urge to rub the sting from the spot where his knuckles landed. Won't give him the satisfaction.

"You think she's into me? I think she's into me."

Of course, he does. But sadly, I think he's right. At least the guy Judith fell for seemed decent.

"I don't think you can anchor that confidence just yet."

He turns to look at me as he's turning into MaMolly's long drive. "What's that mean?"

Maybe I can put some whoa in his go. "A girl like that needs flirting, small gestures, you know, you've got to be a nice guy before you can hit it. Make her want to be there with you. Consensus, you know? It's super possible she's still a virgin. And super possible she wants to stay one."

His brows furrow. "Yeah, right. So, you're telling me to slow down?"

"I'm telling you to think about making sure she wants you to hit it, before you hit it." Maybe Emma will realize Jordan is a cretin. Or Kat can talk her sister out of riding in trucks with boys like this. But I guess straight girls like to ride in trucks with boys like this. He's a moron, but he doesn't seem dangerous.

"Good talk," he says as he pulls to a stop in the circular drive. He puts up a fist for a bump.

Against my better judgment, I touch my knuckles to his.

"Cool."

He peels out of the driveway and I text Kat. Emma is no longer in Jordan's truck. My opinion? Douche.

Bubbles pop up, then her response comes through. A thumbs-up and laughing emoji. Then a second text. Wish she thought the same. But I guess he could be worse. Thanks for your heroics.

A cozy warmth fills my core. Heroics, huh? She did notice. I send a blush smile in return.

"In here, my dear." MaMolly is arranging a bouquet of flowers from her shopping expedition into a cut crystal vase. "Help me put away those groceries, will you?" Then she looks up. "How was the driving lesson?"

"I rolled across a parking lot at five miles per hour."

She plucks a piece of greenery out of the bouquet and tosses it on the counter. "Good. That's a start. If you get up to ten miles an hour, I might put you on the ATV. Actually, teaching you to drive the ATV is not a bad idea. It's very simple. No other cars or trucks to contend with."

"Just hills," I say.

MaMolly sighs and purses her lips. "Piper Kitts. You put yourself into riskier situations every time you work around horses. Cars are machinery. They have no will."

"It's not the cars I'm worried about. It's the other drivers."

"A good defense is the best offense."

I grab an armful of produce and head to the fridge to avoid continuing the conversation.

"How was young Katherine?"

And there it is again, a slight lilt, then dip as my grandmother says Kat's name.

"Fine. She seems nice. Her sister's a little salty, though."

"Ah yes, the dancer. Lovely athlete. I saw her in a modern dance production last spring at the arts center. She's quite talented. Doesn't have her sister's social graces or head for business though."

My grandmother bestowing the compliment of a "head for business" on anyone my age is unheard of. Huh.

MaMolly moves a rose from the front of the vase to the back and my phone buzzes in my pocket. I sneak a peek and my heart leaps, then stutters. It's Judith. And she's FaceTiming me while I'm still thinking about Kat's praise for my heroics. I hold up the back of the phone. "Going to go take this."

My grandmother waves a flower at me and I hit the stairs, the dogs at my heels.

"Hello." I hold the phone up as I walk the thick carpeted hallway to my room.

"Hey." Judith's pretty brown eyes blink at me.

"Hey to you." I flounce onto the bed and look up at my ex-girlfriend's face.

"How was your ice cream? As good as Bedford's?"

Ah, so that's what this call is about. She'd seen the picture of me and Kat with our ice cream and now she's going to circle the subject until she pulls the details out of me. I should have posted a pic of me and Jordan in his truck to really confuse things.

"Ice cream's not as good." I leave a note hanging at the end to torture her with the implication that something else might be though.

There's an awkward pause on her end, and on mine, if I'm honest.

"I just wanted to say thank you for changing your profile picture."

Really? That's what this call is about? A ripple of irritation launches inside me and I work superhard not to let her see it on my face. "Yeah, of course, I should have changed it ages ago. From now on, only pictures of me with horses. That way nobody knows when I've been broken up with." I pause and go for a zinger. "Or when I'm starting something new." That last part was purely to make her jealous, and judging by the quick blinks on her side of the phone screen, it worked. I feel a little bad, but not a lot.

She feigns recovery by fast talking. "I'll text you some pics from the horse show later, okay? But hey." She turns to look behind her as her mom walks into their house. "I've got to go. I just wanted to say thanks. And hey."

"Yeah, hey to you."

The call ends as fast as it started.

KAT

Emma walks into my room wearing a bathing suit I've never seen before. It's a pink and orange floral with chocolate brown strings holding the bottoms together at the sides, and the top together at the back and top. She looks grown-up as hell and way too hot for her own good.

"No."

"What?" She twists. "I work out hard to look like this."

"No, you work out hard because you love dance. That"—I point at her suit—"is boy bait."

She shrugs. "So what? I like boys. I want to look cute. Besides, Jordan's going to be there and I want him to think 'Deeeyamn.'"

"Pretty sure he'll be thinking more than that."

"I swear to Baby Jesus that you either don't like boys or are a total prude. I want to have sex sooner rather than later. But the way you act, you'd think I was going to light on fire or wind up totally preggers."

I lift an eyebrow.

"Oh my god. You do think that. I took health class, you know. We had 'the talk' with both Mom and Dad. Give me some credit. Just because I'm willing to be empowered by my own sexuality does not mean I'm going to wind up a statistic."

"Jordan's graduated and he's dated a lot of girls."

"I'm seventeen. I should be a senior. Can you drop it? I think he's cute and I think he'll make for a fun summer. I'm not ready to get married or serious."

"Fine." I pull my racer tank out of the drawer. Should I tell her that Piper called him a douche? Probably wouldn't make a difference.

"No to you." Emma points at my suit and shakes her head in the negative.

"What? It's comfortable for swimming."

"That's the most unsexy suit ever."

"Which is why I like it." This would be a great time to tell her about my crush. How I *don't* care how I look in front of boys. She wouldn't be surprised. But nope, I'm sticking to my plan. Wait until I have something to tell.

* * *

On Sunday, Dad drives the boys over to Elliot's and me and Emma follow in Delilah so we can hang out longer. There are already cars backed down the street, so we park in front of a neighbor's house and walk the rest of the way. Super casually, I ask questions as we walk. "How was your ride with Jordan yesterday?"

"It would have been better if Freakazoid Horse Girl hadn't pulled some stunt to get him to take her home second. If she hadn't said she liked girls, I would have thought she was trying to put the moves on him."

"Did y'all talk about anything?"

"Like what?"

My flip-flop snags as we step up the curb and I have to stop to push my foot back in. "I don't know. Small talk."

"No. Like I said, she was talking to Jordan, asking him questions about baseball and spouting off Red Sox statistics and all I know is that somehow we were pulled up in front of our house and I was getting out of the car and he was driving off with her. Why do you care?"

I clam up, then divert. "Hey, look at the awesome streamers Aunt Vlada hung in the porte cochere."

Emma skips ahead to twirl under the zillions of fronds in our school colors, silver and blue, then she breaks into a running man, her knees lifting in time with her arms.

The door opens behind her. Uncle Randall sports a pair of coral Bermuda shorts and a Salt Life T-shirt in contrasting baby blue. "Girls! Get on in here, the party's heating up out back. Where's the rest of the family?"

"Here, here." Dad comes walking up behind the twins, who barrel past us and head straight for the backyard.

Randall slaps an arm around Dad and gives him a side squeeze. "Can you believe it? My boy's all grown up." He winks at me. "And Kat will be right behind him. I can't believe how fast time goes."

"Too fast." Dad hands over to me and Emma the card we'd all signed earlier and a wrapped gift of the hair and facial products Elliot loves. "You girls take this to wherever the gifts are being stored. And don't forget your sunscreen."

We walk into the cool of the air-conditioning. Vlada has a big side buffet set up in the dining room with sliders and fruit salad and a cupcake tower. A small folding table is covered in cards and wrapped gifts. Emma places our gift on the pile when Vlada sees us. "Oh, my girls." She opens her arms, then places her hands on Emma's shoulders pulling her in for the kiss, kiss, kiss on alternate cheeks before she does the same to me. "I cannot believe this day, even my waterproof mascara is no match for a mother's pride and sorrow."

Emma's face must twist because Aunt Vlada's eyes go over large. "Oh, sweet dear, your mother will feel the same way. She may be gone but I know you both live large in her heart."

But the damage is done. Emma does the thing where she shakes off the hurt with a flick of her long dark ponytail and straightens her posture. For me, Mom's leaving was a shock, and sad at the time, but I've always been more aligned with my dad's pragmatic ways. Once Mom had been gone for a year, I'd learned to enjoy her absence. I don't need her proximity to know she loves me.

"Thanks, Aunt Vlada." I fill in the awkward silence. "Everything looks great. Who baked the cupcakes? They're perfection."

"Saynara at the bakery in Redfield."

About then Elliot bursts into the room, followed by Jordan and a couple of other guys from their class.

"Hey, hey, hey, ladies." Elliot does this weird more-dude-than-dude thing around the sports guys. "Ready for volleyball? Net's all set up in the pool."

Jordan sidles over to my sister and whispers something to her. She giggles and I have to look away.

What would it be like to so easily let my intentions be known to the world? To flirt and be flirted with right out in the open without worrying about consequences or who might say something? I know things are easy in bigger cities, but that's not where I am. I'm in Harmon, where everyone knows everyone and some people still care way too much about other people's business. I think about Piper and her fear of driving. How irrational it seems to me. But isn't this the same? Like she said at the bonfire when Emma and her friends acted shocked at her pronouncement, it's the twenty-first century. Why can't I just be open that I think I might be into girls? Elliot and Emma would be first in line to try to help me figure it out.

Maybe that's it. Or maybe I'm like a daffodil peeking up through the February soil. A little tease of green. Until my petals find their way into the sunshine, I need to protect myself like that bud pushing up through the earth. I need to be sure I'm blooming the way that I think I am.

chapter eleven

PIPER

My brain swirls with Judith. Is she with Brad? Is she not? Does she regret ending our relationship? Does she ever think about what we had? My body goes hot remembering the way she could send goose bumps over my skin and leave me so weak I could barely walk. How could a girl touch me like that, then dump me? Thinking the dumping thoughts are a surefire way for me to end up back in a psychologist's office, doubting my every move, so I shut them down by walking to MaMolly's barn where Beatriz is cleaning.

Beatriz wipes hair back from her eyes with a gloved hand. "Hey, girl. I'm headed over to my friend's place. You still going? There'll be a few people who ride with Dilara there."

It's the perfect distraction. I need to get my mind off girls and focus on why I'm here. No more Judith thoughts. No more wondering if Kat might be queer.

"Yeah. Let me go put on a different pair of jeans."

Beatriz points at herself. "You don't need to change. We'll all be in breeches or barn clothes. Sunday nights we unwind, even if we all have to be back up at six a.m. You sure you want this life? It's hard work."

"I'm sure." The question snaps me out of my funk. I do want this life. I want to compete and ride and pursue this crazy dream. I don't want to be bogged down worrying if some girl wants me back or not or if some other girl thinks I'm a hero. I grab a manure fork and help Beatriz with her chores so we can head out and I can see what awaits me.

While we finish up, Beatriz peppers me with questions about riding with Erik and the clinics I've done with Lendon Gray and Michael Poulin. We talk about the horses we've ridden over the years, our best tests and worst tests. It's only natural that the conversation veers personal.

"Did you leave anybody special to come down for the summer?"

"It's complicated." I shrug.

"I get that," she says. "It's hard to date when you ride competitively. Or when you're competitive. My last girlfriend stayed pissed off whenever something good happened for me and not for her. I finally got over it and said see ya. She's working down in Wellington now at a jumper barn." She winks at me. "I'm playing the field now and keeping things light."

Cool. Beatriz is queer, too. I'd had a hunch that might be the case based on little things MaMolly said before I got here.

"Yeah." I nod. "My girlfriend dumped me for a guy, though she says it's not because he's a he, but . . ." I sigh. "I wish I could have your chill attitude. My head is all, I could have done more, been better, the whole yadda, yadda."

"Girl, let that brain swirl go. When your grandmother told me you were gay, I figured we'd hang out together some, I mean not together, you're too young for me, plus you're my boss's granddaughter, but, you know, solidarity and all. We can't have you on repeat about the one that got away. You know what they say."

"No, what?"

"Best way to get over a girl is to get under another girl."

"That's terrible." But my mind flashes immediately to Kat and the way she had that cute tilt to her head in the driveway of MaMolly's. What would it feel like to put my hand on the side of her neck and have that swingy hair brush my fingertips?

"Terrible and true. Come on." Beatriz motions for me to follow her to her truck.

I walk and talk. "Thanks for dragging me out. I really

don't want to be stewing in my sorry sauce about Judith. I want to have a great summer."

"Cool. This is a fun group."

We pull up in front of a red-painted barn with an apartment over it. A couple of mini-donkeys flick their ears from the neighboring pasture as we slam the truck's doors. Beatriz reaches behind the driver's seat and pulls out a bottle of tequila.

"Ready?"

"Yep."

I follow her up the steep set of wooden stairs and she pulls open the screen door. "What's up, bitches?" She waves the bottle of tequila over her head and the group of riders erupt into a chorus of "hell yeahs" and "hollas." I hang back, feeling suddenly shy. Beatriz grabs my arm and thrusts me forward. "This is Piper. She'll be busting her tail for Schober with me, starting tomorrow. And she's nursing a broken heart, so be easy on her."

Quick introductions are made. The short-haired brunette is Trinity. The redhead with the multiple tattoos is Jane. The chiseled-looking Italian guy is Lorenzo. There's a Paulie and a Paula and a Stetson. They tell me the farms they ride for, but then I'm forgotten as the talk turns to a highlights reel of the rides they've had this week. Beatriz pours tequila into shot glasses. I sit, listening, as the air fills with each of them trying to outdo the other's story.

An hour goes by and I realize I haven't thought about Judith, not even once.

The redhead, Jane, nudges me and tries to hand me a shot glass. "You sure? Almost gone."

"No, thanks, first day tomorrow."

She throws it back herself. "I hear you. Dilara Schober is a hard-ass. Nice horses though. Me? Dressage is not my thing. I want the adrenaline of cross-country jumping."

"Don't throw shade at the sandbox," Beatriz yells from the kitchen. "Our sport is exacting and analytical and hard work. I control a twelve-hundred-pound animal with my pinkie finger and my ass."

This starts an argument among the group about which riding discipline is best.

Suddenly, my Judith dumping feels like the best thing that's happened to me yet. This is my dream. Being immersed in the competitive equestrian world at levels higher than I could achieve at home.

Beatriz elbows me. "I see euphoria in your face, girl. What are you thinking about?"

I laugh. "Riding, actually."

"Damn, I thought you were thinking about some girl and I'd get to live vicariously through your thoughts. Are you lesbian, bi, pan, or what?"

I shrug. "So far only girls. I'd like to think I'm open to a person, not a gender. I'm for sure not interested in cis guys. But . . ."

"Stop. Don't tell me you're not ready. Didn't we just talk about this? Nobody's looking to get you married. You just need a little someone to get your mind off the heartbreaker. Trust me, there's nothing like the flutter of a new crush to take away the burn. We'll find you a fling before the summer's over."

My therapist would call this projection. Pretty sure Beatriz is painting her own strategy onto my skin. I have to know the person for a fling to follow. Which is why my heart breaks so hard.

She keeps talking. "Don't worry. All kinds of people pass through during the summer for the shows. Nice thing about the Equestrian Center is the bar only cares about your age for drinking. Anybody can hang out, sing karaoke, dance their asses off. It's a fun vibe and lord knows everybody's queer for at least a night."

Paulie or Paula yells from across the room. "I'll be gay for a day for you, baby." Thank god she directed it at Beatriz, not me.

I look at my phone. It's late and I need to get home, but there's no way Beatriz should be driving.

For a second I think about texting Kat and seeing if

she'll Uber us. But she hadn't said yes to the idea of driving me around, and I'd only mentioned taking me to work. If she was freaked out about my being a lesbian, meeting this crew might send her running as fast as she could.

Once I make Beatriz promise she'll either stay put or catch a ride with one of the sober people, I text MaMolly instead and give her the address.

I want to make a good impression with Dilara Schober. Tomorrow's the first day of the rest of my life.

The life I've been dreaming about.

KAT

The pool party ends—too many parents for it to get eventful, even Jordan has to leave with his—so Elliot and I are up in his room building Sims characters to look like people from school. I haven't stopped thinking about Piper since I left to pick up the twins from the creamery yesterday.

"Why are you always trying to get me to check out girls?" I try a different nose on the Elliot character I'm building.

"My nose is not that narrow."

I pick a slightly different one.

He nods his approval, then answers me. "I guess because you've only had friend dates with guys and your sister is as boy crazy as me. I like to dissect people, you know that."

"I could be ace."

"Are you? That would help me understand why you've never told me about any crushes."

I shrug. It's certainly a thought that has passed my mind a time or two. Especially since the one make-out session I'd had with a boy at camp when I was twelve was more of an internal observation of the mechanics of what his tongue and hands were doing and me thinking "Huh, so this is the big deal? I don't get why it's a big deal? Oh, that's the big deal happening in his pants. Better shut this down before it gets stupid." Since then, I'd stuck to friend dates. But the feelings I have around Piper, like the feelings of that almost kiss in ninth grade, are definitely physical. Maybe there's some other neat category for me. But then again, categories are stupid.

The easiest tack with Elliot is to give him what he wants. "Dunno, maybe."

He picks out curly hair for his character. "Not me. Not ever. But I guess it could make life easier."

I change the subject. "So how come I'm up in this room with you, instead of you being out with some closeted sports star?"

"That will come this week. Get it?" He laughs at his own pun. "You were there. Too many parents celebrating their crowning achievements and crying in their own beers because their little babies are all grown up. But Myrtle Beach, baby."

"Please don't do anything stupid while you're there."

"I promise nothing. You don't do anything stupid either." Then he laughs harder because me and outrageous behavior are pretty much never linked. But then, there'd never been a Piper in Harmon before. And even thinking about her was making me all kinds of stupid.

When I get home, Dad and the twins are slung up on the big sectional in the family room watching a show about people that take old vans and turn them into mobile tiny houses.

"How was the party after we left?"

"It wound down. Aunt Vlada and Uncle Randall were all tears in their beers as I was leaving."

Dad chuckles. "I bet they were. It's a damn shame they never adopted a sibling for Elliot. Take some of the pressure off him."

My dad seems to have a pretty clear idea about Elliot being gay even though Emma and I keep our lips zipped. He also has a pretty clear idea about how many of Vlada's hopes and dreams are piled upon Elliot's handsome head. Even though my cousin literally has it all, the car, the house, the clothes, the cash, his mom expects him to be the pride of the entire county. I'll take my absent mom any day over Aunt Vlada.

"Where's Emma?"

Cole speaks up. "Talking to Mom on the computer."

Normally, I wouldn't interfere or I'd wait my turn, but I want to make sure Emma's not being stupid and asking to move to Texas again. She'll only get shot down. I head to the little nook off the kitchen where Dad keeps the desktop computer. There's a full Skype conversation taking place. Mom's talking about some event she's planning.

"Hi!" I step cheerily into the frame. Emma glares up at me.

"Hello, darling." My mother's dark bob is perfectly in place like always. "I was telling your sister all about the big charity fundraiser I was hired to direct. It's going to be massive. Best thing I'll have done yet. And huge payout. Get your wish lists ready."

Buying off her children since her departure, that's my mom. But on her terms. Money to fix my old van, no way. I'd never even bothered to ask because I knew it wouldn't be a glamorous enough spend for her. And sadly, there's no way Dad would let her spring for a better car for us, though I didn't think she had *that* much cash. Money for Ray-Bans or new clothes, sure thing. And maybe, dance lessons? I nudge my sister. This is the perfect time. "Did you ask her about Dance Pros?"

"Is that the one you mentioned here?" Mom's facade wrinkles slightly. She looks at Emma. "We've been through this. Texas isn't the place for you, darling."

I bop my knee against Emma's and rub my thumb against my forefingers like I'm asking for cash. Catching Mom when she maybe feels guilty about leaving us could translate into the dollars Emma needs.

My sister crosses her arms. "Not in Texas." She plasters a sweet smile on her face but I hear the growl in her voice at being so easily shoved aside. "But that's what's on my wish list. Tuition for a better studio. In Greenville."

But it works. Mom's face brightens. "Oh, there. Well, of course, darling. Send me the information and I'll make it happen. How's that? Do you love me? I love you."

Emma grimaces and follows with a saccharine "I love you, too."

"Love you, Mom." But I'm bopping Emma's knee like crazy because we timed that perfectly and Mom went for it.

"Well, darlings, I need to run. We have a wine bar outing planned and I've got to get my lipstick on."

We wave and the screen goes blank on her end.

I grab her. "You asked! She said yes!"

"After she said no to Texas."

"Come on, Emma, you knew that was going nowhere."

"Doesn't mean it doesn't hurt."

I give her a big hug and try to squeeze the hurt away. Eventually she laughs. "Thanks. You are the actual best." She wipes away the moisture from the bottom of her eyes, then her phone buzzes. A smile replaces the mom emotion. She flashes it at me. It's a text from Jordan. Actually, a GIF from Jordan of a panda bear with heart eyes, which is so dorky and out of character it makes me like him for half a second. "Speaking of things that *are* going somewhere."

If there's one positive to Emma being occupied by a boy with a truck, it's that I can explore the Piper thing, in my own time, without outside interference. But still, this is Jordan we're talking about. "Are you sure about him?"

"What do you mean?"

"Come on, Emma. He's not very smart. And he's a guy's guy. Like, dated-and-slept-with-a-few-different-girls guy."

This earns me a huge eye roll. "Seriously? I am not taking dating advice from you, even if you are older. One, smart isn't everything. And two, that means he knows what he's doing. Which is fine. Cherri told me she heard he was a great kisser and was not afraid of kissing"—she points to her crotch and whispers—"the raspberry mouse. Besides, I don't want to be a virgin forever, unlike you."

I'd like to tell her that is unfair. That I don't want to be a virgin forever either. Instead I whisper back, "Raspberry mouse? Do people really call it that?"

This gets both of us laughing so hard that Dad comes in to check if we're okay, which only makes us laugh harder.

chapter twelve

PIPER

Dilara Schober is as scary as her reputation.

Beatriz whispers softly, "Her bite is worse than her bark. But you'll ride better when you're through."

I watch as the trainer shouts in German. I'm not sure if she's shouting at the massive gray stallion pirouetting at the far end of the ring or the petite, blond rider on top of him. When the rider comes out of the small circle and pushes the horse into a medium canter down the long side, Schober shifts her attention to me.

"You are the granddaughter of Malone?"

I nod.

"Speak." She pops the lunge whip at the ground.

"Yes. Ma'am."

"You show up on time. You work hard. You groom. You tack. You wrap the legs. If you are lucky, I will let you on a horse. But first, hard work. You understand?"

I snap my hands against my breeches. "Yes. I understand."

"Good. Beatriz will show you the employee tack room with your chore schedule. Any questions you ask her or Franz."

And with that she turns and starts shouting at the horse/rider combination again.

We leave the big covered arena and walk across a gravel drive to a large white and green barn. Everything is tidy and crisp and clean. It's exactly the type of barn I'd aspire to, if I ever become a professional. Correction, when I become a professional.

"She's something, is she not?"

I nod. But since I don't exactly know where Beatriz's loyalties lie, and also because I already know it's best never to say anything negative about anyone unless it's to them directly, I don't voice an opinion. But I have to admit, I'm terrified. I was comfortable at Erik's barn. I knew my place, which just happened to be in the top tier of his client list. But here—last night's gathering made me all too aware—I'm one of multitudes chasing a similar, and highly competitive, dream. I take a deep breath and tighten my core, physically and emotionally. I can do this.

Beatriz leads me inside the barn to the second door on the right. "First door is the clients' tack room. You'll spend a lot of time in there, cleaning saddles and bridles. Here," she opens the door, "is for the help."

It's a compact room, the walls a soft stained tongue and groove, that includes a fridge, microwave, coffeepot, bathroom, desk, and neat wooden shelves of medications, cleaning, and grooming supplies. There are no tables or comfy lounge chairs which, after meeting my new boss, doesn't surprise me.

Beatriz shows me the work schedule. There's my name. On a worksheet. At a former Olympian's training barn. I take a picture of my schedule. Then I forward it to Kat with the note **Hey, Uber, can you lend a girl a hand?** I think for a second about the going rate for a ride and add a second text. **$8 a trip?** It's way less than I'd pay at home, but I figure she's not having to pay any fees and this is North Carolina. My dad won't care about the charges as long as I keep up my driving lessons.

"Better put that away. If Schober sees a phone in your hand anywhere other than in the staff room, she will send you straight home."

"Right." I turn it off and shove it in my pocket.

"Want to meet the horses while we go find Franz?"

This I can definitely voice an opinion about. Rumor has it that the champion Hanoverian stallion, Dagarron, is retired here and that Schober is selectively breeding a few mares to him each year. I can't wait to see his offspring.

Each stall has an arched yoke front with deep green bars and brass fittings. A nameplate in brass graces the front of each one and meticulously clean leather halters and leads hang on hooks for each horse. There's not a speck of dust or a lone piece of hay anywhere. Horses hang their heads out in greeting as we pass by, and to Schober's credit, they have content eyes and perked forward ears, a sure sign of happy horses. I stop in front of a stall holding a bright young chestnut gelding.

"Who's he?"

The horse walks over and snuffles the side of my face.

"That's Dantoar. A Dagarron son out of an E line mare. He's been a bit of a disappointment to Dilara. But we all love Dan, he's a sweetie."

"What? Why doesn't she like him?" I look the young horse over and he seems perfect.

"She doesn't like anything under 16.2 hands. He stopped growing at 15.3."

My opinion of my new boss drops a notch. I mean, even the famous Valegro is only 16 hands high. Seems kind of shortsighted on her part. No pun intended. But pun all the same. Which makes me think about Kat and her promised dad jokes. Would she have laughed? Judith would have groaned. Why am I thinking about Kat again?

A male voice travels from the far end of the barn as I stroke Dan's velvety muzzle. "Is this our new student?"

"Come meet Franz." Beatriz pulls me away from my new love and walks toward a man with buzzed blond hair, crystalline blue eyes, and a muscular build. He's the male version of Dilara. "Franz, this is Piper. Piper, Franz is Dilara's brother and the farm manager here. If you have any questions, he's your guy."

"Thank you, Beatriz. I'll take over here." Franz has the clipped voice of someone with purpose, but there's kindness beneath it. "I need you to tack up Bristol for her owner, then take one of the sale horses out for some hill work." Beatriz nods, then waves a hand at me before she strides away down the aisle. He looks at me. "Your level?"

"Fourth but schooling higher."

"Good for the ring. But can you ride outside of the ring? We ride on the hills for cross-training and conditioning." He points beyond the barn to the rolling green fields.

My heart leaps. He's going to let me take a horse out with Beatriz? "I mean, some. There aren't many trails where I rode."

"We'll get you there." His eyes crinkle into a smile when he sees the excitement in mine. "But not today. Today, we clean tack. The Dilara way."

I try not to let disappointment bring me down as I follow him through the barn.

He leads me back to the client's tack room and points to a row of bridles on hooks. He hands me spray, conditioner, and sponges. "They must gleam. No residue, no film, butter soft. Chop chop."

Hours later, after I've cleaned a whole row of stalls, wiped down six saddles and ten bridles, and cleaned every halter in the place even though they already seemed immaculate, MaMolly comes to pick me up.

"How was it, darling?"

"Good. Hard. But the horses." I plop my head back against the headrest and put the back of my hand to my forehead in a swoon.

"Yes, she does have lovely stock. Making quite a name for herself with some of those youngsters."

I tell her about Dan and how Franz has promised that he'll get me out doing hill work after a week or two and how frightening Dilara Schober seems but that I'm still really psyched for the opportunity, and then I remember my phone is turned off. I turn it on to check for texts.

My phone blows up.

Mom

Dad

Mom again

But no Judith. And no Kat answering my question about rides.

"Do you mind?" I give MaMolly the courtesy she expects.

"So important?"

"Maybe." The texts are all casual but they all came in pretty close to one another. I decide to call home instead of text. My mom answers.

"Oh, Piper."

A weird buzzing starts under my skin. "Oh, Piper what?"

"Did you talk to anyone from Erik's barn?"

"No. I was at my job. What's going on?"

My mom sighs. "He's quitting. No more physical or stressful work."

"Quitting?" The buzzing turns to a storm cloud. If Erik is leaving the industry, where will I ride when I go home?

MaMolly glances at me and pulls into a parking lot so she can listen in as well. I put the phone on speaker.

"It would be kind of you to send him a text. I know this is very hard on him and he's going to miss his students. But the good news is, a friend of his on Long Island is buying the horses for their program. I guess he gave them a package deal they couldn't refuse."

I'm bummed beyond words.

"Are you there? Piper?"

"I'm here. I'm just sad. I loved riding with Erik. And his horses."

It could be worse. He could be dead. But I feel gutted. He was the best of the best in my town. I'd moved up through some of the lesser trainers. The horse business in New England wasn't nearly as prolific as it was here and further south in Florida, but I'd been happy under his tutelage.

My mother tries to comfort me through the phone line. "You're going to be okay. I know this is a setback, but things work out for a reason. Sometimes one dream can turn into a totally different dream when you reach a bend in the road. We'll figure it out when you get home. Are you going to be okay?"

I sigh. "What choice do I have?" But my voice wavers when I think about all of Erik's beautiful horses moved on to a new owner. I can't imagine how he must feel. There's nothing more to say. "Thanks for calling to tell me, Mom. I love you."

"I love you, too."

When I hang up, my grandmother pats my leg. "I'm sorry, love. Hard knocks for your trainer. But maybe not for you." With that she snorts and mutters, "One dream for another. Hogwash."

150

"MaMolly? Are you okay?"

"Don't listen to your mother's patter. Things will work out, that's true. But if the Olympics are still your dream, you have to work hard and you have to make it happen. Don't let her airy-fairy what will be will be gobbledy goop infect your sharp young mind. Stay focused. Eye on the prize. You're an excellent rider. Opportunities will present themselves to you if you remain open to them. I may have some ideas."

Should I tell my grandmother she sounds kind of airy-fairy herself?

My phone buzzes. It's a text from Kat.

I'm in. Pick you up at 6:40 to take you to work. Driving lesson after I pick you up end of day. And eight dollars per ride is way too much. Maybe just give me gas? Then she types an explosion emoji like she's a middle school boy making a fart joke.

I laugh because it's a joke as stupid as she promised. I send her back some crying laugh faces while MaMolly's focused on the road.

The news about Erik's barn sucks on the grandest scale of suck, but somehow, determination finds a space alongside my bummed-outness. MaMolly is right and so is my mother. When there's a will, there is a way. And I have the will to succeed.

KAT

It's still pitch-dark outside when the alarm goes off but my eyes pop open. I'm seeing Piper again today. Piper who might lead me to actual self-discovery instead of theoretical self-discovery. Piper who isn't from here. Piper who will be leaving at the end of the summer. Piper who laughs at my stupid jokes.

I take my time and try to zen my way through my morning routine. I don't throw my hair into a tie. I don't skip the shower. Instead, I loofah, salt, body wash, shampoo, condition, blow-dry, pluck my brows, file my nails, essential oil, and lipstick before 6:00 a.m. Now to pick out the perfect outfit that will come across as cute without being in your face and isn't too Salon Susie. Should I try to dress gay? I mean, what is that anyway? I know in so many movies the gay girl is either all dark and goth and radical, or they're androgynous and gender-neutral. Where are the Fab Five when you need them? I want more of a handsome yet feminine vibe. I finally settle on cuffed chino shorts in red, an Atlanta Braves girl-cut T-shirt, a worn black belt, and red Vans. No jewelry. I take a selfie to make sure the look carries over into the photos Piper is always posting.

And she is always posting pictures. If I was from her hometown and didn't know how truly dull Harmon can be, I'd be convinced she landed in some kind of cool girl social utopia. The other thing I might assume is that maybe she and I are hanging out more than we are. Some of her friends even commented with things like the fire symbol and who's the new girl? And I might have revisited the comments a time or two. And noticed that she hadn't explained who I was but that she also hadn't responded that we weren't together. Maybe my tingly feelings aren't one-sided. Maybe this can be one of those summers like Elliot always talks about. The one where you meet the hot guy on your beach vacation and make lasting memories to carry around with you forever. My brain voice says, *Yaaaas, queen, that's what I'm talking about.* Why does my inner voice suddenly sound like Jonathan Van Ness?

I grab my keys and head down the steps.

Emma's sitting on the couch drinking a Coke Zero.

"Why are you up?"

She shrugs and points the remote at the television to fast-forward through the commercials. "Someone was stomping on the floor above my head and taking a shower and running their blow dryer and I had a panic attack that somehow I'd gotten confused over the last day of school. Why are *you* up?" She gives me the once-over. "And where are you going all cute and hipster?"

Emma's approval is good even if she doesn't know the depth of my need for it.

"Work." I pour a cup of coffee into a go-cup and add a shot of cinnamon syrup and a splash of half-and-half.

"Work? The salon's not open yet. Dad's still asleep."

"New job. I'm an Uber driver."

"What?" She hits the mute button. "How can you be an Uber driver? That would be stupidly dangerous. Does Dad know?"

I'm not going to be able to wiggle my way around this one. "I'm not a real Uber driver. Piper needs rides to her job. And since Mrs. Malone paid to fix Delilah, I'm up with the dawn."

Emma flops back onto the couch and does her best to hide her smile. "Well, you look really cute. Really cute."

I open my mouth to ask her if she's sure. Are my shorts

too short? My shirt too tight? But I clamp it shut and hold it in.

Besides, Emma's turned her attention back to whatever is on television.

"Thanks," I say, and head for the door.

I pull into the cobblestoned circle at the front of Mrs. Malone's house and text Piper that I'm waiting out front. Just when I'm about to text her again, she startles me, pulling open the van door.

"Hey." Her voice is rough and groggy with sleep. She doesn't even glance sideways at me as she settles in and buckles up.

"Good morning. Ready for your first full day?"

She grunts some sort of response.

"I thought all horse girls were bright-and-shiny-with-the-sun kind of people."

She pushes the palms of her hands against her eyes. "Except when they've been up all night learning the rules of poker with their grandmother and her socialite friends. Did not get my needed eight to twelve hours." She finally looks at me and there's a pause. "You look cute. It's a good chauffeur vibe."

My brain voice whispers. *Nailed it.* Damn if I don't feel the heat creeping into my skin, which means it's no doubt turning blotchy and red. I laugh her comment off. "Well, the way you're so obsessive with your social images, I thought I'd better look halfway presentable. Don't want to give Harmon a bad rep in the Northeast." I get the feeling Piper would prefer a quiet Uber driver but I keep babbling. Maybe if I get to know her better, I can have an actual conversation with her about, well, the gay thing. "What's it like, anyway, where you live? How's it different from here?"

Instead of a grunt, she kind of grunt laughs. "Myriad ways. Too many ways to list."

Even through her sleepiness I sense the tiniest bit of condescension in her voice. "Oh, I get it. You think that anyone who lives anywhere that's not bordered by a big city or a university is ignorant. What's that term?" I rack my brain thinking about what Terry the mechanic had been going off about to some of his buddies. It comes to me. "Coastal elites, that's it."

She shifts in her seat. "Coastal elites, huh?"

I shrug and heat up again. "I listen to the news." Even though that's not where I'd heard it.

She smiles and I'm rewarded with the dimples. "You have layers, Snow White."

"Snow White?"

She does a thing like she's circling my face with her

hand. "Dark hair, pale skin, red lips, interesting eyes."

This feels like flirting. Is this flirting? I try to say something clever. "No dwarfs, though."

Without missing a beat, Piper answers: "Elliot."

Now I'm the one laughing. And tingling. On the inside. Because she's looking at me. She's even given me a nickname, which I hope is not derogatory. Is it derogatory? "Snow White's just about my physical appearance, right? You didn't mean anything else by it?"

She laughs again. "You're a trip. I won't call you that if it bugs you. But no, I was only referring to your looks and your hair cut. No hidden meanings."

Except maybe there are hidden meanings she doesn't know about. Snow White was cast under a spell and was asleep for years. Until the prince came and kissed her awake. It's how I feel. Sleepy and disoriented as the world around me does their easy hookup thing. But now, here I am, insta-crushing on a girl's dimples and arm muscles and slightly deep tone to her voice. It's making me think about things like kissing. And more.

I have to change the subject. "Was it hard to leave home for the summer?"

This time she pauses before answering, and in the pause, it's like I can hear an unspoken catch in her voice. A story below the surface layer that she isn't going to let out.

"Sure. I had plans and stuff. But MaMolly lined up this opportunity for me."

We arrive at the entrance to the farm and I turn in.

I realize she's getting out of the van without the usual photo. The one I'd gotten the Emma stamp of approval on my outfit for. "Hey, what about our selfie?" I unbuckle and run around to meet her on the other side of the van and before I even think about what I'm doing, I pull her into my side and thrust my own phone out to the sky. "Say cheese." I press my cheek up against hers and brazenly put my hand at her waist, drawing her in so there is no space between us. I take at least ten photos before I let go.

"Whoa. Okay. How much coffee did you have?" She glances at my phone. "Cute. Send me your favorite of those. Try to pick one that I don't look like the evil witch next to your Disney shine. I'll say something positive about Harmon for you."

Piper seems pretty unaffected by my photo exuberance, but for me, the tingling lingers. I try to get her to linger as well.

"So, remember, driving lesson later. What time should I pick you up?"

Piper's glancing toward the barn where a chiseled, short, blond guy is standing with his arms crossed.

"Um, I've got to go. Pick me up at six. Unless I need to change it."

"Wow, long day. They take things seriously here, don't they?" I shuffle my toe against the gravel, shoving my hands into my back pockets, trying to look cute in a way that might catch her attention. But it doesn't work.

"Gotta go." Then she turns, her French braid bouncing on her back as she strides toward the man, who motions for her to follow him inside the impeccable barn.

I sigh. Who am I kidding? Why would a girl like her be into a girl like me?

Despite all the photos.

chapter thirteen

PIPER

Shovel. Sift. Wheelbarrow.

Shovel. Sift. Wheelbarrow.

The work turns into a beat inside my brain, each stall reminding me that yes, I am in Dilara Schober's barn, but no, I am not riding any of these beautiful horses or perfecting my seat or nailing down my lateral work. I'm absolutely dying to check my phone to see if Judith has had any reaction to the photo I posted of me and Snow White during my bathroom break earlier. Not that she would, she hasn't so far, though plenty of my other friends back home have. It's a lucky thing that Kat is actually super attractive, and really kind of clueless, and okay, smelled really nice when she snugged me for the photo. My brain drifts back to that moment as I sift through the shavings for stray balls of manure. Maybe the best cure for a broken heart is a hookup? I'd thought she was straight, vertical, horizontal, going in absolutely one direction upon first meeting her—well, except for those hands—but now? Not so sure. This morning felt like flirting. All those pictures. How date ready she'd seemed with her fresh clean hair and fresh clean outfit. I smile thinking about it.

Kat has an interesting aesthetic, definitely femme, but there's a no-nonsense edge to her. And none of her scents, her soap, her shampoo, her lotion are fruity or floral. They're woodsy and warm—something she wore was similar to the oil that Sasha used on her hair. And okay, so that's a major generalization, but maybe a good tell? Kind of like those hands?

"Piper."

Franz Schober's voice is sharp behind me and I jump out of my daydreams. Right. I am not supposed to be thinking about girls. Eye on the prize.

"Yes."

"Put the manure fork down. Dilara needs to put you on a horse for fifteen minutes."

The fork is in the wheelbarrow and I'm out of the stall before you can say giddyup. I follow Franz through the barn toward the covered arena where a huge chestnut is tacked up and the blond rider I'd seen the other day is hopping on one leg.

"Melanie has pulled her muscle. She needs five minutes. But Revario needs warming up. Chop chop."

I slap my helmet on my head and pull on my gloves and climb to the mounting block and throw a leg over before Dilara can change her mind.

"Walk. He needs walk. Loose rein, warm up. At ten minutes, working trot for five. Nothing else."

I'm dying to put this magnificent beast into a shoulder-in or a half pass or something to show her that I know my stuff, but I also know that showing my ass would be the worst thing I could possibly do. Nobody likes a saddle princess. I give the big horse a loose rein and walk. And walk. And walk. Occasionally I give a surreptitious glance into the mirrors that line the short sides to check my position. Then I look to see if Dilara is watching me ride. She's not. A timer sounds and she shouts, "Collect him. Rising trot." At least she'll be able to see that I know my way around a double bridle and can put a horse on the bit, but as I think the thought, the beast has other plans for me. He rips my elbows away from my sides and shoots forward into an ungainly canter from an ill-timed and overenthusiastic nudge with my heel on his outside flank.

"Nein. Nein. Nein. Half halt. Shorten the snaffle rein.

Sit back in the tack. I was told you could ride! What is this circus?"

I scramble to organize myself in the saddle and eventually get the power somewhat contained but Schober is tutting and striding across the ring and grabbing for the rein.

"You are not ready for this horse. Off." She points her whip to the ground and I dismount in disgrace.

I start to open my mouth but I see the blonde, Melanie, making a slicing motion across her throat warning me not to talk. I shut my mouth and take the verbal lashing without defending myself, which I desperately want to do. Schober sends me back to the stalls for the rest of the day.

I just hope it's not for the rest of the summer.

By the time Kat comes to pick me up at six, I'm defeated, tired, glum, ready to fly home and forget about my riding dreams.

"Hey." I shut the door and reach for the seat belt.

"For you." From the cup holder on her driver's door she passes me a vanilla frappé with a smattering of white chocolate curls. "To celebrate a successful day of work."

"Best Uber service ever. Worst work day ever." I take the drink and when her finger touches mine, I remember my daydreams from the morning. If I'm going to be an

163

abject failure as a dressage rider, maybe I should have a summer hookup. Test the waters to see if Snow White is not who I thought upon first impressions. But then I think about Judith. How she'd dumped me. How bad it hurt, still hurts. Plus, Kat seems like the long-term type. I don't get a hookup vibe from her even if, maybe, she was flirting this morning.

I take a sip and let out an appreciative sigh. "You know, if you provide four-dollar drinks with your ride service, your profit margin is going to be abysmal."

She smirks. "Funny. It's not a perk that's sustainable. Especially since we've agreed you're not paying me. But can a friend not bring a friend a treat? Especially if their day sucked?"

My glum mood is lifting with each creamy sip. "Thanks. It's like you knew what I needed. You not only take really cute photos but you're intuitive, too." What the hell, I go for flirty eyes over the top of my cup to judge her reaction. Unfortunately, she looks left to turn out onto the road at the exact same moment. Suave, Piper. Super suave.

But maybe my compliment caused some sort of reaction because her voice raises an octave and she starts talking fast. "Who doesn't need a vanilla frappé? But I am going to make you drive at least twenty miles an hour today and get you out of the parking lot onto the factory road."

Actual anxiety replaces flirting curiosity.

Snow White giggles. "Oh my god, you should see your face." Then she grows serious. "I'm not trying to minimize the very real fear you have around this issue, but I just want to say this. Nobody wants to break the rules of the road. Nobody, well almost nobody, gets in their car in the morning and says, 'Today is the day I'm going to get into a wreck that will injure myself and others.' It's the one place most people do follow the rules and do their part. We've all got to get somewhere and we all want to get there with intact vehicles and bodies. I bet you never get on a horse thinking you're going to fall off."

"True."

"Driving is no different. And"—she smiles at me— "you've got this."

I suck down a big sip and get momentary brain freeze. "You'd make a good coach, Snow White." I risk another glance in her direction. The smile on her face is different, like she's pleased with my compliments, and her cheeks are all rosy again, and I notice the way her breaths make her shirt tighten, then loosen. And for half a second, I don't feel heartbroken. I feel a bit like Prince Charming on a beautiful horse ready to ride in and plant a kiss on those matte-red lips and make her eyelids flutter open into mine.

But I'm still in love with Judith. One hundred percent.

Holding a candle in hope. Right?

That's what I've been focused on. Getting her back. Not getting over her. But now . . .

Suddenly the driving lesson feels like the least scary thing in the car.

KAT

I'm trying superhard to contain my laughter, but Piper's making it difficult. I've never met anybody so anxiety-ridden about something so incredibly everyday. I couldn't wait to drive, and when I started it seemed so easy, but for her it's like Mount Everest or something. My balance between teacherly patience and full-on teasing is growing wobbly. "Oh my gosh. Stick your foot on the gas pedal and go. You. Are. Fine." I wave my hand to the totally empty road, complete with grass growing up through the cracks, in front of us. "There is nothing to hit. No one to hit you. Go, or I'm telling your grandmother you have no gumption."

"Unfair."

"Well, it's important, as she's the only one trying to light a fire under your ass and obviously someone needs to. Do you know I plan on driving my sister an hour away to dance practice? On the interstate? Going seventy miles an hour? And that other people do it, too? Every single day of their lives."

Piper bites down on her lip and furrows her brow, all glorious determined concentration, before slowly easing onto the gas. We start to roll.

"Faster, the snails are beating us." The needle on Delilah's speedometer edges up to ten. "Good, but faster. I told you, twenty miles per hour. We're not stopping till you get there, even if it gets dark."

"God. Who knew Southern girls were so bossy?"

"Bossy ones knew."

Piper steps a bit more on the gas.

"Progress, you're to thirteen. Better get past it. Superstition says thirteen mph is unlucky."

She grips tighter on the steering wheel. "Ugh." But the needle edges up to twenty, then twenty-five.

"You're doing great. See this isn't that bad. Do you feel out of control?"

She shakes her head.

"The road loops back around the parking lot. Just keep going. I'm comfortable with thirty-five if you are."

"Pushing it, Snow White."

"You have this."

And she does. Piper's hands relax, even if her brow stays furrowed in concentration. When we get to the parking lot she surprises me by taking the road again, staying at a steady thirty-five the whole time.

I don't want to end the lesson, but it's getting late and I'd promised Dad I'd grab the brothers and take them for pizza after their practice. On a whim, I decide to invite Piper.

"Do you want to go get pizza with me and my sibs? You don't have to, and fair warning, those boys stink when they get in the van after practice." I'm fairly certain my fluttery feelings are one-sided and that all my detective work looking at Piper's social media is accurate—girlfriend that she's maybe still with or at least hung up on—but I had told Mrs. Malone that I'd not only teach her to drive, but also hang out with her, and I actually want to. She has goals and aspirations and I like that in people, especially in friends.

"You sure you don't mind? I'm smelling pretty extra myself after all day at the barn. Pizza sounds better than leftovers."

"One hundred percent do not mind." Then I tease her. "You're driving us there, right?"

"What?" Her blue eyes get super-wide and she does the blood-draining grip on the steering wheel again.

"Kidding. But you'd be okay. The traffic around here isn't that bad. It's a good place to learn. Way better than a city. I know you must want to drive."

She takes a deep breath. "I do. And I promise, before the summer is over, I will drive you for ice cream or pizza or wherever you'd like."

My brain voice takes over my outer voice. "Like a date, huh?" Then I freak out. What the hell was that? I fumble. "I, um, not like a date, date, but you know, just a promise that you'll drive. A date in the future that you will drive. Somewhere. And I will be the passenger." I can't even look at her as we switch seats.

I take the back way to the ball field and turn up the new Lizzo album to full volume to avoid any further vocal malfunctions. Corbin and Cole are waiting in the lot. They tumble their way into the back seat, throwing mitts and duffel bags as they go. I turn off the music.

"Who's she?" Cole asks.

"This is Piper."

"Hi, nice to meet you." She smiles at my brothers and acts like I haven't made a huge ass of myself.

"You talk weird," Corbin said.

"I'm not the one who talks weird."

"You're outnumbered here, Ms. Massachusetts." I wink at her, like I would with Elliot or Emma, then panic again. Thank goodness, my brother jumps in.

"Oh man," Cole says. "Are you a Sox fan? Can you get us tickets to Fenway?"

"Didn't you just insult her and now you're asking for favors?" I shake my head at them in the rearview mirror.

Corbin holds up his phone. "Emma wants us to pick her up from the house."

"Tell her five minutes."

We pull up in front of the house and there's half a second of awkwardness as my sister reaches for the front door only to realize her privileged place of shotgun is taken. Fortunately, she gets in the back without making a scene.

At Random Pie, the boys head straight for the claw machine while we wait for a table.

"What? No pictures?" Emma has a look on her face that's making me nervous. A little devious. Slightly catty.

"Pictures?" Piper asks.

"Yeah, you know." Emma holds up her own phone. "Seems like you pretty much livestream the exciting time you're having down here with all of us. But especially my sister. So, are you hot for her?" She pulls up Piper's account. "See, you and Kat. Kat and you. You, me, and Kat. Elliot, you, and Kat. Some random horse. You and Kat."

I would be really worried about how I look in this moment—mortified and like my sister just punched me—except Piper looks like she kind of wants to die herself. I'm torn. Throttle my sister. Or see what Piper says.

But Emma keeps talking. "You know, my sister's not gay. If she is, she'd have told me. We're super close. Best friends." She looks at me. "You'd have told me. Right?"

"Emma."

She shrugs. "What? It's just kind of weird is all. Have you seen what her friends are saying about you on here? Total objectification that I would think is pretty anti-lesbian. Definitely not feminist." She repeats herself. "And you'd have told me, right?" Then to Piper, "What exactly are your intentions, Horse Girl?"

Totally tongue-tied. Random Pie is not where I would choose to come out. If I even had anything to come out about.

Piper's keeping quiet, too.

"Emma, we had a driving lesson, that is all. Don't make this weird."

"Me? She's the one taking all the pictures."

From across the room, someone yells "Emma" and my sister bounces off, leaving me and Piper alone with the residue of her implications. Right now, I'd put her on a bus to Texas all on my own if I could.

"Um." I move my keys from hand to hand. "Sorry about that. She can get kind of jealous of my time. She's not used to sharing me with anybody other than Elliot."

"Yeah, no, don't worry about it." Piper pulls her braid over one shoulder, then pushes it back. "I don't mean to make things weird with the pictures. It's just, I am gay, and you are a girl, and some of my friends think you're attractive, and it's just stupid social media stuff. If it bothers you, I can delete the photos of us. I wouldn't want you to feel objectified."

I shake my head too quickly. "No. You can leave them." Then I feel my stupid blush. "I, um, like that you consider me a friend. I mean, I'm sure you'll tell your friends back home they're being ridiculous. But I don't mind the photos."

Piper opens her mouth to say something else but the hostess comes to tell us our table is ready and the boys descend on the breadsticks all talk and chatter and questions about the Red Sox which, surprisingly, Piper knows quite a bit about. The photo conversation goes by the wayside.

Emma leaves her friends to join us right as the pizza arrives from the kitchen.

I reach my hand over and pinch the hell out of her thigh when she sits next to me.

"Ow!"

I whisper under my breath. "Apologize."

She rolls her eyes, but wilts under my stare. She reaches across for the shaker of Parmesan cheese and fake smiles at Piper. "I wasn't serious about the pictures, you know. Just giving you grief because you're the new girl and all. And I love my sister."

Piper smiles at Emma but it's a flat one that doesn't reach to her eyes or show her dimples. "No problem," she says.

But she doesn't even attempt to answer Emma's earlier question.

And I wonder, does she have any intentions?

chapter fourteen
PIPER

I can't help myself.

I text Judith when I get back to MaMolly's.

Maybe it has to do with the things Emma said at the pizza place. Up until the moment I noticed Kat's smile, I'd been obsessively focused on Judith. Her dumping me. My broken heart. My incessant need to get her back. But now I'm confused. Why do I want Judith back so badly? She doesn't want me. What kind of person does that make me that I focus on someone who'd made it clear she doesn't think I'm good at relationships. It seems unhealthy. I don't want to be unhealthy. Or confused.

Hey. Missing the MA life.

I wait a minute and nothing happens, but then I see her typing back to me.

I bet. Is it superhot there?

Wow. Okay, we're going to talk about the weather.

Yeah, but I'm dealing. How's things with you?

Dying to ask directly about her relationship status, but I won't.

I'm okay. My mom signed me up for some physics camp at Harvard. Starts Monday.

Look at you, genius, I respond.

I get smiley emojis in return. Which typically signal the end of our text convos. But I go for another try.

Any big fun plans?

Just the usual, she types. Then, Great to hear from you. Seems like you're doing okay down there. Glad you're making friends.

No, no, no. That's not what I want her to say. I want her to needle me until she finds out exactly the status of said friends. Is she being distant because she wants to be distant? Or is she being distant because she's dying to know what is going on with me but is too scared to ask? Should I put her at ease and say that I'm just friends with Kat? Because that's all we are. Friends. Kat said she didn't mind that I posted a weird number of pictures, even if her sister seemed to see through my shenanigans, because, let's be honest, I hadn't corrected any of my other friends' assumptions. Maybe I haven't wanted to.

Isn't Judith being just as obtuse with me? Like she's

deliberately not saying much because if she tells me she broke up with Brad, or vice versa, she thinks I'll say I told her so or that I'll beg to get her back. I'd never throw it in her face. No matter how much I might want to. And I'm not sure I'd beg to get her back. Not if we're only going to talk about the weather.

Horses are so much easier than girls.

This time I send the emoji. A thumbs-up. That's it. This is stupid.

But then.

Brad broke up with me.

I sit straight up in bed and stare at my phone. I read the text again. My stupid heart, which a minute ago was entertaining the possibility that Kat might be flirting with me and that I might want to flirt back, ratchets up in response. I try to calm down. I need to proceed carefully. Be kind. Thoughtful.

Oh, Jude. He's stupid.

Yeah. I hear her breathiness and sadness in her single word.

Any chance he'll realize how dumb he was?

I get a shrug back.

I type. **Don't want to overstep but I wish I was there to give you a hug right now.**

Me, too, she types.

My heartbeats pick up speed. I want to take it in the

way I want to take it, that she wants me and not just a hug. But I also know I'm probably wrong.

You're probably glad, she types.

Yes, of course I'm glad. But I'm also not. I love her and don't want her to be hurt. Even if I have been trying to make her jealous.

Never want to see you hurt. Like I said, Brad is stupid.

Thanks, she types. Then a blush face. Then a TTYL.

I hold the phone for a long time trying to figure out my next move. Which I finally decide is to send her a GIF of hugging kittens. Just because Brad dumped her doesn't mean she wants to get back together with me. And I'm hundreds of miles away. And I'm focused on riding. Nothing but riding.

My phone buzzes again and I grab for it.

Same time for pickup tomorrow?

It's Kat. An involuntary smile lands on my face. She's a surprise. Nice. I like her. I can see why my grandmother wanted us to hang out.

I type back, Yep. Hey, thanks again for inviting me out for pizza.

Sorry my sister got weird.

No worries, like I said, lmk if you want me to axe the photos. I don't want to embarrass you or anything.

I see dots and no dots. Dots appear. Dots disappear. Then my phone lies dormant. Okay. I get off the bed and gather my laundry into a hamper and am about to take it downstairs to the laundry room when my phone buzzes again. I drop the basket and reach for it. Two texts have come in. The first is from Judith.

Thanks for being so sweet. You're a really good person. And a heart emoji. Then a selfie of her looking up at her phone, her dark curly hair spread out like a halo on her pillow, her soft T-shirt begging me to put my hands up it. Well, this is an interesting development after months of pushing me away to pursue Brad.

The second is from Kat.

You haven't embarrassed me. I mean, maybe my sister did. Because

The phone goes still for a minute. Then, Kat again.

I can't believe I'm going to type this. She wasn't right. About me. Not being. You know. Gay. I think I might be. But I haven't told her. I haven't told anybody.

Whoa. Wait a minute.

What do I do?

My ex-girlfriend, who I've thought constantly about getting back together with since she dumped me three months ago, is telling me I'm sweet and sending heart emojis and a smoking hot selfie and she's single again.

And my new sort-of friend I think just came out to me? No question, the latter takes precedent cause I'm pretty sure she's bound to be flipping out right about now. I text some quick flames and water droplets to Judith. Then I type back to Kat.

First. Your thoughts are safe with me. I will delete this text stream and I would never, ever share this with anyone else. Unless you wanted me to.

Second: You go girl! Is there someone you're into? What made today the day?

As soon as I type that, I get a little nervous. Because all the small moments we've had so far, where she's jumped away from me or turned red or gotten all blotchy on her neck, suddenly my theory that she freaked out because *I'm* gay doesn't hold water. Oh shit. She freaked out because I am gay, but maybe not because she was scared, but because she was actually flirting?

A new photo comes in and Judith is totally making sex eyes at the camera and has her shirt pulled up to show her flawless skin and the tiniest hint of no-bra underboob. What I would give to be able to reach through the phone and push her shirt up the tiniest bit more. Instead I take my hair down and do a fast fluff and snap a quick response selfie and hit send.

Judith sends back her own flames and a wave and then I get a new picture. Her shirt's off, all bare shoulders and chest, but she's bunched it up in the front to hide her breasts and this is cruel because I'm so very far away.

Then I get the text from Kat.

I don't know. Maybe? I mean, there is someone but I'm getting mixed signals.

If I'm not careful I'm going to end up sexting Kat and sending coming out advice to Judith and what in the actual eff is this? I mean, for the past three months I've been utterly heartbroken and now I have two girls texting me at the same time? At a time when I shouldn't be texting girls at all.

Judith sends me an even more revealing photograph. It's kind of out of character, which makes me wonder if she's drowning her sorrows over Brad with a bottle of her mom's rosé.

So you're into this? With me? Positive? I want to be sure having a sext exchange with me is something she's legit into. Because even though I want nothing more than to give the girl all the comfort she needs, I also don't want to get hurt again or have her think I'm taking advantage of a situation.

My phone lights up again.

Okay. Wow. I was that transparent, huh? But yeah, I think I'm positive. I'd be open to it. Are you mad I said something? I mean, I'm fine if you're not into me. But I just had to get it out because I needed someone to talk to and maybe my feelings aren't what I think they are, but omg, I can't believe I'm doing this over text. Are you freaking out? I'm freaking out.

Shit. I sent that to Kat.

So yes, I am freaking out. But not how she's freaking out. And ten minutes ago, I would have definitely entertained this plot twist, but now all I can think about is Judith lying in her bed waiting for my next move and how bad I want to make that move.

I text Kat back.

Don't freak out. We'll figure this out. We'll talk tomorrow. Okay? It's going to be okay. I promise.

Then I second-guess myself. That was abrupt. The girl just came out to me by text, something she said she'd never done at all, ever, and confessed that she was into me and I pushed her off till tomorrow. My fingers hesitate over the keyboard but I can't think of a good follow-up. My sexual energy is replaced by self-doubt and a smidge of self-loathing.

I look at Judith's pictures again, but I can't get the feeling back. I send her a text, making sure it's going to Judith not Kat.

Babe, as much as I love this and looking at these beautiful photos of you, you're too raw. Can we talk tomorrow after I get off work? I don't want you to do something tonight you'll regret tomorrow.

Then I add, **I love you.**

My phone goes completely silent.

KAT

I freak the flip out. What does it mean that "we'll talk tomorrow"? How is that going to go down? I'll drive up to her grandmother's house and wait like a good little Uber driver until she walks outside and then what? She'll jump in the car and say "Hey, congrats on being queer. Here's a rainbow friendship bracelet."

And god, isn't the number one rule of business relationships to NOT get involved with your clients? That's what Dad says anyway, which I've always thought is his excuse for not dating, since pretty much half the town goes to his salon. I mean, Piper is my client. I could have waited to explore this till I left for college. But no, I had to go and open up my soul in a moment of weakness and now I'll have to face the consequences of my reckless texting.

I want to talk to Elliot. But I don't want to talk to Elliot. Besides, he's probably out dancing it off at some club on the beach.

Emma is a possibility. She expects me to tell her before anyone, she made that abundantly clear at Random Pie. But what if the only way I can truly know is if I have an actual queer experience? Beyond fluttery feelings and the warmth of seeing people's comments on Piper's social posts I have nothing. I do not want to lay all my cards on the table if I'm wrong.

I start looking at Piper's social media account again. And then follow the trails out to her other friends. Specifically @judith_judith. Which is where I see a photo of Piper hugging her horse, staring deviously into the camera, and the caption "Messed up the best thing." The girl in the profile pic is super pretty. This amazing nimbus of hair and golden eyes and warm brown skin. Even a beauty mark like that old blond actress from the fifties. No wonder Piper wanted to "talk tomorrow." Why would she be interested in me if she has a girl like that waiting for her at home? I guess this made it easier. Before she even opens her mouth, I can tell her that I'm stupid. That I don't know her well enough to have feelings about her, but I do need someone to talk to about how I'll know if I'm queer or not and that's all I'd really meant with my texts.

I look at the clock. It's almost midnight. She's probably still up but maybe not. The last thing I want to do is send another awkward text. Tomorrow. I'll wait until then. But in the meantime, I can't sleep.

I wander downstairs to rummage through the fridge and am surprised to find my dad awake, hunched over his laptop at the kitchen table.

"Hey."

He startles. "Oh. Kat. Why aren't you sleeping?"

I slip across from him onto a chair and reach for a banana from the fruit bowl. "Can't."

He closes his computer. "Something going on?"

I shrug. "Thinking about things."

"Is this one of those moments where I should pry? Or not pry?"

"Not."

"Okay." He grabs his own banana. "Glad you're choosing healthy snacks tonight."

I smile. Though I don't want to talk about the Piper thing, I can broach something more general. "Can I ask you something?"

"Anything." Dad breaks off a piece of the fruit and pops it in his mouth.

"Does it ever bother you how people gossip around here?"

"You're going to have to be more specific."

"You know, like how people bashed that football coach when he left his car crashed into the tree and assumed he was drunk instead of walking for help, or about how bad a mother Mom was for leaving us. Or the way people think a man owning a salon isn't manly."

Dad chuckles. "Darling, if I listened to half the rumors I hear on a daily basis, I'd have to send every person in this county to jail, the psychiatric ward, or straight to hell. What is it that Natascha says all the time?" He pauses. "'You do you'? It's not a bad mantra, don't you think?"

I shrug again. "I guess."

"Has someone said something to get under your skin?"

More like someone has gotten under my skin. A sun-kissed, muscled forearmed, scared of driving, social media addicted, horse crazy, confidently gay girl from Massachusetts that I'd just made a fool of myself in front of.

"No. It's just this town feels really small at times. People expect people to be all perfect. Grow up. Marry your high school sweetheart. Have two perfect kids and a white picket fence. What if you don't even have a high school sweetheart? What if you don't know what you want?"

Dad nods and I appreciate how seriously he takes my outburst as he gives it a few seconds of thought. Finally he answers.

"I get it. Community is a double-edged sword. It's the best thing but it can also feel like the most confining thing. In general, people don't like change. They like the status quo and the way things feel comfortable to them. Sometimes they forget that what other people do isn't a mirror of themselves but a window to the wider world. That part does feel small and frustrating.

"But people here also forgive each other. They live, they let live, they may run their mouths some, but mostly they only care if you're good people. They learn to accept and the love never stops even as they adjust." He puts his hand on my hand. "We're good people. Your mother is good people. You kids are good people. Wherever this life takes me, or you, or your siblings, we are surrounded by love. It might not seem that way to you right now, but one day you'll see. You have to trust people to love the real you."

"That's why you took the chance of opening the Orchid even though people thought it was strange?"

Dad smiles. "Yes. I know what people say about me, Kat. And they may not be wrong. They may not be right either. For now, my truth is that I loved your mother very much. We had four beautiful children together and it worked for a while. Then it stopped working. That's okay. One day I may find love again and I'm not so fool-headed to think I will one hundred percent know what that looks like. I'd like to think I'm open to the possibility of the great infinite, and the great infinite can take many different forms." He pauses. "I hope I'm not freaking you out."

He is. Totally. Because this sounds like my dad saying he's pansexual or something. And, well . . . cool. I stutter in response. "Maybe. A little. But it's okay, it'd be good for you to find love again one day. And, thank you. I wondered. Because, you know . . ."

He finishes my sentence. "People talk."

"Yeah."

I roll my now mangled banana peel into a napkin and pause. "Dad . . ."

"Yes, pumpkin?"

But words won't come. They're locked at the back of my tongue and no matter how hard I try to just open my mouth and say, "Dad, I think I like girls. You know, for romance and stuff," the words won't budge.

Coming out to Piper was enough for one day.

I stand up and take his banana peel and kiss him on the forehead. "I love you. You're awesome. Mom was lucky to have you. She still is."

He pulls me into a side squeeze. "We're the lucky ones to have great kids like you and your sibs. Now, get some sleep. Don't you have to be up early tomorrow?"

"Ugh," I say. "Don't remind me."

He chuckles.

I wish I could find the humor in it. Despite our good talk, I still have to live with every minute replaying Piper's text, my texts, her return texts, and what the next day will mean.

Will it be the beginning of the rest of my life?

Or just a colossal disappointment?

chapter fifteen

PIPER

I'm pulling on breeches and an old Ariat polo when my phone buzzes. It's too early for Judith, too early for Sasha, so it can only mean one person. Kat.

I'm on my way to take you to work, but I'd like to back pedal from the things I typed last night. I'd like for this not to be awkward.

I blink a couple of times, then rub an eye. Okay. Not sure how it's not going to be awkward, because I think she kind of confessed to having a thing for me, but not really? I'd already decided to tell her about Judith. It had been fun to play that I had something going with her on social media when she didn't know, but now that she was potentially into it, I had to be honest.

I type back, No worries. Seriously. Not awkward. See you in thirty minutes.

Downstairs, MaMolly plates two poached eggs with a spread of avocado, sprinkled with everything bagel seasoning.

"Delicious. Thank you."

"Every athlete needs a shot of protein in the morning."

I grumble. "I'm only a farmhand after my horrible exercise ride. My luck in the horse department seems pretty abysmal these days."

"May I remind you only bad riders focus on their bad rides? Working at Schober's is giving you an opportunity to ride some big movers. I'm guessing that's the kind of horse she put you on and its action took you by surprise."

I nod through a mouthful of my breakfast, rolling my eyes a little in the process.

"Don't be condescending in your response to me. I rode internationally. Your mother could have. You will. But, Piper . . ." She waits for me to look up. "You need to shore up your fighting spirit. I don't know what's happened to you in this past year, but between your ridiculous reticence to obtain your license and this moping about, you are going to get left behind. Other riders are willing to fight for it. Not whine."

The air tightens in my lungs and my muscles go hot.

No wonder my mother gets irritated with my grandmother. But I bite my tongue and search for the internal steel I use at horse shows. This is what I'm here for, I tell myself. MaMolly's drive, her lectures, and the opportunity to ride with an Olympian. I eat my eggs in silence. When I put my fork down, I'm powered up.

"I drove yesterday. I'm driving again today. I'm going to get past it."

"Good. Now get out there and do your best. Even if Schober only lets you ride at a walk all summer, you'll have this experience to put on your CV." She chuckles and the deep lines in the sides of her cheeks crinkle. "Your last name may be Kitts, but you're still a Malone. And Malones are winners. Not just in competitions."

I'm still thinking about MaMolly's tough love pep talk when I get outside. Kat is waiting for me in her van. Today she's got her hair thrown back in a short ponytail and is wearing a school T-shirt, a pair of Nike shorts, and flip-flops. It's a stark contrast to her glamour of the day before. A little flutter of, hmm, this girl likes me, makes me look twice. My friends are right. She's fire symbols and now that I know she's questioning, I feel like I should have known from the start. But it doesn't change my morning's resolve. Horses, riding, not girls. I am here to grow as a rider, not have a summer fling to make myself feel better about getting broken up with. Even if she is cute *and* nice.

I break the awkward. "Hey, thanks again for the ride. And look"—I hold up both hands in surrender—"no awkward. In fact, there's something I need to explain."

Kat pulls out of the driveway. "You don't need to explain anything to me. I, well, god. This is awkward."

"No, stop." I think about the inner steel my grandmother swirled up inside me and draw it into my words. "It's me that needs to apologize. I had no idea you were into girls, which, my bad on making assumptions, but I've been going through an awful breakup and all those pictures I took of us, well, they were kind of to make this girl back home jealous. If I'd known I was giving you the wrong impression, I would have toned it down. But I thought you were straight, saw what I thought was a harmless opportunity, and took it. I didn't mean to lead you into the wrong impression. I really like you as a person, Kat, but I have to concentrate on my job, you know?"

Kat wrings her hands on the steering wheel and lets out a bunch of short breaths like she's yoga meditating or something. Damn. She's upset. I turn my body toward her.

"Please don't feel bad. I like you so much more than I thought I would." As soon as the words leave my mouth, I know they're wrong. "God, that sounds horrible."

Her widened eyes confirm my thought but she's still not saying anything.

I try again. "My *grandmother* connected us. You can't possibly think that's cool."

At this she finally says something. "Yeah, but your grandmother's not your average granny." And she smiles.

I let out a breath I hadn't realized I was holding. "True. And you're awesome and some girl's going to be so lucky. But I'm not ready to pursue a new relationship." I don't mention that I've been pretty desperate to rekindle my old one.

She's quiet for a minute as she drives, but then she shakes her head. "There's no way I could make that girl jealous."

"You don't know her. You could."

"But she's so gorgeous." Kat reaches the palm of her hand to her face and groans. "Oh my god, I made it awkward again. Now you know I was stalking you."

I can't help it. I start laughing. "You are seriously ridiculous. Don't we all do that? And yeah, Judith is gorgeous, but you are, too." Now I'm the one that feels awkward because I've made Kat's neck go all blotchy again with my compliment. I divert. "But what you said, about being queer. Is that legit?"

Kat sighs and turns onto the highway toward the farm.

"How would I know? I've kissed one boy. And I've never kissed a girl. And it's not like there's this huge pool to draw from in this tiny town. But yes, I think so. When I tell myself that I'm into girls, all these moments of my life kind of fall into place and make sense."

"I get that. The intense friendships? The one girl you couldn't stop obsessing about because she seemed so perfect? The way you noticed the smallest details about her and didn't notice boys the same way?"

Kat nods. "Yes. That's it."

"Am I the only lesbian your age you've ever met?" That would explain a lot. It seems like most of my friends had fallen for the first girl who they'd ever had the mutual confession with. Even if it only lasted for a few hours.

"I mean, there's this girl that works for my dad but she's a few years older than me and not really somebody I'd be into dating. She's kind of shallow." She groans again. "That makes me sound awful. I'm sorry. It's just, you're actually smart and interesting and motivated. Can we please rewind?"

Her compliments don't go unnoticed but I can't linger in my ego stew at a time when I know it'd be bad for both of us. Kat's becoming a friend and I don't want to do something stupid just to make myself feel better because the opportunity is there. Even if everything she just said is exactly the kind of thing I like to hear.

"We can rewind. Or . . ." A new idea begins to form. "You can teach me to drive, keep making Judith jealous in photos, and I can help you find an available girl to test your theory on. In all our spare time."

Kat laughs. "I've lived here for eighteen years. You think you can pop in for the summer and find an eligible girl?"

"Yes. I've been meeting some of the other riders in the area. It's a diverse group of people. I could introduce you to different people than the ones at the bonfire. People you might not ever meet in your circles."

Kat's expression changes to a grimace.

"What? Did I say something wrong?"

She shakes her head. "No, it's just horse people. I don't ride. I don't talk the talk."

"But you listen. And most of us just want someone who's willing to listen to us obsess about our perfect canter departure. Besides, we're talking about finding someone for you to kiss. You don't have to ride to make out with a rider."

She pulls into the barn driveway and comes to a stop, then drops her forehead onto the steering wheel. "This is so fucking awkward." Then she lifts her head up and shrugs. "Okay. I'm in."

"Really?" I didn't expect her to go for it. Now that she has, I kind of want to take it all back.

Kat points to the barn. "Guess you better get to work. Pick you up at six?"

"Yes." I take a huge gulp of air. "And make me drive again?"

Kat raises her hand and I high-five her waiting palm.

Just as she's getting ready to drive off, she yells at me through the open passenger window. "I promise to wear something picture worthy upon my return."

What I don't have time to say is that she's the kind of person whose inner light would shine through in any photograph.

But then, that probably would have been . . . awkward.

KAT

My inner turmoil has calmed, sort of. I've had a week of driving Piper to work, giving her driving lessons, and she hasn't made me feel strange. And giving voice to the thing I've been thinking about off and on for the past year or two feels good. I'd told a girl that I was potentially into her. The sky hasn't fallen. The ground hasn't split open. And weirdly, it feels right. So, okay, Piper isn't into me. Which is a bummer, a major one, but there has to be a girl somewhere? That horse girl from the coffee shop had smiled at me, she had been cute. Maybe she's one of the people Piper plans on introducing me to. But then again, I doubt I can just randomly hook up with someone. I'm not the kind of visual person like Elliot or my sister where

I can see someone and immediately lock lips with them. I need conversation, a tiny window into their soul, a true connection.

Which brings me back to Piper. I can imagine the moment.

My brain voice laughs. *You* have *imagined the moment.*

I give Piper a driving lesson. She goes out on a real road. We park the car to switch seats for me to drive us home and as we cross paths in front of Delilah, she puts her hand on my arm to stop me. She smiles. Says thank you. I never thought I could drive. You've made it all possible. Then her dimples deepen and a sweetness settles into her eyes and her hand is still on my arm and then she steps closer. I don't move. I stand there. I smile back. She leans closer, hesitates, to make sure it's okay, and I nod. Then we both move toward the other until our lips meet and maybe I put my hand on her arm and pull her closer. Maybe we even need to get into the van to kiss more. I touch my lips as the fantasy unfolds for about the twentieth time. A previously unfamiliar tightening pulls at my core.

I open my eyes wide to stop the daydream. This is stupid. Why even go there? She made it clear that kissing me was not something she thought about, at all. Now I have to imagine kissing someone else after it'd taken me so much to work up to thinking about kissing her.

Ugh.

Emma breaks the spell as she pops into my doorway. "Is this good?" She twirls in an aqua fitted tank, sparkly jazz shorts, and a pair of leg warmers and half socks.

Something in her voice makes me smile. I guess it's that she actually does care enough about this audition to worry about what she's wearing.

"You look like their next lead dancer."

"Doesn't work like that."

"Don't get snippy. Can't you let me compliment you when it's due?"

She flops onto the bed next to me. I pull on my cute orange socks that have lemon slices printed on the fabric and grab my white Vans.

"You look like a Dreamsicle."

"You may be able to dance circles around me, but my personal style is perfect for me, and you know it."

She flips over onto her back and steeples her fingers. "A unique cross between hipster librarian, Future Business Leaders of America, and middle school. What's your first tat going to be? Pikachu?"

"Doubtful. You'll get one before me. It'll be a late night, drunk, tramp stamp. Oh, I know, infinity symbol above your butt crack."

Emma's brow wrinkles and I fall back on her, laughing.

"Oh my god, I'm right! You're already thinking about it."

She pushes me off. "Stop. You know I love infinity symbols. Are we going or what?"

"Going," I say and grab the keys off my dresser.

On the way to Greenville, Elliot calls and Emma puts him on speakerphone. "Hey, cuz, what's up? How's Myrtle?"

"Disgusting. Over it. Ready to come home," he answers.

I'm surprised. "Really?"

"No, of course not. There are actual people here. From all over. Celebrating freedom. And debauchery. And beer pong."

"Then why are you calling?" Emma always cuts to the point.

"Because . . . been seeing pictures of Kat and new girl from the North. Wanting the report."

Emma's stare is hot on me as she waits for my answer, but whereas last week I would have freaked out over this question, today I have a whole new, and honest, perspective.

"New girl is nursing a broken heart and she is using our imagery to create a faux scenario to cause waves of jealousy that ripple across the country and make said heartbreaker regret the moment they parted ways. I am nothing but a willing pawn."

I can't look at Emma cause I'm getting on the interstate

but I hear her quiet "whoa."

Elliot laughs through the phone. "Ooh, subterfuge. I like it. Count me in when I get home."

Emma finds her voice. "Oh, I love a good catfight. I'm in too."

"I have to drive, y'all. Bye, Elliot. Be safe."

"If you see my parents, tell them I met a nice girl from Ohio named Bill."

When we hang up, Emma is all questions. "If you knew why she was taking so many photos, why didn't you say something at the pizza place?"

"I didn't know then, plus you weren't exactly being friendly enough to merit an explanation. You called out her friends for being anti-feminists. She told me the whole story when I took her to work the next day."

"And you're okay with being used like that?"

"I mean, now that I know the whole story it's not weird. Besides, what's wrong with a little ego boost?"

"So you do like girls?"

"Why do you keep saying that?" I know I should just tell her. She might freak out at first, but only because I'm her sister, not because she's a homophobe. Am I internally homophobic? Is that what's keeping me from admitting it? No. I hold firm to the way I've been feeling. This is mine. I need it to keep being mine. At least for right now.

Emma lifts her palms up in the air. "Because it boosts your ego to have queer girls calling you hot? You've never had a boyfriend. You've never even really cared about it. And, I dunno. You do get sort of perky when Piper's around."

"Perky? Just because your hormones started popping when your boobs did, doesn't mean I'm the same way. And wouldn't you get an ego boost being called hot?"

Emma smirks. "Jordan called me hot like five minutes ago." She flashes her phone screen.

"Can we please drop it? You know things are different for me."

"Fine." Emma turns toward the window and mumbles. "I'm only trying to help. I only want to see you happy."

Me, too. I want to see me happy, too. But for now, I only have daydreams.

chapter sixteen

PIPER

I've had two whole weeks with Dilara Schober. Two whole weeks of mucking stalls and not being allowed back on one of her horses. Wicked frustrating, but at least the other parts of my Harmon summer are turning out okay.

Today I'm going to drive on an actual road. It's a private road in an undeveloped subdivision and has zero traffic, but Kat's dad has agreed to meet us in his car so I get the feel of passing and approaching another moving vehicle. It's my version of training wheels. I'm only a fourth as anxious as when we started.

"Piper." My mom picks up on the first ring.

"Just wanted to say hi. And let you and Dad know I'm driving on a road today." I don't bother telling her all the boring details. "Any barn leads?"

Mom has sent me links to a few training stables I can ride at when I return home, but MaMolly has scoffed at every one. The only one Mom's found with a trainer MaMolly trusts is an easy hour and forty-five-minute drive from our house when you factor in traffic. Mom nixed that one. It seems like my riding career will be over for the rest of high school if we don't come up with something soon.

"Not yet, but I'm asking around. You can always go back to Fair Winds."

"They don't have a dressage trainer."

"Can't you switch disciplines for a year?"

"And throw away all my hard work?"

Mom sighs. "I'm doing what I can. You are in Harmon for the summer, aren't you? I did agree to that."

I want to tell her that it's great and that MaMolly's offer is really panning out but considering my last few weeks of work, it'd be an even bigger lie than letting them believe I was driving on a road that might have traffic.

"I know. Thank you again."

This seems to mollify her. "You're welcome. I'll let your dad know about your driving. He'll be thrilled."

We hang up and it only takes about a minute before Dad sends me a string of Big Papi GIFs, and lots of way-to-go-girl's. Dad's favorite Red Sox player gets me thinking about Kat's brothers, which gets me thinking about Kat.

After tonight's driving lesson, I'm dragging her to a party. It's a horse show weekend, so the party's going to be big. When I shared with Beatriz that I had a friend who was looking for her first girl-girl kiss, Beatriz got excited to help and invited us. I feel a responsibility to help make this happen even if I still feel conflicted about it actually happening. Kat is cool. She's a great driving instructor and a great listener and if I were looking to get involved again, definitely a consideration.

Example. Yesterday I had her stop at the local tack shop so I could get a new pair of lighter weight gloves that don't make my hands sweat. She took the location and found fun photo opportunities around every corner. She staged a mock fencing duel with the dressage whips, then had us try on the blingiest helmets ever and made sure to use the makeup filters for optimal sparkle. All in the name of making Judith jealous.

And the photos *are* creating some kind of impression on Judith. Her texts come regularly throughout the day, even though she knows I can't even look at my phone while I'm at work.

Maybe we're kind of back together?

There are lots of "I miss you" and "I love you" and "I was really stupid to break up with you to be with Brad" texts, but she hasn't come right out and asked if I want to get back together with her. And since she's the one who did the breaking, it seems like she's the one who should do the mending.

And then there's the other part. The impression Kat is creating on me. Example. When she slipped the perfect show coat on over my shoulders, then brushed the tops of my arms to straighten the folds. I'd be stupid not to notice how I froze up and couldn't move with the perfection of it. Or when she popped up next to me with that silly stuffed hobby horse and whispered, "Haaaaayyy, neighhhhbor" into my ear, then laughed at herself, but all I could do was focus on how warm her breath was on my neck. It's making me question this whole party idea.

My grandmother peeks her head into my room and breaks up my thought process. "Up for a ride?"

"Sure." The distraction will be perfect.

We walk to the barn in companionable silence. I remember one time telling Judith and some of her friends about MaMolly and how she was in her seventies and still riding her horses. To me it isn't a big deal because I grew up seeing my mom and grandmom astride. In fact, equestrian events are the only Olympic sport where men and women compete as equals in the same programs, a fun fact I love to mention. But I guess for kids whose families aren't horse afflicted, they think of grandmothers as ladies who shuffle around and bake cookies or something. My grandmother is a badass.

We saddle up Fonty and Jester. Though neither is sound enough to compete in the show ring anymore, they both enjoy a hack out around the farm a couple of times a week.

"Meet you at the mounting block." MaMolly's even faster than me when it comes to tacking up.

We walk the horses out the grassy lane that leads to the back pastures, then cut across a small wooden bridge to the community trails. Under the trees, the heat isn't as bad, though I brought the little horse hair swatter to keep the flies and mosquitoes at bay. That's one thing about summer in the South I don't like. All the damn bugs.

"Fill me in. Tell me about Schober's." My grandmother slows Jester to ride alongside me.

"She runs a tight ship. Everything is immaculate and her training program is disciplined. She also really pays attention to the horses' needs. She's quick to shift a session if any little thing seems off." The last thing I'm going to do with MaMolly is whine. She needs to see that I am truly in this. That I listen and understand.

"The Germans always did have a way with horses. Good classical riders. How are the horses? Any of them stand out?"

I tell her about the big gray mare that's moving into Grand Prix work, and the young stallion Franz said would be Dilara's next international horse, then I mention Dantoar. "She has a cute five-year-old she claims is too short for her program. But I've seen him move. He's lovely. And sadly overlooked."

The horses prick their ears as a doe bounds across our path and MaMolly and I watch as she disappears into the underbrush.

"Another fool decision in my mind. All this emphasis on giant dressage horses with legs just ripe for injury. In my day, hardly anyone rode the dinosaurs they pass for show stock now. Is he for sale?"

"MaMolly." My grandmother spoils me rotten. Always has. When she asks this my mind immediately leaps into overdrive and I know my parents would expect me to engage the brakes.

"Don't scold me. It's a reasonable question if you think he has talent. Maybe if I purchased a horse from her she'd actually let you on top. If the Olympics are your dream, you can't get there without riding. I'm not going to second-guess her program, but I can do what I can to make sure you don't fall further behind."

We come to a grassy part of the trail and the horses break into a little trot in anticipation of a good run. When we rein them back to a walk, I question MaMolly.

"I thought you said simply working for Dilara would be good for my future."

"It is. Invaluable to soak up as much as you can from someone of her caliber. But I'm also serious. I've thought about this. I could invest in a horse, and you. There'd be some maneuvering that would need to happen with your parents as far as the school year, but if you know what you want, why not leap into it now? Other girls have been traveling the show circuit for years already. Homeschooled and such. You have talent. Now's the time to leap. Get into the scene before it leaves you behind. Missing a year by riding at some hack stable back home won't help you a bit."

Fonty lifts her head in synch with the shock I feel inside. "Are you saying what I think? That I don't go back home? That I stay here and train with Dilara?"

MaMolly grins from under her helmet. "I knew I raised a smart one."

This would be the time I mention that she didn't raise me, my mom and dad did, but my head is literally reeling.

"Now I know your mother will argue about the schooling thing. But surely we can internet school you through your final credits. And if you want to go to college, there's Converse nearby. But even that little Olympian Laura Graves only went to cosmetology school and I don't think she ever finished. If you're going to be a horse professional, why not start now? You can take business classes along the way. In the meantime, let's hone your God-given talents. What do you think?"

I think I want to squeeze Fonty's dark bay flanks and break her into a gallop and scream wildly through the woods because it's a pretty amazing opportunity.

But.

There's Judith. And my parents. And finishing out senior year with my friends. And culture. And Uber. All the Uber. And my grandmother's kind of intense, though she does give me a tremendous amount of freedom.

But.

"You'd really buy Dan for me?"

"For us. I'd own him. You'd show him. Of course, I'd want him fully vetted and to get a few other opinions on his viability as a potential high-level horse, but if he panned out, then why not? If not him, then another." She reaches over from her saddle and pats my thigh. "I missed the moment to really push with your mother and I don't want to miss it again."

And unlike my mother, I don't mind the push.

KAT

I don't know how I'm going to get through this night. I'd agreed to go to a party with Piper. A party with horse people and strangers and potentially kissable girls. But now I have all the regrets. What am I doing? I'm not some jet-setting New England to the Carolinas to Florida multimillionaire homeschooled girl. I'm the daughter of a hairdresser and a party planner and I've never left the country and even though I have very high hopes about a brilliant and interesting future for myself, this doesn't really seem like the start of it.

Am I wrong?

Piper had been so excited at our driving lesson. She'd done great. Her grandmother had given her some secret bit of good news that she said she couldn't talk about yet and she hadn't even seemed nervous behind the wheel, she was so pumped up. Afterward, I dropped her off to shower and eat but now it's time to go pick her up for the party. The one where I'm supposed to find a girl, kiss her, and discover if this feeling inside is legit. How am I going to simply kiss some random girl? Is this really the way it works?

"No." I move a hanger to the side. "No." Another. "No." None of my clothes seem right. They're too girl-from-Harmon-County and this party is definitely people-from-elsewhere and they are probably all going to be in technical polo shirts and utilitarian jeans with the occasional polka-dotted belt. I finally settle on my go-to short jean shorts, gray Vans that have a strip of lavender along the sole with lavender laces, and a deep purple V-neck fitted tee. I wing out a dark cat-eye but leave the rest of my face makeup-less except for some coconut moisturizing lip balm. Lip gloss seems like it might be gross for kissing.

"Have fun." Emma's voice chirps the minute I step out the door onto our front porch.

Who's sitting on the porch swing with my sister? Jordan. She was right, between Jordan and dance I've hardly seen her. But what's even worse is my dad and brothers are sitting with them, too. Family time that I'm missing out on to go hunt random females.

"Thanks. But . . ." I glance between the five of them.

"But what?" Emma waves her hand. "You look cute. I like the purple."

"Is there a party?" Jordan asks.

Huh. It does feel good to know about a social event not on his radar. "Yeah. Out-of-town people here for the big horse show."

He nudges my sister in the side. "She's getting all fancy on us."

"You sure you don't want to go to the batting cage?" Dad grins, knowing I love watching baseball and cheering for baseball, even following a few of the Braves' players, but I am pretty hopeless when it comes to connecting bat to ball.

"I'll pass." Though it sounds like the perfect escape from this torture I've set myself up for.

When I pull up to Mrs. Malone's house, Piper's waiting on the front steps. I do a double take. She has her hair down and I've never seen it that way, long with soft waves that curl around her shoulders. Her green button-up shirt is the perfect color to complement the not-quite blond, not-quite brown, not-quite red of her hair. I hope Judith knows how lucky she is to have such a total-package girl still in love with her. If only.

"Hey, hey, hey. You ready to get your groove on?" Piper bounces into the front seat and turns her back toward me so she can snap a quick video for her story. "Where we going, Kitty Kat?"

"Party!" I smile into the phone.

"Are we going to have a blast?"

"A blast," I parrot back, then I remember I'm supposed to keep the maybe, maybe not part of our charade going, so I reach forward and twirl a piece of her loose hair around my finger. "Your hair looks amazing like this. You should wear it down more often." I look into the video. "Hey, Piper's friends up north. Hair up? Hair down? Let her know in the comments." I turn my face and smile in her direction and she lets go of the button to end the video.

"That was good." She looks down, then scoots toward the door and away from me.

Which, okay, ouch, but who cares because all I can think about is how good she smells, clean with only the slightest hint of horse, and how soft her hair felt in my hand. I've felt plenty of hair, having spent more than my fair share of time at the shampoo bowls at the Tousled Orchid, but none of those heads of hair have made my hands tingle. Who am I kidding, this whole situation is a farce. I like Piper. Piper likes someone else. End of story. Or is it? We've been having fun. She texts me with rider jokes and horse ads she likes at least every other day. She still hasn't disputed any of her friends' comments online and the way those dimples deepen when she smiles at me. I'm a puddle. How can this not be something more? How can she not feel the way I've been feeling?

Piper types the address of the house into her phone and we're off. The closer we get the sicker I feel to my stomach. This is a mistake. All of it.

When I back the van into an empty spot near a huge barn, I exhale dramatically.

"You're going to be fine." Piper reaches over and squeezes my hand.

But I don't let go. My brain voice fires up inside. *Take the moment, girlfriend. Take it. Just do it. See what happens. Life isn't worth living without some risk.*

Really? I think. *Really,* the voice says.

So, against my better judgment and based off my delirious daydreams, I listen to my stupid inner voice. And pull Piper toward me, and before I can rethink anything I lean in and press my lips to hers.

Piper pulls back and the look on her face is fire. "What are you doing? You need to stop."

I knew, the minute I put my lips on hers and they were braced in return, what a miscalculation I'd made. You never kiss anyone without their consent. Without checking in to make sure they're okay with it. But I can't go into the party with the intention of hooking up with some random stranger without having tried to kiss Piper at least once.

"I needed to know before we went in there."

"Know what?"

I wish I could categorize the look on Piper's face but it's flipping through so many things, anger, hurt, surprise, that I look away.

"If coming to this party was the right thing to do."

"Was it worth doing *that* to figure it out?"

"No," I whisper, even though every one of my cells screams yes, yes, yes. Because here's the thing. Even though it was awkward and not what Piper wanted, to me, her lips feel like what I've been missing. "But I do think I'm gay."

"Well, I'm glad that one-sided, nonconsensual kiss could confirm things for you." She sighs and fidgets with her phone case. "I forgive you. This once. I guess I kind of get it." She opens the car door and glances over her shoulder at me. "But I wouldn't throw you into a lion's den. I have friends here. I'll be here. You don't have to do anything you don't want to do. You're sweet, and smart, and funny, and cute. If you lived in Massachusetts, you'd have kissed twenty girls by now. You don't need to kiss me."

But that.

That's where she's wrong.

chapter seventeen

PIPER

I march straight ahead into the party and filter a thousand thoughts at once. Snow White just leaned over, out of the blue, and kissed me straight on the lips. I did not see that coming. At all. And now? Seriously conflicted. I'd wanted to lean into that kiss. I'd wanted to lean in bad. Which would make me a cheater. Kind of? I don't know. Technically Judith and I are not back together. But isn't that my intention? Isn't it hers? Bottom line is I'm not a cheater and I can't kiss Kat, or let her kiss me, until I know what's going on with Judith.

I've been playing with fire when I should have had all this girl stuff on the back burner. All the flirtatious videos and photos and general shenanigans have come back to bite me on the ass. Or kiss me on the lips, as the case may be.

"Hey, Piper!" Beatriz is the first person I see as we walk into the room. I recognize a dozen or so of the riders and grooms and vet techs I'd met in the past couple of weeks and over at the apartment get-together. But there are a lot of new faces, too.

"Hey." I swing to my right. "This is my friend Kat I was telling you about."

"The driving instructor." Beatriz totally checks her out. "I've heard a lot about you."

"Hi." Kat reaches out her hand and Beatriz lifts an eyebrow before refusing the hand and pulls Kat into a hug.

"I would have waited to learn to drive if I'd known the instructors were so attractive." Beatriz's Southern accent deepens to gravel.

I stare at Kat's neck and there it goes, the blotch giveaway when she's embarrassed.

"Come with me for some introductions." Beatriz loops an arm around Kat's waist, winks at me, then leads her away into a crowd of girls.

Holy hell. I hadn't figured Beatriz was adding herself on to the list of possibilities. I'm not sure how I feel about that. Besides, she's twenty-four, kind of old to be interested in a high school student.

"Hey, Piper." Melanie, the blond rider from Dilara's, walks over.

I glance one more time in the direction Kat was led away. Beatriz's hand is still firmly on Kat's waist as she's introducing her to a group of people. Kat looks back in my direction for a second but just as quickly turns away. The need to march over and break it up surprises me. What the actual. But I don't. The whole idea was for Kat to meet someone who is not me. And now she has. Beatriz may be too old but she's a good person, and besides, Kat's not a pushover. She's proved that more than once. She proved it just a few minutes ago. I reach a hand to my lips, before turning my attention to Melanie. "Hey." People slide past us to the big wooden dining room table and fill up small plates with cheese and deviled eggs and other snacks.

"Come meet my boyfriend and some of the other local dressage students. Heard a rumor you might be with us for more than the summer."

"What?"

"Your grandmother stopped by the barn this afternoon to talk to Franz. I just happened to be there."

"Wow. She works fast. It's not a sure thing. At all."

Two guys bump into me, then apologize before moving away. I realize one of them is a well-known eventing trainer. "Is that . . . ?"

Melanie nods. "It is. And how amazing is it that this might be your world soon? I wished I'd had this kind of support when I was your age. I'd be so much further along in my riding. Between you and me, I think Dan is hella talented. In the right partnership, with the right rider, he'll go far."

"My grandmother asked about him?"

Melanie smiles. "She did. Didn't sound like it was a secret. Hope I didn't drop a spoiler."

I shake my head, then hold out my hand when she presents her boyfriend. "This is Alex."

I'm not into dudes, but that doesn't stop me from sucking in a breath. He's like the slightly older, slightly darker skinned version of Judith's Brad. So good-looking, in fact, that I'm immediately thrown into self-doubt. Are Judith and I back together? Is that what we've been doing? I mean, will I even be back in Massachusetts to be her girlfriend? I glance back but don't see Kat. I think about the way she'd leaned over and kissed me. And how I'd frozen, then gotten upset. Okay, so upset was maybe okay for that moment, but now? Am I an idiot?

The need to text Judith and get some answers pounds against my brain. I make small talk, meet a couple of other riders, glance around to make sure Kat's not looking for me, then slip into the nearest bathroom.

Hey. I wait for a few seconds and thank god, she's typing back right away.

Hey! And a heart.

I'm going to ask. I'm going to ask in a text. Because this dance we've been doing is messing with me and I have to know.

Can I ask you something?

Anything, boo.

What are we doing? I mean, since you told me about breaking up with Brad, it kind of seems like we're acting like girlfriends again. I need to know.

Someone knocks on the door.

"Wait a minute," I shout and wait for a return text. It comes immediately.

Why? Why do you need to know?

This unglues me.

Then her next text.

Is it because you want to date that girl? It kind of seems like you guys are into each other. She's pretty, I guess.

Another bang on the door.

Can I call you? It will take me a second to find a quiet place.

I open the door and a drunk girl throws her arms around me. "I thought you were never getting out of there. I have to pee so bad." She pushes me out of the opening and squeezes past. I make my way to a back porch that overlooks a small pond and dial Judith's number.

"Hey." Her voice is soft.

"It's good to hear your voice. I wish you were at this party with me."

"You're at a party?"

"Yeah, horse show people."

"Ugh, the worst."

I laugh, because I know what she means. We're our own brand of intensely pretentious. But I'm not calling her to make small talk. "Do you really think I want to date someone else?"

"I mean, maybe. That girl is in, like, all your pictures. It seems like y'all are into each other."

"You mean like Brad was in yours."

I hear her suck in a breath on the other end of the phone.

I ball my free hand into a fist because I know I shouldn't have said that. But my insecurity sometimes gets the better of me.

"Don't get mad. I just, there was a guy here who looked kind of like Brad and it brought all my stuff back up and it just seemed like maybe we'd been flirting again. I mean, we have been flirting, right?"

She sighs on the other side of the phone. "Yeah, I guess so."

A door opens and someone has cranked the music inside and I hear Cardi B rapping about her money moves. A couple smokes weed near the railing and I slink back into a corner and turn my back to them and the party that's starting to rage inside.

"You guess so?" I try to keep the irritation out of my voice.

"You're not dating that girl?"

"No." I lean against the wall.

"It sure seems like something was starting to happen from all your posts. Like you're really moving on. Away from me. That's why I wasn't sure. It seems like you've wanted to make me jealous or something. To pay me back."

Even though that's been my goal, hearing her say it out loud makes me sad. I don't want her to feel bad. I don't want her to think I've been flirting with her while starting up something else. "I'm not dating her. She is really nice, in a small town kind of way, but she's vanilla. She's not traveled, she doesn't ride. She's not anything like you." As soon as the words come out, I want to take them back. They're disingenuous. Kat is cool. She'd boldly kissed me in her van, which was totally not vanilla at all. Why did I feel the need to paint her as less than just to make Judith feel secure?

"But Piper. Do you remember how it was before we

broke up? You barely had time for me. You have big goals and I'm just normal. I have hobbies. You have aspirations. I'm going to college so that I can get a good job and have a family one day. You want to ride in the Olympics. Besides, you're there for the summer, and I'm here."

"I love you, Judith. I was so happy when you were my girlfriend."

Something about the words don't seem right though. Was I happy at the end? Any person who's going to be with me is going to have to figure out how to fit into my world in a way that works for both of us. I'm not going to be an easy partner because of my riding, but I know I'll be a good one. Judith never could see that. Why did it take until this exact moment to finally understand?

I stare up at the stars before I answer her question. All this pining I've been doing hasn't been because I missed our relationship. Our relationship was not right for either of us. I'd just been pissed off that she betrayed me. Pissed off she left me for a guy, even though I'd tried to be okay with it. Brad could just as easily have been a girl and I know that. She doesn't deserve my anger.

It's time for me to truly let things go.

The music quiets as the door to the porch closes again. I clear my throat and add, "But yeah, I do remember how it was. We fought. A lot. You weren't happy."

"And you're not going to change, Piper. It's what makes you amazing."

"Just not right for you."

"No." She hesitates, then adds, "I don't think so."

"So no more flirting?"

She laughs. "Well, there's nothing wrong with flirting if we both know it doesn't mean anything. I still think you're cute as hell."

"That's definitely flirting."

"Habit. What can I say."

"So, that's that?"

"Seems like it," she says.

There are a few seconds of silence and I think we're going to end the call, but then Judith speaks up again. "Tell me about this rumor I heard from Sasha that you might not be back in the fall? What's that about?"

I slide down the wall and pull my legs to my chest. It feels good to be able to really talk to Judith without the weight of our hurt cutting into our words. I tell her about driving, and Dilara Schober, and MaMolly's offer. How if my grandmother and I get our way, I won't be back for senior year. It's a good talk, the best talk we've had in months, and when I hang up an hour later, I'm ready to go find Kat.

KAT

I make the mistake of eating one of the gummy worms Beatriz hands to me, only to figure out it's spiked with tequila.

"It's good, right?" Her hand hasn't left my waist and at first, I thought it was super nice, but now it feels a little predatory.

"I don't really drink. Besides, I'm the designated driver."

She laughs. "Such a pretty driver."

I twist away from her hand. "Look, I've got to find the bathroom."

"Sure, sure." She points toward the kitchen. "See the line." Then she leans in. "But come back and find me, okay?"

"Okay."

Somebody turns on the music and I notice a group of people, in the den with the furniture pushed back, doing shots and grinding to Cardi B. I look around for Piper while I stand in line but can't see her. The girl in front of me bitches, "They're taking forever in there."

I decide to come back when the line is shorter and wander into the kitchen. Still no Piper.

A door is open out onto a deck, so I step outside. At first, I almost turn back around because there's a guy and a girl smoking weed, but then I hear a familiar voice. Thank goodness.

I walk closer to where Piper has her back turned and see she's talking on her cell phone. I start to turn around but then her voice raises and I hear her say, "She is really nice, in a small town kind of way, but she's vanilla. She's not traveled, she doesn't ride. She's not anything like you."

My feet freeze in place and my stomach plummets. Vanilla? Small town? Not traveled? I want to die. Obviously, she's talking about me. Then I hear her whisper in a pleading voice, Blah, blah, love you, something, something, be my girlfriend. I don't hang around to hear anything else or let the knife that just planted into my gut twist any deeper. Wow. Okay. I really should not have kissed her. My bold interior voice goes strangely quiet, like it's embarrassed at what it pushed me to do. Well, fuck it.

I'm here for a reason, aren't I?

Inside I bypass the bathroom and go straight to where I'd left Beatriz. So yes, she is probably too old for me. And yes, I don't know her. But she's obviously into me. Definitely not from here. And chances are, she won't blast my pictures all over the internet in order to have a hush hush reunion phone call on some random person's back deck.

"Want to dance?"

Beatriz snakes her hand onto my waist again.

"I thought you'd never ask."

A girl with dark spiky hair walks by with a tray full of little Dixie cups. I grab two of them and down them in quick succession. Fortunately, whatever it is, is sweet and tastes like peaches.

"Well, alrighty then." Beatriz grabs two for herself. "Ready to have fun?"

"So ready."

In the den, we thread through dancing bodies. All I can think about is Elliot's teasing over the years and Emma's eye rolls and now Piper's "vanilla" piled on top. What good has being the good girl gotten me? Nothing, a big fat goose egg. Screw it. I'll show Piper just how vanilla I am. Having a sister who's practically a professional dancer has at least rubbed off on me a little and I can shake it with the best of them.

At some point after we'd danced so hard I'm glistening, Beatriz leaves to use the restroom and the spiky-haired girl who'd been doling out shots dances up to me. "Lou."

"Kat." I smile and undulate my hips to the beat. She grins and opens her arms and we start throwing dance moves at each other and laughing.

When the song ends and Beatriz still hasn't returned, Lou motions toward the kitchen. "Let's go get another drink."

A tiny rational voice, not the ballsy internal voice, whispers "not such a good idea" but is immediately shushed by the ballsy one shouting, *Vanilla!* "Sure," I say and follow her. When she reaches back and grabs my hand like it's the most natural thing in the world, I don't pull away.

In the kitchen, she moves between cabinets easily, throwing things into a blender that seem to be there solely for her.

"Here." She hands me a cup filled with a frothy drink and a pineapple slice on top. "Piña coladas. Super cheesy but everyone loves them and most of these riders like to pretend they don't drink so we call them slushies for code. So where are you from? I haven't seen you around." She pours one for herself.

I suck through the paper straw. "Oh wow, this is good. Slushies are my new favorite." From the other room, I hear a musical trill. "Where's my little Kitty Kat?"

My eyes must get big because Lou's crinkle in response. "Want to get out of here?"

I nod. "Yes, please save me." Beatriz's voice is getting closer.

Lou grabs my hand again and pulls me out a door, opposite of the one leading to the deck where I'd heard Piper's stupid conversation with that stupid Judith girl, onto a stone patio where a few people are hanging out.

"Great party, girl."

"Thanks." Lou nods at the group, but then focuses on me. "Come on, let's go talk so I can find out more about my cute mystery guest."

"This is your house?"

She nods. "Yeah, I mean, my parents and mine. But they pretty much never come except for the big shows. They're down in Wellington or up in Connecticut. So." She guides me to a low stone wall and jumps up onto it in a sitting position, then pats the spot next to her. "What about you?"

Suddenly, I'm overcome with impulse. I lie. Sort of. "I'm Kat. Here for the summer visiting my cousin Elliot from . . ." I hesitate, thinking about how horribly true it is what Piper said, and finally land on Dallas because at least I have been there to visit my mom. "Dallas. Headed back to UT in the fall." I think about how old I should be to be drinking. "For my, um, junior year, but my parents got a divorce so I needed a chill summer. A friend who's into horses brought me to this party."

"So, you're not a horse show person?"

I sip through my straw and look at her over the top of it. "Is that a problem?"

She swipes her hand back through her short hair and looks sideways at me. "Not a problem at all."

Then she smiles again and I notice how her upper lip lifts up higher on one side than the other and even though she doesn't have dimples like Piper, her jawline is really amazing. I lift the cup to the side of my face as the air grows hot around me. She doesn't seem to notice.

"If you're not into horses, what's your thing? Besides stellar dance moves." Lou adjusts herself on the stone wall and now her leg is a mere fraction of an inch from mine. My brain voice chooses to slur her way into my consciousness. *Look at that leg. It's right there. You could touch that leg.* I lift my hand but then remember the trouble my stupid voice caused me in the van with Piper. I reach for my straw instead.

I take another sip even though I'm definitely feeling all the alcohol I've put in my body. "Business, I guess. I know that sounds boring. But both of my parents are entrepreneurs and I think it's cool to get to make all your own choices. And I really love baseball, watching it anyway." Then I label myself because no one knows me here, and it seems like as good a time as any to try it on someone besides Piper. "I'm a terrible lesbian when it comes to actually being able to hit a ball with a bat."

Lou laughs. "You're really cute. You look a lot younger than you are. But that's cool. I did two years of community college. Also business." She holds up her fist for a bump and I manage to tap knuckles without totally missing her hand. "But I'm taking a break to ride the circuit for a couple of years, then see what happens."

We fall into silence. Okay, awkward silence. Then she clears her throat and swings her legs against the stone wall. "So, I know we just met and all, but after dancing like that, I really want to kiss you."

My mind briefly flashes to how I didn't ask Piper that same question.

But this is what I've come here for, isn't it? And Lou seems cool. And I am attracted to her, I guess. Or at least my inner voice likes her leg. And sure, I've just told her a zillion lies and I'm pretty sure I'm drunk, and none of this is a great setup for getting involved with somebody. But this is only a kiss. The kiss. The beginning of the rest of my life. What the hell. If not now, then when?

I whisper, "That'd be okay."

"Cool." She inches closer so there's no space between us.

When we turn to face each other, our mouths connect immediately. Her first kiss is gentle, like the brush of wings. I close my eyes and get slightly spinny. We part, smile, then lean in again. This time Lou's mouth opens and mine follows suit and her tongue finds mine. A giggle works its way up my throat. She smiles against my mouth. "What's so funny?"

"It's nice, that's all."

She hops off the stone wall and turns to face me and pulls me toward her so my thighs are on either side of her and her hands are on the small of my back. This time when she kisses me, it's fierce. I put my hands on her back and hold her as tight as she's holding me and surprise myself with the breathy groans that come out of my mouth. I feel her smile again as she kisses away from my mouth to my neck and I tilt my head to give her easier access. Maybe not the best move. The stars start to circle.

"I can't believe you came to my party," she whispers into my ear and her hand moves from my back toward my side and to just below the sides of my bra.

I'm having a hard time focusing on anything between the spinning stars and the mouth on my neck and the hand that has now moved up and the thumb that grazes my nipple and makes me gasp.

"You'll stay tonight, won't you?" Her mouth moves back onto mine and she's warm and soft and tastes like pineapple and I think I might be turned on if I wasn't spinning and her hand wasn't now fully on my breast, which feels super good but also super foreign. But my breath is a traitor and keeps coming out of my mouth with tiny sounds like a mewing kitten and my legs are pulling her closer and my hand somehow goes under her shirt where it becomes enamored with soft skin, until suddenly my brain clicks into a moment of clarity and . . .

"Wait, what?"

Lou enunciates each word between kisses. "Stay. The night. With me."

"Oh." I pull my hand off her back and lean away from her mouth. I push her curious hands back to her sides. "I . . ."

"Kat?" A voice sounds from near the house. "Are you out here?"

Piper.

I hop down from the wall. "I'm so sorry. I've got to go."

"Noooooo." Lou reaches for me and her bottom lip pushes out in an extravagant pout. "I can give you a ride home later."

I lean in, give her a kiss on the cheek. "Tempting."

Then the dancing stars take over and I blurt, "Rain check?"

A grin comes back. "Promise?"

"Yeah," I say even though I have no idea what the hell I'm doing.

She lets go of my hands and I turn around as Piper comes into view.

Under my breath, I whisper to myself and the stars. "Vanilla, no more, baby."

And even though I'm mad as hell at Piper, I'm still glad to see her come down the walkway.

chapter eighteen
PIPER

My guilt for leaving Kat for so long evaporates as I see her untangle herself from the girl who's hosting the party. Well, I guess her night took a turn for the interesting while I was stuck in a deep heart-to-heart with Judith. A heart-to-heart where I essentially freed myself to maybe, at some point, return Kat's interest. Except now? My heart, which had been a leaping, soaring thing a minute ago, quietly retreats into a cave of self-loathing.

Looks like I missed my moment. As I walk toward them I have a quick chat with myself that this is best. Kat gets to discover herself and I can focus on my sport. It's all as it should be.

But is it?

Yes, I tell myself, it is. What makes Kat any different from Judith? I'm still a focused equestrian, and she's a girl who's not even out to her family. Let her figure things out with somebody else.

The girl, Lou I think, glares in my direction and swipes a hand up through her hair. She latches a finger into Kat's jean shorts and pulls her back. "Ah, don't go. Your friend won't mind, right?" Lou winks at me and oh my god, seriously?

Kat giggles and turns back to face her and whispers, "I can't stay. But, rain check? Remember?"

Stay? She can't stay. Her dad would kill her, I'm sure. There's some kind of negotiation happening and I am over it.

"Kat. I have to go home. Now."

She whips around. "Fine."

Another girl wanders around the corner and calls out, "Lou, where's another bottle of rum? You told me to keep the drinks flowing."

Lou places a hand on each of Kat's shoulders and pulls her forward and I witness what I can only describe as hot sapphic action. When she ends the kiss, Kat kind of wobbles and giggles, then punches her number into the girl's waiting phone. When Lou breezes past me, she winks again. "Make sure she gets home in one piece, will you?" Gross.

When she's gone, I walk over to Kat. "Well, damn. I only left you for a second."

She rolls her eyes. "You left me for an hour." She holds up a finger, then adds a second, and a third. "Probably two, and I fought off Beatriz, and ate gummy worms, and did shots, and met Lou, who gave me a very tasty piña colada. Oh, and also her tongue."

"You're drunk."

Kat puts her hands on my shoulders. "I AM drunk. I had peach shots and pineapple drinks and berry gummies and nothing, nothing at all that was vanilla." She locks fierce eyes on me until she burps a fruity alcoholic burp. "And I made out with a girl and I feel very, very weak in the legs. Is that normal?"

Shit. She must have overheard me on the phone if she said that vanilla thing. I am such a bitch. But I can't think about that now because one, Kat has her head on my shoulder and is humming Katy Perry's "I Kissed a Girl," and two, the realization has hit me that there's no way she can drive.

"We're going to have to call my grandmother to come get us."

This snaps her head up. "We are not calling Mrs. Malone. I am responsible. Responsible for you. Hey . . ." Her eyes light up. "I know, you can drive us home. I can talk you through it and we can go very, very slow."

Her phone buzzes and she looks at it and giggles again before looking up. "She's so CUTE. Right? Lou. So cute." She shows me the text. Can't wait for that rain check. Then she puts her hand on my shoulder and leans forward toward my face. "And here I thought you were going to be my first and we were going to be this nerdy happy couple and I'd support your business while you rode all the fancy horses and we'd look fabulous doing it, but instead Lou wanted me to stay in her bed tonight and teach me her ways. And you only wanted to get me kissed. You are a low achiever, Piper from Massachusetts with some long-distance girl-friend."

Wow. If I didn't feel shitty enough about myself already, I feel extra shitty now. Because I have no long-distance girlfriend, and the local girl who just drunkenly confessed she had some fantasy of our future AND kissed me earlier is now calling me an underachiever. There's only one thing I can do in this moment to feel bigger. Tackle a fear. Which means I'm going to have to tackle my biggest fear, at night, on curvy roads, with a drunk girl.

"Give me your keys." I hold out my hand and Kat bounces, then wobbles, on her tennis shoes, while she digs her hand deep into her pocket before pulling her keys out with a flourish. The silver charm shaped like the state of

North Carolina catches between my fingers.

"Voilà." Then she dances her way toward the van singing that stupid song at the top of her lungs.

Once inside, she leans her head back against her seat and pats the dashboard. "Be sweet to Delilah. She was my first girl, you know."

"You're going to stay awake, please."

"Yes. Absolutely. Awake for you. But . . ." She puts a finger to her lips and makes a shhhh sound. "I will also be thinking about that kiss. It was not my first girl kiss, but it was my best." She glances toward me. "No offense."

I take a deep breath and start the engine. Now, I'm not the kind of girl who can't be alone. But if this wackadoodle plan my grandmother has come up with works out, I sure did blow my opportunity for not only a life built around riding, but for an in-the-flesh local love life as well.

"Take me home, Jeeves!"

Luckily, Kat had the foresight to park with our nose facing out to the driveway so I manage to crawl toward the road without impediments. I push away the anxiety and give myself tiny goals. That big tree at the corner of my headlights. The end of the fence running along the road. The stop sign where I have to take a right onto a main road. My breath picks up.

"Kat, this was not a good idea."

"Piper. Girl. You are a rock star. You got this. You're driving. You're taking me home safe and in one piece. You got me kissed and you got to talk all mushy to that girl on the phone. Does she love you? She better love you. I mean, I shouldn't say this, it's probably too much for me to say but it looks like she was loving on some hot guy on her page." She giggles again. "Oops, stalker confession. Take a left."

I get a lucky break and there's no traffic coming in either direction so I turn slowly out and to the left. I speed up to twenty-five miles per hour.

"She loves me, she just doesn't want . . ."

Kat flings her hand out to my arm and I flinch.

"Easy peasy, girl. Anyway, of course she loves you. You know, I would have totally been your girlfriend, but now I've got Lou." She hums again. "Lou of the dreamy lips and the dreamy hips. Did you know she put her hand on my boob?" Her head drops to the side and she laughs hysterically. "It felt so good but it felt so weird. Is it always weird?"

This might be the time to mention that Lou is probably twenty-one or twenty-two and maybe not even the girlfriend type and yeah, the first time things happen it can be weird, but all I can focus on is the headlights that have crested the hill in front of me.

"Shit, Kat. Shit."

She sits up taller. "You are a great driver. You are fine. Hands on both wheels. I mean both hands on the wheel. Breathe. Easy. Look straight ahead."

The car passes us.

"See. You're fine."

I don't feel fine. I feel like I'm on the verge of dying. But I am driving. And eventually, and very, very slowly, I pull the van into Kat's driveway and park.

KAT

A tiny man with amazingly big fists awakes inside my brain. I put both hands to my head and try to stop him from pounding my skull. Eventually I realize it's the alarm on my phone. I fumble for it and hit snooze, dropping back to the pillow.

"Fuck." Flashes of last night come back to me and I cringe thinking about the kissing I did in that backyard. "Double . . ."

"Keep your fantasies to yourself, party girl, I have to go to work."

I jump at the voice I don't associate with being in my bedroom. I crack open one crusty eyelid. Piper sits in the chair at the foot of my bed. She looks irritated.

"What are you doing here?" The words stick to the roof of my trash can of a mouth.

She throws a crumpled-up T-shirt at me from the laundry basket at her feet. "I drove you here. You wouldn't let me call my grandmother to come get me and your dad suggested I should just stay over."

"Oh my god, you didn't call MaMolly? I'm going to be in such trouble with her."

"Don't be ridiculous, of course I called her. But you probably *are* in trouble, with your dad, though he's grateful you refused to drive home."

"That's right. You drove. On the highway. With the traffic. I'm so stupid."

"You think?"

"Well yeah." I don't want to admit how stupid I feel for making out with Lou. "You hardly know how to drive."

Piper rubs her temples. "You are far more complex than I thought you were. Don't worry. Just because I drove on a road doesn't mean I think driving is fun . . . yet." Then she sighs. "Seemed like you had fun."

I put the heels of my hands on my eyes and press. I take a few seconds to skip through the events before I look at her again. I did have fun. But then I also didn't. Partying is not my thing and even though I'd done exactly that, it isn't going to become a regular part of my identity. Plus, there were those things I'd overheard her say out on the porch. I remember those all too well. Which kind of sucks.

Lou, well, that's interesting, but she isn't going to be into me if she knows I'm still in high school and a local girl to boot. But Piper doesn't need to know my doubts and she doesn't need to know Lou is probably a dead end. Let her think I'm complex. Better than vanilla.

I sit up slowly and stretch my arms over my head. "Yeah, I had a blast. Super fun." Then I grimace. "Ow."

"Take some B12, a couple of aspirin, and a ton of water. I'll be downstairs waiting for you."

"Um, Piper?"

She stops at my door. "Yeah?"

"Where'd you sleep?"

She scoffs. "Don't worry. I slept downstairs on the couch."

Why would she think I was worried?

After I take Piper to change at her grandmother's, so much silence, then drive her to work, even more silence. I text Elliot. **Are you back?**

His reply is swift. Come over.

As I drive to his house I contemplate what I'm going to tell him. How much? Anything? Now that I've labeled myself, it seems easier to go ahead and tell him. He can be gossipy, but not when it comes to things that matter. Maybe it's time I let someone besides Piper in on how I'm truly feeling. Nothing risked, nothing gained, or something like that. There's a lot to be said for living authentically, even if it does mean putting yourself out there for small-town scrutiny.

Elliot meets me at the door. He looks horrible. Red patches cover his arms and cheeks and neck.

"You got sun poisoning?"

"I tried to stay out of the sun, but it's kind of hard at the beach when there are wet Speedo competitions and practically naked concerts by the pool. Anyway, you need to come upstairs with me . . . now." He glances furtively in the direction of the kitchen.

Once in his room, he shuts the door and locks it.

"Um, what's with the security?"

He grabs my hands and leads me to the bench at the foot of his bed and sits me down. "I told them."

"What are you talking about?"

"I told my parents."

I clap my hands to my mouth, forgetting all about my own revelations. "You finally came out to them? Elliot, that's amazing."

He shakes his head. "Not amazing."

"Oh no, your dad . . ."

He plops next to me. "Actually, no. Dad is fine. Said maybe we'd expand the pool business into Charlotte after I graduate from UNC and go after the LGBTQ dollars. Said he could care less about my private life as long as I'm happy and still willing to make Pool Pardners his Pool Pardners and Son reality. It's my mom who's the basket case. She's downstairs crying. Something about how she'll never have grandchildren now."

"How could she not have known?" I realize the irony of my own statement as soon as it comes out of my mouth.

Elliot groans. "She's so dramatic, too. I mean, I'm almost nineteen. But still, what is she even doing thinking about grandkids?"

I laugh. "I would think Aunt Vlada would be thrilled she didn't have to compete with another woman for your attention."

Elliot sighs. "Right?"

I lean my head on his shoulder and pat his knee. "She'll come around."

"Yeah, I hope. Just bums me out is all."

"Hug?"

He opens his arms and we squeeze each other tight. When I let go, I say: "The last thing you should be is bummed out. This is huge. I'm so proud of you. And how cool about your dad."

"Honestly, I think he knew and maybe he was pretending for Mom's sake. Anyway, enough about my family drama. What about you? What's been going on while I was off taking in too much sun and too many men? Anything good to report?"

Nerves march their way up my body. Elliot has just been exceptionally brave. Shouldn't I be, too?

"Ah come on, baby cousin." He elbows me. "Something's stirring beneath those pretty brown eyes."

"Emma did great at her audition in Greenville. They totally wanted her. And she's officially dating Jordan."

"Wow. Okay. Your sister's always liked the truck driving ones. But I have the spidey sense that you're avoiding. What's going on with the horse girl?"

I run my hands over my knees and back again. "Well . . ."

"Well?" Elliot nudges me.

"It's not the horse girl you think."

"Shut the front door."

I ball my fists up in front of my face and nod, then whisper, "I kissed a girl. You were right."

"I knew it. I knew it. I knew it. But, wait, not Piper? I thought you guys were into each other and just playing some weird hard-to-get game. Does Emma know?"

"No," I hiss. "Emma doesn't know and you can't tell

her. I'm not sure what's happening yet. Anyway, this girl, Lou, is like twenty or twenty-one and she thinks I'm going into my junior year in college. Also, I got hammered."

Elliot falls off the bench onto the floor in a heap and laughs hysterically.

I kick him with my toe. "Stop. It's embarrassing enough."

"I would have loved to have seen you out of control, that's all. You going to see her again?"

I groan. "I don't know what to do." I hand him my phone open to the text from last night and the one from this morning asking when Lou could see me again.

He hands the phone back. "Seems simple to me. Figure out a time. She's not local, is she? What's wrong with a white lie if it means you get to have some fun?"

So many, many things. But Elliot won't understand because random sex is totally his thing and totally terrifies me. And Lou definitely wanted to have sex. Isn't that what stay the night means?

He laughs again. "I can't believe it. I knew I was right about you." He quiets down. "Are you going to tell your family?"

I slide down onto the floor next to him and lay my head on his stomach and look up at his ceiling. "Yeah, eventually. It's so stupid that coming out is even still a thing, you know? Why can't we just grow into whoever we are and that's that. No big heteronormative bullshit to deal with."

"Agreed."

"Labels bug me. I guess that's why I've been hesitant to name this part of myself."

"If you did have a label, what would it be?"

I turned to look at him. "Definitely not asexual. Maybe demi-romantic? Pretty sure I'm a lesbian. Kat. I'm one hundred percent Kat."

Elliot grins. "You could always get together with that Lou girl again for the sake of experiment."

"What kind of experiment?"

"The see-how-lesbian-you-are kind. Or, you know, is it about the romance or the sex?"

"I don't know, Elliot. She seemed pretty . . ." I hesitate, looking for the right word. "Forceful."

Elliot's smile cracks open. "Well, you know what Obi-Wan would say."

"Ha. Ha."

But I do know what he would say.

May the Force be with you.

chapter nineteen
PIPER

Work is torture. The horses are all inside because it's wicked hot out and the stalls need constant cleaning. My thoughts aren't helping either. Thoughts of Kat pressed up against that girl. How comfortable she'd looked. How it could have been me. But instead, I'd gotten upset when she'd kissed me in the van, then she'd overheard what I'd said to Judith, and I hadn't even found a good moment to explain it away.

I wipe the back of my hand against my sweaty brow and try to talk myself out of feeling so bummed. Explanations never work out like you want them to work out. They end up sounding like excuses. Besides she'd found a girl to kiss. She didn't need me.

"Piper Kitts."

I jump to attention as Dilara Schober stands in the entrance of the staff room and am reminded I am definitely, most definitely, not supposed to be thinking about girls. "Yes." I'd tried a Southern "ma'am" on her once and that had not gone well at all.

"You are to ride Dantoar today and show me if you connect. Only then will I consider this plan of your grandmother's. So far, your riding seems more a liability than an asset for my program."

Today of all days? Today she wants me to ride? When I'm feeling so tormented?

"Finish your lunch quickly. Tack up the horse. Meet me in the arena at 2:15." She turns and marches off down the rubber-tiled aisle.

I glance at the clock on the stable wall. I'm going to have to hoof it, pun intended. I take deep breaths and fill my center. I do a quick sun salutation to send the frustration out of my body. I need to be 100 percent present when I ride.

I fast walk it to the other barn where Dan is stabled. He greets me with perked ears and a deep nicker.

"Hey, buddy." He drops his nose to allow me to slip the leather halter over his ears and I buckle the latch before leading him to the grooming stall. The feel of his coat and the earthy smell of the barn work better on my calm than any yoga pose.

It takes me about thirty minutes to groom him as close to perfection as I can, find his tack, and put on his leg wraps. By the time we get to the big indoor arena, I have exactly one minute to spare. I'm surprised to see MaMolly sitting on the observation platform. She lifts her fingers in a subtle wave, then lifts her thumb. I nod and lead the gelding to the mounting block. I can do this. I can right my riding wrongs and show Dilara Schober I have what it takes to ride with her.

Dan looks back as I place a foot in the stirrup and I pat his neck as I throw my other leg over. Once I'm settled in the saddle, I ask him to walk off. His stride is quick and animated as we warm up. When it's time to move him up into a trot, I concentrate on keeping my aids subtle and do all I can not to look to see if Dilara is watching.

At some point, she decides my warm-up is over and starts barking commands.

"Shoulder in down the long side.

"Leg yield from the quarter line.

"Good. Collect him more. Play with the reins when you ask for collection. But only from your wrists. Don't move your elbows! Keep the steady connection!

"Four loop serpentine into an extended relaxed trot."

So far, she hasn't barked at me or told me I'm a terrible rider. And Dan. He's a dream. He's easy to put on the bit. His back rounds naturally into my seat. Excitement builds inside me, which of course translates to the horse.

"Settle him. Slow your seat."

I breathe deeply and calm my inner thoughts. She has us do canter transitions, then back to sitting trot before she calls out, "I've seen enough. Cool him out."

I let the reins hang long and Dan drops his nose as he walks. When we pass the observation deck, MaMolly is smiling. "Did it feel as good as it looked?"

I pat the gelding's neck again. "Amazing."

"Good. We'll talk more when you finish with work."

Once I wash Dan and put him back in his stall, I find Franz to work out the remainder of my day's job duties.

"All good. Your grandmother is waiting and will give you a ride home. Ah, but walk with me to the end of the aisle. Someone else for you to meet."

I follow him and we approach a horse being held by someone while a farrier trims its hooves. The mystery groom turns as we approach, and I slow down. It's the girl from the party. The one tonsil locked with Kat.

"Piper. Meet Lou. Lou. Meet Piper."

Lou lifts her chin. "Hey, what's up."

"I thought you were into jumpers."

"Close. Eventing. But dressage is my weak link, so my parents helped me connect a few days a week here with Franz and Dilara."

The horse she's holding gets restless so she refocuses her attention and I turn to go find MaMolly, but before I walk away she calls out, "Hey, tell your friend to text me. She's just your friend, right?"

"Yep," I say. "Friend." But I don't say I'll pass along the message.

When MaMolly and I get back to the house, she decides it's time for *the* phone call. The one to my parents where I propose MaMolly's radical idea. We go into the study with the dogs.

"They're not going to say yes." I tuck my legs up and curl into the corner of the leather sofa.

MaMolly bundles Jill into her lap while Jacque pushes up against my thigh. "You certainly won't get to yes if you never ask the question."

The pretty chestnut gelding, and his potential to take me to the top, gives me the nerve to dial the home number. I put it on speakerphone. Dad answers.

"Well, hello, child of mine."

"Hey, Dad."

"Hello, David," my grandmother calls out. "I'm here,

too. Can you get Erin on the line as well?"

My mother's suspicious voice joins in. "I'm standing here, Mother."

MaMolly leans over the phone, her voice a bit louder than necessary. "I'm going to ask that you listen to everything I have to say before you answer."

My mother makes a throat noise on the other end of the line. "I can already tell you I'm not going to like whatever you're going to say if it's starting this way."

"Please, Mom," I interrupt. "I really want both of you to listen to what MaMolly has to say. You're right, you're going to say no." I pause. "At first. But maybe, can you wait to say no? Can you hang up the phone after we tell you and think about it? Talk about it. Give me a week or so to fantasize?"

My dad answers, "We can do that. Right, hon?"

My mother sighs. "I suppose. Go ahead, Mother."

And MaMolly does. She lays out a succinct, yet comprehensive plan on how I will go into partnership with her on this new horse, work and ride and compete for Dilara's breeding program, and finish up my high school degree online. I'm surprised to find out she's already approached the local community college to find out about both dual enrollment and their GED program.

When she finishes talking, I add my two cents. "Mom,

I know what you're thinking. That I should finish high school with my friends. Be at home with you guys. And I would have if Erik hadn't retired. But I really want to ride professionally. It's my dream. There are so many more opportunities for my riding career here. And Dad, I drove last night. On a main road. With other cars. Which I'd never have the guts to do up there."

MaMolly mouths silently, "You didn't tell me that."

I shrug. I hadn't told her all the gritty details about staying over when I'd called last night because she might question me getting future rides from Kat when I have a perfectly serviceable truck to use sitting out by the barn. But I could be as doggedly focused as my grandmother when it came to achieving a goal. And in this case, my goal is to put off getting my actual license for as long as possible.

And, if I'm being 100 percent honest with myself, the longer I can push out the license thing, the longer I get to hang out with Kat, even if she is seeing somebody else. There's nothing a new girlfriend can protest about when Kat's getting paid to teach me to drive.

KAT

I pull up to the barn at 6:00 p.m. and wait for Piper to appear. Six fifteen comes and goes and there's still no sign of her. There's no point in texting because I know her phone gets locked away in the staff office until she's done, but I start to worry. I also have to get home in time to meet up with my brothers at their practice. When the clock hits 6:20, I get out of the van to go find her.

A longhaired tabby cat greets me at the entrance to the barn Piper usually comes out of and twines itself around my legs.

"Hey, kitty." I reach down and pet its head while it butts against my hand. A door opens off to the right.

"Piper?" I call. "Is that you?"

A voice answers. "Uh, no, she left a few hours ago." A

figure emerges from the door and I suck in a breath. It's Lou. From the party.

One side of her lip arcs upward. "Well, hey there. And here I thought you'd been avoiding me." She lingers in the doorframe, propping one hand up against the side of it as she locks eyes with me.

I open my mouth to say something, then close it. I'm woefully unprepared for this moment even though I've spent pretty much every spare minute since I left Elliot crafting imaginary texts to her. I sputter something unintelligible, then manage to say, "I was going to text you back."

She drops her hand and scoops up the cat, which had walked over to her. "Good. Because I hate feeling avoided. What were you going to say?" The cat purrs in her arms.

I guess it depends upon which imaginary text. There were the ones that said Oh hey, about last night. I'm really only eighteen and still have a year of high school or the ones that said Look, you seemed really nice but I think you've got the wrong impression of me. Not a partier, still a virgin, and not sure I'm into you without consuming a bunch of alcohol, or the ones that said I'd love to hang out. What do you have in mind?

Erring on the side of nice and Elliot, I answer, "I was going to say that'd be cool. To hang out sometime."

She puts the cat down. "What about now?"

"Oh. I, um, can't." But I also can't tell her I'm picking

up my brothers because I'm not supposed to live here. "I'm supposed to do something with Piper."

She looks around. "Don't see Piper. Like I said, she left. Gone. Kaput. And me . . ." There's the smile again. "I'm standing right in front of you."

"I . . . um . . . can't."

"Okay. Got it. Well, no harm, no foul. We had a minute of fun. I'm sure I'll see you around." She thumps her hand against the doorframe and starts to turn to go back in the room she appeared from.

Wait, is she blowing me off? On the one hand, that would be the easy way to figure this out, but on the other, I'm not sure what I want.

"Wait. No. I don't mean. Gosh, I don't know why I can't talk around you. I'm not blowing you off."

The grin comes back. "You actually can't."

"Right." I smile and exhale. "I actually can't. Not tonight."

"When?"

I twirl my car keys between my fingers. "How about day after next?"

"Cool. Remember how to get to my house?"

I nod.

"Come by around seven. Bring a swimsuit." She winks. "Or not."

Oh damn. May the Force be with me.

When I get back to Delilah, I text Piper. **Are you okay? Came by to pick you up.**

She responds immediately. Oh shit, I'm so sorry. MaMolly came to the barn and things got distracting.

As I'm texting her that I'm glad she's okay, a thought comes to me. I keep typing.

Do you want to hang out, maybe tomorrow night? I could use some advice.

Is it weird that I would even consider talking to Piper about my encounter with Lou? It's just that, I know the advice Elliot gave me, which is basically go for it and get dirty. And I am curious, especially after running into her again today, but maybe there's more I need to think about. Maybe I need a better plan. Piper has experience. And if she can't be my girlfriend, at least she can be a friend.

Piper sends me a smiley face in return. Then, Yeah, that'd be great. We can watch a movie or something.

As I start the car, another text comes through, from Emma. It's a picture of condom boxes and a question mark.

What the hell.

I don't bother texting back. I call.

"What are you doing?"

"Exactly what you think I'm doing. I don't want to be unprepared. His parents are out of town and we're going to chill at his house."

"Emma."

"Your voice is judgy."

I watch as Lou saunters down the aisle of the barn and glances back with a smile in my direction. I put the phone on speaker so I can drive away. I don't want to judge Emma, but she's my baby sister and it's Jordan we're talking about and shouldn't I be the one to lose my virginity first? I mean, in the long line of firsts this is a big one.

"Sorry," I say. "Really? You're really going to do this tonight?"

"If it feels right. I have to lose it sometime and he's got great abs."

My mind cannot even comprehend choosing your first sex partner based on the strength of their abs.

"I'm getting this. The Trojan Pleasure Pack. Twisted, Sensations, Intense, and Warming." She's not even whispering into the phone. "That's got to be good, right? A pleasure pack? There are twelve of them in here. Do you think that's enough?"

I'm going to have a wreck if she keeps talking.

"I have no idea. Are you coming home first? Can we talk? I've got to pick up the brothers but I feel like we need to talk."

"Stop it. I'm having sex tonight. With Jordan. Get over it."

Desperation takes over. Or maybe it's my own nerves

around this issue, because my sister seems completely at ease with her own decision. "Emma. No. Please come home. I have something I need to talk to you about. Something serious."

I hear the cashier asking her if that will be all and my sister's voice all perky. "No thanks, this is great, thanks so much." How can she not know that half of Harmon is going to know she marched her ass into the CVS and bought condoms? How can she not care?

"Unless you're finally going to tell me you like girls, there's nothing stopping me from getting into Jordan's truck right this very minute."

"Wait, what? Jordan sent you in to buy the condoms?"

She laughs. "No, he's not here, but it was worth a try."

I swallow a huge gulp as I turn the van into the ball field.

"Okay."

"Okay what?" she asks.

"I'm going to tell you something you want to know if you please come home first before going to hook up with Jordan."

She screams on the other end of the phone.

"OMGIKNEWITCOMEPICKMEUPFROMTHE-SALONASAP." Then the phone goes dead.

chapter twenty

PIPER

After MaMolly and I finish the call with my parents, I head out to the barn. Beatriz is busy cleaning up.

"Hey, girl. Whatever happened with your friend from the party?"

"She walked right into Lou's arms."

Beatriz clucks. "Oh man, I should not have let her out of my sight. Lou's a piranha."

Pretty sure Lou's not the only piranha, but I skip over that opinion. "Kat's only eighteen. Still in high school. Lou wouldn't go after somebody that young, would she?"

Beatriz shrugs. "Eighteen is legal. I would have hooked up with her. Total hottie." She side-eyes me. "Thought you weren't interested in her?"

"I shouldn't be."

Beatriz laughs and hangs up the pitchfork on the barn wall. "Should have, could have, would have. There are no rules in love, baby girl. Besides, sometimes the frying pan feels real good after the fire. Between the devil and the deep blue sea and all those other sayings. One girl breaks your heart, another one puts all the tiny little pieces back together. There's nothing that says you have to have a set number of days between relationships."

I pull my braid over my shoulder and re-plait the end of it. "Thought you were into staying free of encumbrances."

"That's me. But you." She wipes her hands on her breeches. "You seem like the type of girl who does best all encumbered. What do you say we go get some food? Have plans? We can get all deep and emotive over carbs and protein."

I think about it for a second and quickly come to yes. Beatriz actually is turning into my Southern Sasha, slightly older, slightly wiser, definitely fun, and somebody to talk to about the ways of the girl-loving heart. "I have zero plans and carbs sound great."

I climb into Beatriz's truck and as she drives toward town, I lose myself in dangerous thoughts. Kat and Lou. Kat doing something she might regret. Kat doing something she might not regret. I take a quick scroll through my posts and look at some of the very first photos I'd taken from the night at the bonfire. If only I hadn't been so hung up on Judith. My friends back home were right. Kat was fire to look at and fire to know and interesting despite not being a horse girl. And I can't stop thinking about that thing she'd said when she was drunk, about our imaginary rosy future. I'm such a sucker for a romantic dream.

Beatriz slows at the entrance to the BBQ Barn. Outside the tables are crowded with people sweating it out.

"Good?" she asks.

"Sure."

We park and make our way through crowded picnic tables and I side-eye people's plates of ribs and pulled pork. We're almost to the order window when a familiar voice calls out, "Massachusetts. What's up?"

"You know that guy?"

I look. It's Kat's cousin, Elliot, waiting for an order. "Yeah, he's cool." I wave, then hold up a finger in a universal wait-a-sec pose. When we finish ordering we thread through tables and I make introductions. "Beatriz, Elliot. Elliot, Beatriz. We work together at the barn," I explain.

"Oh." The word is weighted. "Been hearing stories about you horse girls."

I'm not sure how to take that so I skip on past. "Heard you were at the beach."

"Was." He stretches his arms up above his head and cracks his knuckles. "Got back this week." He drops his hands and winks. "Didn't stop me from creeping on your account, seeing all those cute, cute pictures of you with my sweet little cousin."

Beatriz eyes us. "Oh, so you're the brunette's cousin?" She digs an elbow in my ribs.

"Yep. You don't know how many years I've been waiting for some girl to come along and make her wake up and smell the roses, and here you are."

I feel my face getting warm. What is even happening? What have they talked about?

The guy at the counter calls out Elliot's order number. He stands. "Y'all want to come back to my place? Eat by the pool? Continue this conversation?"

Beatriz elbows me again. "Say yes, frying pan."

"Um, yeah, sure."

After we all get our food, we follow Elliot back to his place.

We settle under the covered lanai and spread the food out on the table. "So," Elliot says as he picks up his sandwich. "You are from where?"

Beatriz eats a sweet potato fry. "Concord. Outside of Charlotte. But I lived in Germany for a while. Spend part of the year in Wellington when Dilara takes the horses down for the season."

"And you are of the LGBTQ variety?" He motions between himself and me. "Like us?"

She stares at him, then laughs. "You're a trip. Yes. Q. I'm down for just about anything except toxic masculinity and unhealthy relationships."

"What do you think of my sweet not-present-so-we-can-talk-about-her-but-only-with-kindness Kitty Kat?"

Beatriz doesn't hesitate. "Hot."

Elliot steeples his fingers and looks at me. "And I understand you have expanded her universe?"

I about choke on my chicken wing. "What?"

"She said you took her to a party, which proved interesting."

Beatriz leans back in her chair. "Oh, it was interesting all right." She leans forward and jerks a thumb at me. "This one has been pining away about some girl back home while the whole time, your sweet, cute, available-for-the-picking cousin has been right under her nose. But no, rather than explore her options, she hands your cousin on a silver platter to the biggest player this little community has seen in a couple of summers."

I start to say something about how Beatriz would have willingly gotten in there herself but Elliot interrupts.

"And you did this because?"

I can't take it anymore. "OMG. Stop talking about Kat like she's an object. She has agency in this. She makes her own decisions. The girl is wicked smart, and wicked self-assured, and you two are talking about her like she's some sort of sex toy. Stop it."

Elliot smiles. "I like you, Massachusetts."

Beatriz nudges me. "Frying pan."

"How are we going to fix this?" Elliot looks at Beatriz.

She purses her lips. "Karaoke?"

He laughs. "Karaoke fixes everything."

I have no idea what they're talking about.

But I start thinking about songs.

KAT

I park Delilah in the driveway and Emma practically pushes me upstairs and into my room.

"What are we eating?" the brothers yell.

Emma yells back, "Dad said order pizza."

Whoops and hollers echo off the stairwell as she shuts my door and spins around, throwing her CVS bag onto the floor.

"Spill. It. Right. Now." She shoves my clothes off my desk chair and sits with her arms hanging over the back of the chair facing me.

I sit on the bed. Now that I have her here I'm tongue-tied.

"I, uh . . . let me see what you bought."

"No. This is not how this works. You do not get to use sly manipulation to get out of the conversation you promised me we would have in order to delay the inevitable sweet death of my virginity."

"Jordan McMasters."

"Yes." She rolls her eyes. "He of the great abs, average mind, and questionable future. But he is sweet. And not the douche his truck would imply. But. You are stalling. Tell me."

I grab a handful of my comforter, then release it. I think about sitting on the stone wall and Lou's hands on my body. Then I think about Piper's face when I kissed her against her will and feel kind of sick. I blurt it out. "Okay, you and Elliot were right. I like girls. I want to kiss girls. It's why I can't begin to conceive of a Jordan in my life because, just . . . gross."

"I knew it." Emma claps her hands together.

"That's what Elliot said." As soon as the words leave my mouth I know I've made a mistake. Emma looks stricken.

"You told him before you told me? I can't believe you." She turns her back to me for a second, then turns back around waiting for an explanation.

"Emma, don't be mad. It was an impulse kind of thing. I really did mean to tell you first."

"How long have you known, can you at least tell me that?"

"A while," I say. Because even though I didn't have substantial proof like my body's recent reaction to Lou's kissing, it is something that's been simmering under the surface for a few years now. I can think back on all these moments of feelings. The cousin of a friend who I met at the swimming pool and got irrationally attached to in seventh grade. The almost kiss freshman year. The way, even though Cassidy Phillips was never my type, I would study her in the halls of school. My obsession with any show on Netflix that has two girls in a relationship. I'd managed to convince myself it wasn't because I'm queer, just openminded, and who wouldn't think it's hot when two girls are into each other? But now, I know without a doubt, that it's so much more than that.

"Are you into Piper? Was I right about that?"

I shrug. "She's not into me. I told you she's hung up on some girl back home."

"The Judith one from the internet."

"Yeah." I take a deep breath. "But she wants to help. She took me to a party. The night you went to the batting cage. I met someone there."

Emma jumps up from the chair and leaps onto the bed and starts tickling me. "Tell me, tell me, tell me."

I push her off. "Stop." I turn to look at her. "You're okay with this? With me being . . . you know . . ."

"My sister? Please. I love you. Even though I get super

sad about Mom leaving and think how great it would be to live in a bigger city, it's you I could never do without. Whoever you are." She boops my nose. "Now spill. I want details."

I take a relieved breath. "Well . . . I was walking around the house and this girl started dancing with me." I leave out the part about getting shit-faced and overhearing Piper's conversation about me. I don't deep dive into exactly what happened out on the stone wall, but I do mention the kissing and how she wanted me to stay the night.

"Damn." Emma's eyes grow wide. "That girl moves fast."

"I might have told her I was older than I am."

"You did not."

I nod.

"What happens next?"

"It may be happening night after tomorrow night."

"Shut up."

"She invited me to come over and go swimming."

The doorbell rings and the brothers yell up the stairs, "Pizza's here!"

"Swimming sounds innocent enough."

I tuck my hair behind my ear. "Just the two of us. Suits optional."

The boys yell again. "We're going to eat it all!"

I start to get up.

"Wait." Emma grabs my arm. "If I tell Jordan I can't come over tonight and go over the night after tomorrow instead. And you go swimming with this Lou girl. Then the two of us, well, we can kill our v's on the same night. How perfect is that?"

"Kind of weird. Plus, for it to really be fair you'd need to wait an entire year from this date."

"Please." She bounces up. "I may be younger in age, but I'm way older in experience." She stops before she leaves the room and her face gets serious. "Are you sure you want to go over to this girl's house?"

"Shouldn't I be asking you that about Jordan?"

"You already did and yes I do. But you, Kat. You're different from me. And that's okay. And just because I think I'm ready doesn't mean you have to be. What's this girl even like? Is she nice like Piper?"

My eyes flare open. "I thought you hated Piper."

"I never said that. Only that her obsessive photo taking and posting was strange since she didn't know us. She's cool enough. At least I've met her."

"I, uh . . ." I don't know Lou, not like I'd spent the last month getting to know Piper. Maybe this whole going over to her house for a rain check is a stupid idea. Do I even want to?

Emma opens my door to head down for food. "Well,

whatever. This is a big week for us. You coming out. Me losing my virginity. It's going to go down as epic." She laughs. "Get it, go down. That's what you'll do, right?"

As she disappears down the stairs laughing hysterically, I hesitate.

What will I do?

What will Lou and I do?

How does it all even work?

chapter twenty-one

PIPER

I think a lot about the conversation with Beatriz and Elliot. I can see what they're trying to do, be matchmakers, hook me up with Kat. But I'd been trying to force the situation with Judith for the last four months and what had that gotten me? A flattened heart and battered self-esteem. I need to stick with what I'm good at. Riding. Time to woman up. Time to get my driver's license and take care of my own needs. That way I won't focus on distractions and Kat can be free to pursue Lou and find herself. Even if I like her, which I do, how would it seem if I came back around now after saying bye to Judith. "Um, yeah, so I've been trying to make Judith jealous since I met you but now that you like somebody else, suddenly I like you." It would seem desperate and pathetic, that's what.

I text her. **MaMolly's driving me to work this morning.**

Her response is instant. Oh. But are we still getting together tonight?

I hesitate in my answer because getting together is not letting her have her space. It's not me avoiding distractions.

She texts again. I need advice, remember?

Right. She had asked for that. It'd be rude to change plans. **Yeah. Okay, so pick me up. But I want to drive home from the barn.**

What? OMG! You're a badass. I should get drunk more often. Look at you go. Oh crap I better delete this text before anyone sees I was drunk.

The smile breaks through before I can stop it. She's so cute in her innocence. Which makes me think about Lou. Not innocent. A player, Beatriz had said. Probably a breaker of hearts. Wouldn't it be better if I stop Kat from getting a broken heart? Some other voice in my head pokes through. It sounds kind of like Judith. It scoffs. *You, not break her heart? Once you focus on riding and showing, how will you even make time for a girlfriend? She'll be sitting in the stands holding your cell phone and water bottle all by herself. And she's not even into horses. Be honest with yourself. I wasn't the one who ended us. It's you.*

I push my hands against my head. No. No. No.

??? Where'd you go.

Sorry. See you at six?

I get a horse emoji in return. Pretty perfect choice.

I walk to the kitchen to find MaMolly.

"Kat's coming over later tonight and I want to drive the truck to work. With you in it, of course."

MaMolly smiles from her corner desk. The truck comment definitely registers—I see her blink—but she doesn't make a big deal. "Wonderful. There are some salted caramel cookies in the pantry and plenty of microwave popcorn. Maybe you can take her on a dusk farm tour. Does she ride at all?"

"I don't think so."

"Well, there's always a first time. Fonty would be a good choice."

I doubt Kat is going to want to ride, but I'll offer. You never know.

The truck is a different beast from Delilah, but it's an automatic and even though I see MaMolly's hands grasp the seat a time or two, I get us to Dilara's inside the lines, at the speed limit mostly, and in one piece. I put it into park and unbuckle my seat belt. "How was that?"

"Not ready for NASCAR yet, but give you another week and I think we can talk about that license. It's part of the bargain for living here."

"Did my parents . . . ?" We'd only talked to them last night, there's no way they've said yes.

"Not yet. But I am very persistent. And this driving thing may be an excellent bargaining chip."

The day goes by quickly. I do my regular cleanup and then am pleasantly surprised when Franz comes and gets me to hack out horses with him. It's not schooling work, but at least I'm allowed astride. I see Lou once from across the barn. She waves, even smiles, and a flicker of guilt hits me. I don't really know her. Rumors spread about people without warrant and if Kat likes Lou, she likes her. It's better this way. I'm going to keep telling myself that until I believe it.

Fortunately, Lou's nowhere to be seen when Kat comes to pick me up.

"I knew you'd figure out this isn't so bad." Kat is already out of the driver's seat and handing me the keys. "Wait," she says and reaches for my phone. "Let me be your social husband and get a pic of this momentous occasion. Hold up the keys."

Judith hated when I'd ask her to take pics for me and here Kat is offering it up like she enjoys it.

I hold up the keys and smile. Okay, so I flirt with my eyes a little. We never explicitly said we were ending our internet ruse. I've never even had a chance to talk to her about the conversation the night of the party. The one where I'd both insulted her and let Judith slip through my hands for good.

Kat lowers her lashes when she hands back my phone.

She is really, really cute. My breath catches in my chest and there's a warm buzz under my skin.

Stop it, Piper.

Kat heads to the passenger door oblivious about my internal struggle. "Why the big change of confidence?"

Can I answer her without giving myself away? I take a huge breath to make the feelings subside before I speak. "I decided a little fear is okay. It's what keeps us safe. It's like riding. I'm aware my horse is a sentient being with its own mind, but I prepare. Driving is the same thing. Besides, you're probably going to be super busy with driving your sister to dance and stuff. And like you've made abundantly clear, Uber's not an option."

She hesitates. "Well, yeah, I am, but I'd planned on making time to drive you." She fumbles with the seat belt. "Gosh, that came out wrong. I don't want to discourage you from this. It's why we've been working on it. But, we're still going to hang out, aren't we?"

I am overcome with the urge to crawl across the console and kiss her. But I don't. Because that'd be stupid.

And the exact thing I'd gotten so upset at her about. And what the fuck is wrong with me? I'm not the girl who has to always have a girl, am I? Can I not just let it slide and be on my own? Not pining. Not crushing. Not looking beyond myself and my riding for something to complete me. I think about what Beatriz and I had talked about and how maybe some girls do best in partnership and maybe that's okay, too? Fuck me. Just shut up, Piper. Just be her friend. That's all.

"Yeah, of course we're still going to hang out. But I figured you'd be hanging out with Lou some, too."

The splotches come back to her neck. "Yeah, of course, me and Lou."

Right.

I focus on the van. Turning it on. Backing out. Staying between the lines. Going the speed limit but not a mile over. I don't talk while I concentrate and she's quiet in the passenger seat.

But I'm so, so aware that she's there.

KAT

Piper is incredible on the road. It's like all the little pieces of our almost daily lessons over the past weeks have added up to a big win and now she's actually driving. Still cautious, not so fluid, but she gets us home and she never acts scared and her hands don't even have their usual death grip on the steering wheel. I like her determination. It's super attractive.

"How was that?" Her dimples spring into action when she smiles.

"Amazing. You'll be ready to take your test when you get home from the summer. We're getting close to the forty hours you said was required. By the way, your grandmother's more devious than I thought. I can't believe she agreed to sign off on the hours I drove with you like she was the one who'd done it."

Mrs. Malone comes walking down the steps to greet us as I'm talking. "Not devious. Just maximizing my time and there's really no harm. You've done a good job as her instructor. But more importantly, you've not heard? I hope to keep my gorgeous granddaughter from going back north at all."

"Really?" This is big news. Piper's not leaving?

"MaMolly. You know it's highly unlikely."

Mrs. Malone kisses the top of Piper's head. "Your grandmother has the determination of a bull." She turns to me. "Now, it's time we got you on a horse, young lady." She looks at my sandals. "I believe I have some boots that will fit you."

I start to protest. Horses are very nice from the ground, but being on top of one of them has never been high on my agenda of things to make happen in this lifetime.

"Nope," Piper says. "You can't say no. At least not this one time. If you hate it, we'll never make you do it again. Right, MaMolly?"

She waves us off, her gold bangles clinking together. "Whatever you say, my dear, but I'm hoping if you live here that my friend Kat is going to be a very frequent visitor." Then she winks at Piper and me. What the actual? Is

Mrs. Malone trying to set us up?

Piper either doesn't notice or ignores her grandmother. "Come on," she says. "Let's go find you those boots."

In the barn, Piper moves with utter confidence, handing me a pair of boots, pulling two horses out of their stalls, putting them in something called cross ties, which are basically ropes that connect to their face collars and hold them in place so we can brush them.

"This is Fonty." Piper leads me to the big brown horse. "She's very sweet."

"She's very huge."

"Yeah, but she's like riding a couch. I swear I wouldn't put you in danger. We'll stay at a walk the whole time. Promise. Here." She hands me a pair of gloves that have little massage nubs all over them. "Put those on and then rub in a circular motion over her body."

I slide the gloves on and lift my hand to the horse's side and hesitate.

Piper stands next to me and takes my hand in hers. She's very close as she moves my hand in circular strokes over the horse's coat. It's like Lou on the stone wall, but better, because I'm not drunk and it's Piper. I feel the heat from her body and for a split second, she shifts so that her leg is touching the back of mine. My hand freezes. Is this on purpose? I start to pivot to face her, but she moves to my side, taking the heat with her. "Like this," she whispers, then coughs and takes another step away from me.

I clear my throat in an attempt to focus on the horse, not the girl standing next to me. I won't kiss her again. Not after what happened the last time. And not after those things she'd said about me. I'm not her type. I'm too home-spun. Not someone she'd be interested in romantically. I know she hadn't meant for me to hear, but I had. I'm not stupid. I won't keep throwing myself at her. Besides, Lou is definitely into me as more than friends. Or at least parts of me.

When we finish the grooming, Piper brings out saddles and bridles and gets the horses all dressed. She hands me a helmet and puts one on her own head. She adjusts the foot things for me and we walk outside to a little stack of steps that helps us get closer to the horse so we can get on.

Once I'm actually standing on it next to the horse's side, something huge catches in my throat. "I don't think I can do this."

"Remember what you asked me that first time you took me driving? About how I'd teach you to ride a horse?"

I nod.

"Okay." Piper holds the horse's bridle and looks up at me. "Breathe."

I take some deep breaths.

"The next thing I'm going to ask you to do is put your

left foot in the stirrup and swing your other leg over. Go slow and be gentle. Fonty will not move a muscle. I promise. Are you ready?"

I am not, but Piper has been brave with me so I'll be brave for her. "Yes."

She tells me again and the next thing I know I'm sitting on top of the horse. Piper helps me get my other foot in place, then shows me how to make the horse stop by sitting deep, breathing out, and if I need, gently tightening the reins. She explains that turning is more about moving my hips, not yanking on the mouth, and to go, I only need the lightest squeeze with my calves.

Once she's mounted, we walk out side by side down a wide grassy path around the pastures.

"Are you breathing?"

"I am."

"Do you like it?"

I smile. "It's not bad. But . . . I'm not sure I ever want to do more than walk."

Piper laughs. "Don't worry, these two are retired and that's all they want to do, too."

We grow quiet and it's nice, riding side by side, listening to the birds, and the gentle clop of the horse's feet. Piper looks like an empress on her horse. "You might be staying?"

She shrugs. "It's my grandmother's pipe dream. My

mom quit competing after she married my dad and really blew MaMolly's hopes for an Olympian. She's transferring those hopes to me."

"Wow. Sounds like a lot of pressure."

Piper absently scratches at her horse's neck. "I don't mind. It's a nice dream. I'm nowhere near good enough yet, but I'm willing to do the work. I'm not afraid of trying."

"That's really cool. To have a big dream like that. I bet you'll get further than you think."

She rewards me with a flattered smile.

We grow quiet again and I mimic Piper's affection for her horse and scratch Fonty on the side of her neck. The way the horse moves underneath feels rhythmic and soothing. I can see how people get into this. When we get back to the barn, I manage to get off without falling.

"That was fun. Thanks."

Her face lights up. "That's awesome that you liked it. Maybe you'll come over and ride with me again one afternoon." She stops. "If you're not busy, of course."

"Yeah, sure." I turn away as I take the helmet off so she can't see my smile.

When we've cleaned up and gone inside, Mrs. Malone has steaming bowls of pasta ready for us. "I'm off for bridge. You girls eat up. Stay for a while, Kat. I know Piper would enjoy that."

I swear it feels like Mrs. Malone is trying to hook us up. Which is insane.

"So, um." Piper uses her spoon to roll her noodles neatly onto her fork. I try to copy her and end up splattering olive oil all over my hand.

"Crap." I wipe it off with a napkin. "Sorry, what were you saying?"

Piper demonstrates her pasta technique again and I follow each step. This time I manage to keep the angel hair neatly on the fork before I open my mouth.

"You needed advice?"

I'm super glad I have a mouthful of pasta because it gives me a few seconds to think. Yes, I'd asked for advice. I'd specifically come over here to get advice about Lou. But I'm not sure now. Maybe I need to figure things out for myself. There's always the internet. Hah. That'd be some interesting search history. What makes a great lesbian kiss? What exactly is lesbian sex? How soon should you have sex with someone after you meet them? Should you ask the girl you really like for hookup advice with a different girl?

I swallow, take a sip of water, and clear my throat. "I'm trying to make my social media account say more about me. You seem so good at it. Maybe you can help me curate the pics I have on there? I've heard colleges look at that kind of stuff and I want to make sure my image reflects the me I want to be. That I'm more than some small-town girl."

Complete and utter bullshit but the effect on Piper is interesting. She coughs on her forkful of pasta.

"I, uh, you know I don't think of you as that. I mean, maybe I did, at first, but you talk about my determination. You've kind of got your own fire going. If anything, I said, or did, or that you might have overheard, made you feel like I was looking down on you, I'm really sorry." She takes a sip of her iced tea, then smiles over the glass at me. "But yeah, I'd be happy to go through your pictures with you."

I roll more pasta onto my fork and this time I do it perfectly. All on my own.

chapter twenty-two
PIPER

As we go through Kat's photos, I figure out a few things. She loves her family. Like a lot. Her dad is awesome. I've never met anyone whose dad ran a hair salon. Actually, I've never met anyone who owned a hair salon. It meant that along with family photos, Kat knows a lot about fashion and makeup and products, but what is cool is that her vibe is natural and understated and not what I think of when I think of beauty bloggers. Not that she is one, but she could be the way she promotes the products she likes and frames them perfectly. She has an eye. For the way colors go together, for the juxtaposition of ideas, for the unexpected in visual form. It's those photos that really make me excited.

Example one. She has this photo from what looks like a Fourth of July celebration. Her sister, Emma, in a star-studded tank top, stands with her arms out and her palms up, and the photo is framed in such a way that there's a Mennonite family, all buns and hair coverings and suspenders, resting in one palm and an elderly African American couple in their Sunday finest holding one set of hands and ice cream cones in each of their other hands resting in Emma's other palm. In reality, they're just in the background, but Kat framed it so perfectly the illusion of them being cradled is wicked real. It's like the jumble of what makes this country great all in one shot.

Example two. It's a picture of a woman leaning over the counter at her dad's salon. Behind her, on a chair, is an infant in a carrier. The baby is the main focus of the image and it's staring straight at the camera. The mother, oblivious, has a scowl on her face as she talks to the woman behind the desk. There's something unsettling about it. Like the baby knows something is off.

"What's this one about?" I ask.

Kat leans over and her hair brushes against my arm. I hope she can't see the way it makes all the fine hairs on my arm stand at attention.

"Oh, that one." She sighs. "It's kind of a portrait of my mom. That's not my mom, but it could have been. Maternal instincts weren't—aren't—her thing."

I can't imagine. My mom is a tigress when it comes to me. Always there, always wanting what's best for me. My thoughts flick away from Kat's photo and I think about what I've asked my parents for. A stab of homesickness hits me. Staying with MaMolly will be a sacrifice. MaMolly is more like the woman in this photo. She'll feed me, house me, clothe me, and kick my ass across four states and back if I don't practice discipline in my sport. There will be no more coddling. But it's what I want. I need to let my mom know how much I'll miss her though. Not as a point of manipulation, but for real. If she understands that I truly get what I'm asking for, new horse aside, she might think about my staying in a different way.

"Must be tough," I say.

She shakes her head. "Nah. Not for me. My dad is plenty maternal. And he's cool. It's been harder for Emma but I think she's starting to realize it really isn't about her."

"What about your brothers?"

She laughs. "I think by the time they were born, Mom was so absent even while still here, that they looked to Dad as the mother hen. They like that she sends expensive gifts and takes them on a once yearly trip to Disney. She's not out of our lives, just recognized that actual parenting was not her calling."

I look at the photos again. "Do you consider yourself a photographer? Some of these are excellent."

I glance over and notice how her neck blotches start when I compliment her. Maybe all's not lost. But then I remember my talk with myself. No frying pan. Let some time pass. Let me figure out me and Dan. Me as a serious student with Dilara. There will be time for me as girlfriend again. I have to trust.

"No." The blush makes its way to her cheeks. "I don't know much about cameras. I like to observe people though. How they interact. How they connect with the world around them. My business teacher at the high school seems to think I'd be good at marketing because I like to tell stories with my images. Another person suggested journalism, but I'm not a good enough writer for that. One day I'll get out of Harmon, see more of the world, and figure out who I want to be."

Her phone interrupts and beeps in my hand. A text comes through from someone she's labeled as Swoon, Heart Eye Emoji times four.

Tomorrow=Rain Check=Anticipation

"Oh." I hand it to her as she's grabbing for it. Her blush deepens as she reads the screen.

My reality sinks in. "Lou?" I ask.

She nods and shoves the phone in her pocket.

"Don't be embarrassed. You wanted to meet a girl and you did." I don't want to hand her to Lou on a silver platter. But what right do I have to intervene? The more I've thought about Judith, the more I think that nagging voice in my head may be right. I wasn't the greatest girlfriend. Judith was strong enough to stand up for herself and let me go. I need to be strong enough not to grasp at the next available straw. Kat is into Lou. I get it. I need to let it be.

I clear my throat. "I sort of thought that was the advice you wanted. About you and Lou."

Her voice comes out chirpy and overbright. "What? Really? No. I'm good. I'm just going over to swim. It's not that big of a deal."

"Okay," I say. "But, if you did want advice, I am your friend."

Then my phone buzzes. It's my mom asking if she can call.

I stand up. "Hey, um, I'm sorry, but I really need to talk to my mom."

Kat jumps up, too. "Yeah, sure, of course. I need to head home anyway. Thanks again for the horseback ride. It was fun."

"Repeat?" I ask.

"Totally."

But the way she's rushing out of the house feels like maybe I've blown it at even being her friend.

KAT

I'm waiting outside the dance studio for Emma to finish rehearsal so that I can go home and shower and try on the clothes I'd picked out for the zillionth time. Tonight, I'm going to Lou's. Alone. No party, no other people. Me, her, a swimming pool, and . . .

There's where I get lost. I remember making out with her. I remember the way my body felt. I remember being flattered and silly and open to possibilities. I even remember thinking, this, this is what I've been missing. So why am I feeling hesitant and nervous and like I'm going to throw up?

Come on, I text Emma from the van. **What's taking you so long?**

One word comes in response.

Chill

Ugh. She's infuriating. Finally, she pushes through the darkened glass doors, sandwiched between two other dancers, all of them laughing at something on one girl's phone. For a second, I forget my anxiety, because my sister looks happy and relaxed. She's excited about dancing with this new school and since the last couple of calls with Mom, who did cough up the money to pay for the studio fee, Emma seems more emotionally settled. Maybe having Mom support her in something she cares about so completely is enough of a maternal statement to make my sister feel whole. I hope so.

Emma waves goodbye to her friends and turns toward Delilah with a frown as she flings open the passenger door. "Why so rude? Your virginity can wait an extra five minutes, can't it?"

"I thought yours couldn't."

"Don't be mad."

"What?"

She peels off her shoes and leg warmers and pulls her legs up into a cross-legged heap. "I had sex with Jordan last night when you were at Piper's. I'm first." She doesn't sound happy about it.

"You seem upset about that."

She rolls her eyes. "I'm not upset. I just thought it would be monumental or something. Like stars would fly out of my hair and I'd feel electrified. It wasn't that at all. It was kind of sweaty and awkward and it hurt and it was over really, really fast."

"He hurt you? I'll kill him."

"God, no. He was super nice actually. Kept asking if I was okay and if I was sure and was it okay and I was like, yeah, let's just do it, but it was hard for him to get it inside me and then when he did it was sort of push, push, grunt, grunt, unghhh." She acts it out with her hands including flinging her hands open and looking skyward with the final grunt.

I can't help it. I start laughing. "Oh my god. That sounds awful. Maybe you going first is totally okay for this milestone."

"Can we go get a frappé now? My vagina needs soothing."

I pull out of the parking lot and turn toward the coffee place across from the dance studio.

She keeps talking. "Maybe you're the smarter one. I was looking online this morning to figure out what we did wrong and apparently girls have way more orgasms with other girls. He had no clue either—raspberry mouse rumors were totally unfounded—therefore I had very little lube once he got started, which according to the internet helps things down there. So that's my advice to you for tonight; if you're going for penetration, make sure things are moist. Demand your foreplay."

I mutter under my breath, "I want to die in so many ways right now." Then I get in the drive-through line.

"Well, I want a double mocha caramel frap with an extra shot and don't worry, I still like the D. But I expect you to report back with the ways of the ladies after your big night."

Who knew my younger sister would become such an expert?

Two hours later I am spit-shined and polished in a simple white T-shirt, a pair of soft, gray, girlfriend-cut chinos, and flip-flops. Underneath I'm wearing my favorite red bikini and carrying a bag with my towel and dry underwear for after swimming. My stomach heaves as I pull into Lou's driveway and I have a serious case of need-to-put-it-in-reverse-to-leave. But she opens the door and walks out onto the front porch to greet me. There's no turning back now.

"Well, hey there." She's doing that lean against the doorframe thing again and I recognize it as a bit of Jordan-esque cheese, but in girl form it's so much less douchey.

"Hey."

When I get to the top of the steps, she grabs my bag from my hand and surprises me by leaning forward and kissing my cheek. "Glad you're here. Come on, I made a big salad for us."

The house looks different from the night of the party. Less mysterious, airier, more like a home. Lou leads us to the kitchen, whistling as she walks. When we get there, she sets my bag down on a stool and turns and takes my hand, pulling me forward into her arms and a close, long hug.

"Hey," she says again, her voice deep and sort of throaty. "Wasn't sure you were going to show."

Nervous laughter bubbles up in my throat. Grow up, I say to myself. People do this all the time, I say to myself. Where is that ballsy inner voice when I need her? Problem is, I don't know what I want. I wish Piper were here to deliver a play-by-play in my ear.

What is the matter with me, why am I thinking about Piper when Lou looks like she wants to devour me?

Lou must sense my unease because she lets me go and simply touches her thumb to the edge of my jawbone. "Let's eat. Then we can swim."

I hope she doesn't hear my exhale.

It doesn't seem like it as she moves around the kitchen like a pro.

"It's pretty cool your parents let you take over the house like it's yours."

She slides a bowl in front of me and grinds fresh peppercorn over the heaping Caesar salad. "Yeah, well, it's cheaper than me renting a separate apartment. And nicer. Except for the occasional party, I take care of it. Your parents still don't trust you?"

I remember my imaginary age. Older. Independent. "Not with their houses."

"Ah, right. Divorce. That must suck."

I swallow the bite I'm chewing. "Not really. They were a train wreck. Everyone's happier."

We keep making small talk, about families, and school, and the weather. I do my best to find the smallest lies possible in the telling. When we finish the salads, Lou opens watermelon-spiked seltzers and motions out in the direction of the pool. "Got your suit?"

"I'm wearing it." The blush creeps up my neck as I remember her offhand comment from before. "I mean, my swimsuit. Under my clothes."

"Mine too."

At the pool, she peels off her shirt. She wears boy short trunks and a sports bra kind of top in chocolate brown that shows off her tan and lean muscles. "Come on." She turns and cannonballs into the pool.

With two brothers, cannonballing feels like familiar territory. But when I emerge from the water, she waits for me and pulls me into her arms. This time she doesn't ask for permission, just leans in and kisses me, like it's a given.

I kiss her back. Because, well, it's what I came here for, isn't it? But the rush I'd felt the other night isn't there. It feels like mashing my lips against a stranger's.

She doesn't seem to notice and floats me over toward the side of the pool, until she finds our seltzer bottles. She hands me one and takes the other. "To us," she says and touches the edge of her bottle to mine.

What I want to say is, there's no us. Instead I smile and take a small sip. Then I set the bottle down. I don't want to get drunk again. I don't want to stay the night. I don't mind being here. She's nice and definitely attractive, but I've set this whole thing up on a lie and I've already come out to my sister and Elliot so the whole internal monologue of I need to know for sure before I apply a label to myself is now total bullshit. There's no need for me to hook up with Lou simply to prove something to myself.

Lou must see my release of the bottle as a sign I want another kiss, because she puts hers down, too, and pulls me close again, leaning in and touching my lips softly with hers.

I push her back. "Stop."

"Stop?"

I bounce back a few steps along the pool's edge. "Look, I'm sorry. You seem like an awesome person, but I totally gave you the wrong impression the other night."

Her expression clouds. "Jesus, not another straight girl."

"No." I shake my head. "It's not that. I'm not straight. I'm just, completely inexperienced. And you're, well, you obviously are. And all this . . ." I point at the drinks, her, back at the house where she'd served up seduction salad. "It's too much, too soon. I don't usually drink, and I was kind of drunk at the party, and I was trying to prove a point to someone, and it was absolutely fun in the moment, but now it feels . . ."

"Awkward?"

I breathe out a huge breath of relief. "Yeah. Awkward."

She turns and rests her arms on the side of the pool, kicking out her legs behind her. She doesn't say anything for a few seconds and I start to worry I've really pissed her off when she turns her head sideways to look at me and grins. "How inexperienced?"

This makes me laugh. "The most. I'm the most experienced at inexperienced."

"But you're into girls?"

I nod. "Affirmative."

She grins again. "Okay. I'm patient."

Hmmm. Maybe I can kiss her again, after all.

chapter twenty-three

PIPER

It's been a week since Kat's rain check with Lou. I bite my tongue every time I'm around either of them, wanting to ask, terrified to ask, but neither of them is talking about it. Until now.

"Hey, coming out tonight to the horse show?" Lou passes me in the barn aisle, the big gray mare behind her.

"Maybe. Have a driving lesson first."

"You're doing carriage work, too?"

I laugh. "No, in a car." Leave it to a horse person to jump to the alternate meaning of the word.

"You don't have a license?"

"No." Now's as good a time as any to probe. "Figured Kat would have told you. My grandmother hired her to teach me to drive this summer."

Lou puts the mare in her stall and fishes a peppermint out of her pocket that she lets the horse lip off her palm. "We haven't had time to talk about that." She smirks.

I look at loose strands of hay on the barn floor. Of course, they've been seeing each other. Why wouldn't they have been? But Kat has been letting me drive her van home every day she's picked me up. And she's never gone out of her way to see if Lou is around at the barn. She doesn't talk about her. She doesn't tell me she's had some great big girl-kissing epiphany. But then, she wouldn't. Not her style. Kat's not a gossip. Not someone to flaunt her private life. It's yet another thing I seriously like about her.

"Right, of course," I say.

"Heard through the grapevine you're sticking around."

"Really?" Since I'd only been given an extremely tentative maybe after a week of begging and pleading, it can only mean one thing. MaMolly must be in negotiations to buy Dan. Bubbles of excitement work their way up through my body. She wouldn't buy such an expensive horse if it didn't mean I'd have a future riding him, would she? "I mean, yeah, maybe. If it all works out."

"Cool. Well, see you at the horse show maybe."

She leaves and I sweep up the offending hay before hurrying to saddle Dan. It makes sense now, how Dilara put me on the schedule to ride him, with her as my instructor.

"Hey, sweet boy." I croon to the horse as I curry his coat, bringing dust to the top that I sweep off with a bristled brush. I pick out his hooves, spray no-tangle spray on his mane and tail and brush them out, before giving him a quick spritz of fly spray. His eyes are half closed in pleasure as I work. I can't believe he might actually be mine.

Once I have him tacked, I lead him over to the covered arena. Dilara is finishing up her own schooling session, so I mount and stay to the inside of the ring to warm him up. I want to pinch myself. I'm riding a horse in a ring with an actual Olympian. God, I hope my parents say yes.

She finishes her ride, hands the horse over to a groom, and turns her attention to me. She puts us immediately into transitions. Walk to trot to walk to halt to trot to canter. Speeding and slowing each gait. She barks when I use too much bend with the rein or let my body sit heavier on my right seat bone. I'm so focused on the work that I don't notice the observation deck.

Until I check my position in one of the mirrors lining the arena.

And I see Lou.

Who's leaning in saying something to Kat.

Who is smiling and looking extra cute in a Red Sox T-shirt I'd given her as a thank-you. She's got her eyelids tilted down and her lips, in their usual matte red, lifted slightly.

"Get out of your head!" Dilara barks from center ring.

Lou's eyes meet mine in the mirror before I refocus.

I make my shoulders tall and sink my body into the saddle. This is why I'm here. To ride. To train. To become a star. I need to get the stars out of my eyes when it comes to love.

I finish the lesson with laser-sharp focus. When it's time to cool down and I once again look at the observation deck, it's only Kat I see. She's leaned forward, her chin planted on her hands, watching me with a huge smile. She sits up, waves big, and gives me two thumbs-up. But of course, she would. We're friends. It doesn't stop my traitorous breath from catching in my chest though.

After I have Dan untacked, with not even a hint from Dilara about the quality of my ride or the possibility of him being mine, I make my way to the front of the barn where Kat is sitting on a bench with one of the barn kittens in her lap. Is she looking intentionally adorable?

"Hey." She lifts her head. "You looked amazing out there. Super fancy." She stands and puts the kitten on the cushion. It pounces at a loose piece of string before leaping away and running down the aisle in pursuit of one of its littermates.

"Not that fancy. But thanks." Is it bad that I love that she was watching me? And had an opinion on how I looked?

She hands over the van keys. I notice she's added the Red Sox charm I gave her at the same time I gave her the T-shirt, even though she protested that she was a Braves fan and could never put it on her key ring. She nudges me with her elbow. "Don't be modest. Aren't competitors supposed to know they're fierce?"

Like Lou, she's got the fierce thing down cold. But yeah, Kat's right. Fierce. I should be fierce, too.

"I guess I'm not half bad."

"Half bad is half good. You're definitely more than half good. And your driving? You're practically a pro now. I can't believe the difference between our first lesson and now. You will nail your driving test."

"Thanks."

I back us out of the parking spot and head to the main road.

"Are you going to the horse show thing tonight?" Kat points to a car approaching from the left. I brake, but the approaching car rolls obediently to a stop when it's supposed to and I reapply the gas.

Lou had asked the same thing. I guess she'd asked Kat to go. "I hadn't planned on it."

Every weekend riders came from all around the Southeast and further afield to compete at the Equestrian Center horse shows for enormous purse money. Because the classes are speed jumping with huge jumps, the Friday night shows are a draw for the locals, horse people or not. Everybody can understand the adrenaline of pushing horses over such substantial jumps in a timed event.

Plus, it's something to do in the otherwise sleepy community. There are a bunch of restaurants and shops, even an open-air bar that, though I've heard they aren't slack about checking ID's, do allow not quite legal drinkers to hang out in the hammocks and at the picnic table benches and sing karaoke. As long as you don't try to imbibe.

"Lou was saying there was karaoke at the Sunset Bar after the show. She asked me to come. Said a bunch of your kind would be hanging out."

"My kind? Isn't that your kind too now?"

Kat turns crimson. "That's not . . ." She blows an exasperated breath. "You know what I mean. Riders."

I turn on my blinker and look twice before turning left onto MaMolly's road. Karaoke. Isn't that what Beatriz and Elliot had talked about? If Kat's going to be there and I can find the perfect song . . .

Gah. What am I doing.

Everything doesn't have to be about having a girlfriend.

And now I might even have a horse. My own amazing competitive dressage horse. Focus on the horses. It's what MaMolly would say.

"Well?" Kat asks again. "Are you going?" Her smile is shy as she reaches out and puts one finger on my arm before pulling it back. "I'd love it if you were there."

My arm buzzes where she'd barely touched me.

My mom always says that MaMolly doesn't know everything.

"Yeah." I put the van in park in front of my grand-mother's house. "I'll try and make it."

Kat's smile is all I need to solidify the rightness of the decision.

KAT

"Come with me." I can't believe I'm actually asking my sister and Jordan to come with me to meet Lou, but I am. Lou's been supersweet since my confession about being inexperienced, but her texts and innuendos and looks have gotten increasingly laden and I'm still not sure I'm ready to jump into it with her. But I'm not backing out of tonight. Especially since Piper said she might come.

"Where do you want us to go?" Jordan can't stop touching my sister. Her thigh. Her arm. Her shoulder. Her side. And Emma, she looks like one of those googly-eyed cartoon characters. I guess whatever she'd discovered on the internet is working because together they are gross.

"To the Equestrian Center. There's karaoke. It will be fun. I swear."

Emma mumbles something to Jordan and he mumbles something back and she giggles and—

"God, just forget it."

Emma puts her hand on Jordan's thigh and nestles in closer to him. "I'm sorry. It's just tonight is the last night Jordan's parents are gone and we . . ."

"Lalala, I can't hear you." I put my fingers in my ears like a twelve-year-old.

"Call Elliot," Emma says. "He'll go with you."

She's right. An hour later I have Elliot in my passenger seat and we're headed out of his driveway.

"So, the girl you drunk kissed is going to be there?"

"Yes."

"And Piper?"

"I think so."

"And who do you want to drunk kiss tonight?" Elliot turns to face me.

"They card. I'm driving. There will be no drunk kissing."

"Answer the question."

The problem is I don't 100 percent know. Lou is a good kisser. And she is attractive. She's experienced and a good listener and gentle with me. She hasn't tried to kiss me again, but she's been texting and even called one night and

I look around. I hadn't thought it through that I might actually blow my own cover by coming out to meet Lou and Piper tonight. But isn't that what this is about? Owning all of me? I look again. "Do you see Piper?"

Elliot scans the area. "Nope. Want me to text her?"

"That's okay."

Lou spots us and jumps up from the picnic table and walks over to where we stand. "Hey." She gives me a hug and holds it. "Glad you came." She releases me with the lightest caress against my waist.

"Um, this is my cousin. Elliot."

She puts out her hand. "Nice to meet you. Lou."

They shake like dudes.

She grabs me by the elbow and stewards me toward her group of friends. "Ready to sing? Can I get you something from the bar?"

I hold up my soda. "I'm good, thanks."

"Really? For karaoke night? Come on, let me get you something."

Getting me something would involve my ID, which would blow my cover, which I don't want to happen. Not yet.

"No, really, I'm good. You go ahead."

"Suit yourself." But she doesn't head to the bar. Instead, introduces me around the table to her friends. I see a

we talked for an hour about her parents and she listened as I'd told her about my mom, even if I still hadn't divulged the entire truth of my situation. Lou would be easy to kiss again. We could go on a few dates and I could learn how to be a queer girl.

But then there's Piper. Piper with her dimples and weird combination of self-assured and insecure. Piper, who loves the Red Sox and has an amazing grandmother and who let me teach her to drive and taught me to ride a horse. She's also a girl who, when she fell in love, she fell hard and didn't let it go. It says something about her level of commitment to a person. I'm not sure I can ever move forward with someone who isn't that way. She might not be into me now, but if she's sticking around, maybe there's a someday? And I swear, that evening we went riding, there'd been some sort of spark. Our energy reminded me of that almost kiss three years ago. Was I going to let another opportunity like that pass me by?

"I wish I knew."

"Karaoke test," he said.

"What's that?"

"Hard-core judgment based on what songs they choose. The best girl wins."

"It's not that easy."

"Judging others is always easy."

I groan. "You are impossible. Anyway, that's not what I meant."

He points to a car about to back out of a prime parking spot and I stop.

"So why isn't it easy, dear cousin of mine?"

"Piper's in love with someone else."

"Are you sure about that?"

"Pretty sure."

"Hmmmm." Elliot gets a smug expression on his face.

We walk across the parking lot, past the tack store, toward the big arena in the center of the grounds. I glance sideways at him. Does he know something that I don't?

A woman in tight jeans and a crisp polo rushes past us. "Hurry up," she says. "You don't want to miss the jump-off. The purse tonight is seventy-five thousand dollars."

"Damn." Elliot whistles. "These horse people don't mess around."

Lou had explained to me that dressage riders don't ride for money like jumpers. That they were more of the get-sponsorship variety, but it's all still kind of an expensive mystery to me. But we hurry after the woman to the arena to watch the final riders do their thing. Elliot disappears for a minute and comes back with big cups of crushed ice and a giant orange soda.

"Thanks," I say as he pours half of the soda in my cup.

In his own cup, he adds fortification fr
he pulls out of his pocket.

"If you get caught with that, we'll g
here."

"I need it if I'm going to sing."

He has a good point. Karaoke is h
you're hanging out with friends and fam
front of a bar full of strangers. But still,

When the final horses have ridden a
been awarded, we make our way to the
where the Sunset Bar is located. They'
in a big metal silo to create a bar in the
industrial cool. Around it are picnic ta
chair hammocks under a shaded cano

I see Lou before she sees me. She'
picnic table entertaining a group of ot
story, her hands waving and her prese

"That's her." I elbow Elliot and
direction.

He looks over the straw he's sipp
Can see the attraction. She still thin

"Yes."

"Don't worry, I won't blow y
around. "Don't see anybody else th
from school at least."

couple of people casually check me out, but it only lasts a second before they all are engrossed in their own conversations again. Some guy in a straw hat pats the open spot on the bench next to him and Elliot immediately plops down.

Lou hands me a sheet of paper. "You have a go-to song? They can pull up pretty much anything. Put down the song and your name and they'll call you up for your turn."

"Oh." I take a step back. "Me and singing, alone, in a public place, not such a thing."

"Ah, come on. Nobody cares here. It's fun." She steps closer to me so our upper arms are touching. "What about a country song? Those are fairly easy. We could do a duet. Like 'Don't You Wanna Stay.'"

"I don't know it. But a duet would be okay, I guess."

Her grin lifts the corner of her eye into a mischievous twinkle. "Oh, you'll love it. And it's perfect. Just follow my lead."

She scrawls down the song name and our names next to it.

I look around one more time, but there's still no Piper. How can I pick a girl based on song choices when there's only one choice?

chapter twenty-four

PIPER

I head upstairs to change out of my barn clothes and take a shower. What the hell. I'll go to the thing at the Equestrian Center. Even though I can't sing that well, and even though the thought of karaoke embarrasses the hell out of me, it's for the greater good. I'll make a fool of myself but isn't it worth it? So yes, the timing is bad. And I will be busy with training and work. But Kat seems like she gets it. It seems okay to her. And if she is into me, even a little, aren't I better for her than Lou? Wouldn't it be fun to see where things might take us?

"Piper," my grandmother calls from down the hall. I stop outside the door to my room.

"Yes?"

"I just got off the phone with your father. We've had a little change of plans."

My heart plummets. She's not buying Dan. I'm not staying in training with Dilara. "Oh." My shoulders drop and I feel my body sink into my heels.

The dogs circle my feet and look up with worry in their round brown eyes.

"Don't look like someone stole your lunch money. Get packed."

"What?" The dogs jump, planting their front paws on my calf and nudging at my knee with their noses.

"You heard me. I'm taking you to the airport."

"I don't understand. I thought I got to at least stay the summer."

"With any luck, you get to stay more than that. But you need to go home and convince your mother. You also need to take your driving test."

"I can do that here."

"No, you can't. You're on your parents' tax returns and you can only get a license in the state where you reside. Technically it's still there. If you're staying, you'll need to be driving sooner than later. Your fine chauffeur will start back to school in the fall and as you've already discovered"—my grandmother winks—"there's no Uber."

This feels defeating. I can drive in rural North Carolina,

but taking a test in Lincoln, Mass? A whole different level of traffic. And that doesn't even add the convincing my mother part into the equation.

"Quit standing there with your jaw dropped. Take a shower and get going. Your flight leaves at nine and we need to hit the road to Charlotte."

"Right." I turn and head into my room. As I throw clothes into a bag, I send off a quick text to Kat. Sorry, can't make it tonight. Have fun. My fingers pause on the phone. Should I say more? Even though she'd hooked up with Lou after I'd rejected her, we still had this incredible energy. And she'd specifically said she'd *love* if I came out. But what would I say? Something like, "Don't get with Lou. I made a mistake. I'd like to try us as more than friends." But it feels weird to text it. And she's already been with Lou, and they're both being super quiet about whatever they have going on. No. I need to know that story before I press into it. Personal rules for starting relationships and all. I put my phone down on the bed, strip off my dirty breeches, and head for the shower.

Two hours later and I'm through security and getting on the plane, it feels like some kind of reverse déjà vu. So much has happened in such a short amount of time. And now, with any luck, the next time I fly back to MaMolly's, it will be for good. I check my phone once more before putting it to airplane mode, but there's no response from Kat. Guess she took that "have fun" to heart.

It takes two hours to fly and when the plane bumps onto the runway at Logan, my heart is twisted in my chest. I've spent the whole flight working myself up over my driving test, the possibility of Kat and Lou, my driving test, and Kat and Lou. It even sounds cute, Kat and Lou. If I fail my driving test, I won't have to go back. I won't have to face another loss in the girl department. But then, I lose the opportunity to ride Dan to the medals. Horse over girl. Horse over girl.

As I exit the security area, my heart catches and does a weird flop in my chest. At the bottom of the escalator I see my dad . . . and Judith.

They smile at me and as I walk into my dad's arms for a bear hug, I'm still staring at Judith. What's she doing here?

Before the words are out of my mouth, she provides the answer.

"Your mom called and said she was sure I'd been missing you and wouldn't I like to ride to the airport with your dad to see my girlfriend."

Right. I'd never shared the breakup. Because I thought it was temporary. And now my mom was trying to use subterfuge to undermine MaMolly's plans. Except we're broken up. For real and for good. Guess I should have said something.

My dad lets me go and practically pushes me into Judith, who, at the last second, opens her arms and catches me in a hug. And there it is. The smell of her hair, the way her body curves against mine in familiar patterns. I can't help myself. I bring my arms up and capture her between them. "Hi," I say into her curls.

"Hi," she says back, then with a question, "girlfriend?"

"Long story?" I answer and then step away because my dad's there and even if it were true it's still awkward to hug your girlfriend too long in front of your parent.

"Shall we?" Dad takes the bag off my shoulder and turns toward Central Parking.

"I can't believe you didn't have me Uber."

"Figured you could practice driving on the way home." I slam my walking brakes. "What?"

Dad grins over his shoulder. "Kidding. But I am craving late-night pancakes and your girl Judith here was game for the adventure, and what can I say, I missed you."

"Me, too," Judith says as she grabs my hand and the yo-yo feeling comes back, but only for a second. The game is up and I'm happy about it. But before I even have time to take my hand away she's snapped a selfie of the three of us.

"What are you doing?"

"Documenting."

"Don't post that."

Dad strides ahead of us.

"What if I do? Will it make that girl jealous? Isn't that your play?"

"That's not fair. You broke up with me. It was normal for me to want to make you jealous. Besides, she doesn't follow you." I hesitate. Not that it's any of Judith's business, but, "And she's not my girlfriend."

Judith taps on her phone. "Then it won't matter. Posted it." She reads, "Just like old times. Late-night pancakes with the dad."

Dad gets to the car and unlocks it, throwing my bag in the trunk. "You two can sit in the back and catch up. I'll chauffeur."

Judith grins. "You're the coolest, Mr. Kitts."

He winds out of the parking garage and turns up the talk radio station so that Judith and I can have some privacy.

She whispers, "How come you didn't tell them about us?"

I slump back against the headrest. "You know why. I thought we still had a chance and I didn't want them to think less of you."

She twists the silver band she wears on her thumb. "That's sweet."

"I am sweet," I say.

She sighs. "You are. But you know I'm only here for the pancakes. And to find out why your mom still thought we were together. And because I do want us to be friends. I'm sorry I hurt you, Piper, but like you said, it really is for the best."

I put my hand on hers, as a friend. "Yeah, I actually finally think it is."

KAT

I've listened to an off-tune rendition of "Bad to the Bone," a hilarious reenactment of "Old Town Road," and three passable attempts at various Taylor Swift songs, when the emcee calls Lou's name. I scan the crowd one more time and still no Piper. Like a dumbass I left my phone in my van, and even though Elliot finally texted her to see if she was coming, his battery died before she responded. His new friend lent him a charger—lord knows the boy can't go five minutes without his phone—but it doesn't help us now. I hope she's okay.

"Lou and Kat." The emcee grins at the crowd. "Well, if that doesn't sound like a country duo already I don't know what does. And they're singing 'Don't You Wanna Stay,' the Aldean and Clarkson classic." Then he fans himself with his sign-up sheet. "Going to get steamy in here."

I whisper to Elliot, who's prodding me to get up. "What does he mean?"

"You don't know the song?"

I shake my head.

Elliot drops his face into his hands, and his shoulders shake as he laughs.

"You ready?" Lou holds out her hand to help me up from the picnic table. I look back at Elliot, but all he can do is wave at me to go on as he keeps laughing. Lou's friends start whistling and screaming as I follow her up to the wooden platform.

"Got a little gender twist on this one, folks." The emcee winks at us as he hands each of us a microphone.

I look around at the crowd. There's the out-of-town folks, the horse people, but there are also a handful of locals. Nobody I'm close with and nobody from the high school, but I'm pretty sure that's Debbie from the bank in the hammock chairs and maybe the salon's window washer over by the back railing.

The music starts, some soft piano, then guitar. The teleprompter scrolls the words and I realize I do know this song. Before I have time to really process, Lou picks up the microphone. She takes my hand and looks at me.

"I really hate to let this moment go." She winks. "Touching your skin and your hair falling slow . . ."

The implications of the type of song and who I'm singing it with start to settle into my skin. Then my telltale blush starts creeping up my neck and beads of sweat gather at my hairline. Holy shit. I'm singing a love duet, with a girl, onstage, in my hometown. I take a deep breath. I guess I'm doing this thing.

It gets to the part where I'm supposed to come in and Lou squeezes my fingers. Sing? Or bolt?

About that moment, Elliot yells "Get it, Kat!"

What the hell. I can camp it up. If people choose to make something of it, they choose to make something of it. I'm not doing anything wrong. At all.

". . . don't you wanna hold each other tight . . ."

". . . we can make forever feel this way . . ."

Lou doesn't break her focus from me and as the music plays and I realize she can really, seriously sing, butterflies start up inside me. The guitar stops and it's my turn again.

The line is true to me, about taking it slow, making a love that lasts.

Then she joins in, singing about me wanting to fall asleep with her tonight and even though this is karaoke and I don't sing as well as her, the moment begins to feel too real and the stage begins to feel both too small and super-duper exposed. When it gets to the part where we're doing some sort of back and forth with long notes, I break and start nervously laughing. Lou doesn't let go of my hand. She keeps singing her part, looking at me with sexy eyes that only makes me more nervous . . . but in a good way. The crowd whistles and cheers and nobody seems to give two fucks that we're two girls, only that we're putting on a damn fine show. The song lasts forever until finally the last note sounds and Lou's crowd of friends jumps to their feet, clapping and doing some sort of fist pump whoop thing.

I stumble off the stage after her, but she never lets go of my hand. One of her friends high-fives her as he walks past to the stage but Lou doesn't hang around for accolades. "Be back in a second," she says to the tattooed girl at the far end of the table. She keeps walking, me running to keep up.

"Where are we going?"

She holds up a finger to her pursed mouth and winks again before taking a left toward the show barns. When we hit a dark spot in a crevice along a back wall of the stables, she turns and pushes me toward it, her mouth on mine, her hands cradling my hips as she rotates me in her direction. "God, that was sexy," she says when she breaks the kiss. "You can sing."

"Not like you." But she's right. It was sexy. Hot even.

She tucks my hair behind my ear and kisses me again, her hands back on my hips. I think about the words to the song and the way she looked at me onstage. She likes me. Maybe for more than just an overnight thing.

"Where are you? You seem kind of lost in thought." Her hand moves from my hip to my shoulder to my neck where she draws silken circles on my skin with her fingertip.

"I, um . . ." I really need to tell her the truth. That I'm still in high school. Only eighteen.

But she doesn't wait for me to answer. She lightly touches her lips against mine and whisper-breathes as she dots my lips with a series of gentle kisses before I involuntarily open my mouth to her warmth. I shut off my thought and lose myself. Lou is an excellent kisser and after our duet, me onstage singing a love song with a girl for the whole flipping world to see like I'm some sort of LGBTQ warrior, I'm kind of into it. I feel deliciously alive.

Lou shifts, positioning one leg between mine so that when my body arcs in response to her kisses, I find solidity. She pulls my hips toward her, while her other hand circles over my bra, my body electric beneath her touch. Her mouth tastes my neck, my jawline, my lips as she rocks her leg against me. This, this is what everyone gets so worked up about.

Warm air hits my midriff as Lou pushes up my shirt.

She nips gently with her teeth and keeps up the slow easy rhythm of her thigh between my legs. I move my hand to the wall and splay my fingers. The world shifts underneath me. My other hand grabs Lou's back pushing her into me as she gently rocks, my breath coming quick and rapid into the night air. Pressure builds low inside me and a feral sound comes out of my throat that I barely register. I take my hand off the wall and put it on the back of her thigh, pressing her harder into me as my body convulses. What the hell. I don't let go until the waves slow.

"Did you?" Her expression is bemused.

Oh my god. I did. I shrug and try not to be embarrassed.

She kisses me sweetly. "Guess you can't say you're the most experienced at inexperienced anymore."

A flood of unnameable feelings and emotions wash over me. I just totally got off. With my clothes on. With a girl I've only known a little while. From freaking kissing. This means a few things. I'm more like Elliot than I thought. I'm definitely, most definitely, into girls. And Lou won the karaoke battle.

Hands down.

chapter twenty-five
PIPER

Dad drives us home after we're full on pancakes and laughter. When we get to Judith's house, I walk her to her door. She turns and takes my fingers in hers and I lean forward and kiss her on the cheek.

"Friends?" she asks.

"Friends." I nod. She turns to go inside and I stop her. "Yeah?"

"I, well, I just wanted to say I get it. I understand why you broke up with me."

She waits.

"I wasn't there for you. I know I was pretty much all about my goals. But I did care about you."

"I know that." She smiles. "But thanks. I appreciate

you saying that and not just making it about Brad."

A light comes on at the neighbor's house and a car backs out of the garage. Judith glances over, then looks toward her own front door, then at my dad waiting in the car. "Are you going to tell them we're broken up?"

"Yeah. Tonight."

She wraps her arms around herself. "They're nice. Make sure they know we're still friends."

"I will."

"Well." She drops her arms. "See you around. Thanks for the pancakes." She turns and walks in through her front door.

In the car, I buckle the seat belt. "Judith's not my girlfriend anymore."

Dad cocks his head.

"We haven't been for a while. I didn't tell you guys because I didn't want you or Mom to hold anything against Judith. She likes the two of you. We're still friends."

He starts the engine. "Okay." Then he adds, "Hope tonight wasn't uncomfortable. Your mom thought she was doing a good thing. Seemed like the two of you enjoyed seeing each other."

"It was great to see her. But c'mon, Dad, we both know Mom orchestrated this to make me want to give up the North Carolina thing."

Dad chuckles and pulls onto the turnpike. "Not so subtle, huh?"

"Nope." I fish my phone out of my backpack and check it. Still nothing from Kat, but finally a few texts from Elliot asking where I am. Huh. She must not have gotten my text. I check to make sure it had gone through. It has, but she hasn't responded. I click over to her feed but there's nothing new. Then I go to Elliot's and that's where I see it. A video of Kat and Lou onstage. I pop my earbuds in and unmute the volume. Lou's singing to Kat about wanting to stay with her tonight and Kat is six shades of red and laughing uncomfortably on the stage, but they also look super into each other. The next post is later and Elliot's videoed the group and Lou has her arm around Kat and Kat is looking at Lou with stars in her eyes. Like something happened between the awkward stage singing and this video.

I want to immediately jump to the obvious conclusion, but I'm well versed in the cluster of making assumptions based on social media photos so I text Kat.

Hope you had fun tonight. Hope you got my text. Ended up flying home unexpectedly. All's okay. I get nothing in return, but then again it is past midnight.

I text Elliot.

Sorry I missed you guys.

Bubbles appear. Disappear. Then

Oh, you missed it all right.

I send back some question marks but Elliot doesn't answer.

The next morning my mom is at the door early. "Wake up, sunshine. Time to go for a drive."

I grab my phone before I get dressed but there's still no word from Kat. My mind starts to spin but I stop myself. It's time to focus. On getting my license. Getting a horse that can take me to the big ring. Getting back to Dilara's barn. I leave my phone in my room as I head downstairs to meet my mom.

She greets me with a hug, but there's stiffness, too, and I know I haven't won her over to my side yet.

"Do you want breakfast?"

I shake my head. "No, I'm still stuffed from pancakes. I'll just have an apple."

I walk to the little desk cubby next to the fridge where we keep the fruit bowl and grab a gorgeous Fuji from the top. Laid out in a pile are a stack of photos from my mom's showing days. I flip through the first few. She looks regal in her shadbelly coat, white breeches, and top hat. "Is this Sultan?" I know it is. He was my mom's favorite horse.

Mom looks over my shoulder. "Yes. We got a decent

score at that show. Above sixty percent. It was our first Grand Prix level test so I was thrilled."

"After you got your silver?"

"After we got our silver."

Mom had gone all the way through her Dressage Federation medals with Sultan. When she switched to international competition she rode Fonty, the mare I'd let Kat ride at MaMolly's.

"You looked amazing."

Mom put a hand on my shoulder. "I loved it. Like you do."

I look at her. "So, you understand? You'll let me stay? Let MaMolly buy Dantoar for us?"

Mom sighs. She sounds frustrated. And maybe a little sad. "You're so young to be leaving home."

"Mom. Please. I want this so bad. It's all I want to do with my life. At least in the near future. Please, can't you understand?"

I throw my arms around her in a hug. "Don't be sad. I'm not choosing MaMolly over you. *You're* my mom." My voice thickens and I step back. "I'm still going to get a high school degree. And I will go to college, but maybe not right away. You of all people should understand. I love you, Mom. But I love riding so much. I want to make us proud."

Mom's eyes glisten. "I know you do. That's what worries me. The competition can be fierce. It can crush your soul if you're not careful."

"I'll be okay. I have a devoted support system. And if I fail, you'll be there to pick up my pieces."

Mom smiles at that. "Indeed, I will." She wipes at her lower lid. "I believe before this can become official we need to get you in a car and out on these roads." She grabs the keys off the hook behind me and hands them to me. "No time like the present."

I swallow down air and search for the familiar feeling of fear only to realize it isn't there.

In its place is resolve.

And excitement that is off the charts. I'm going to do it. I'm moving to North Carolina to finish out high school while I ride competitively. It's more than I ever dreamed could happen.

I can't wait to tell Kat.

About everything.

KAT

Lou keeps her arm around me the entire night. I forget about Debbie from the bank and the window washer guy because I am high on pheromones or whatever it is that happens in your brain when your body lets itself go. Elliot keeps taking pictures of us so that he'll have a record of what he calls my fresh-fucked-face. I want to strangle him, especially since I seem physically incapable of wiping my face back to neutral.

"Hey." Lou lifts her beer. "Let's go back to my place for a late-night swim."

The group pounds on the picnic table in response. One girl shakes her head. "Can't. Night check at the barn. But you have your usual fun." She looks at me when she says it.

"Come after," another girl yells.

"Come again," Lou whispers in my ear, but not so quiet that the tattooed girl who'd been watching us doesn't smirk and roll her eyes.

The pheromones skip and falter but then Lou hooks her finger in my belt loop and wiggles me closer.

Dad's window washer saunters past the table right then. "Good duet, ladies. Tell your dad I said hello, Kat."

Elliot's eyes widen. Guess he hadn't thought about the implications of my duet. Or maybe he's just looking out for my cover story.

"How does that guy know your name?" Lou asks.

Elliot jumps in. "Kat's dad grew up here. With my dad. That guy's a family friend."

The explanation seems to satisfy Lou, but it also solidifies my decision to tell her the whole truth. She obviously likes me. Otherwise what happened earlier wouldn't have happened. It's not like I'm a minor. I've had my eighteenth birthday. Surely a detail like me being in high school won't stop her from wanting to hang out with me.

"Come on." Lou stands up and the group follows suit. I reach for her hand but she moves hers, raising her arm to motion for everyone to head to the parking lot. My hand closes around a push of warm air. But then she grabs me again. "Riding with me?"

"I drove."

"Let your cousin drive."

Elliot reaches for my keys.

"You've been drinking," I say.

He scoffs. "Not that much."

Lou interrupts us. "Well, so have I, but it's not that far. He'll be fine."

If there's anything my dad has hammered into my brain it's not to get into a car after drinking or with anyone who has been drinking and since I'd already had a lifetime of being the designated driver, I'm not stopping tonight. "Why don't you let me drive you both?"

Lou shrugs. "Sure. You can always drive me back here tomorrow to get my truck." She gets the wicked grin again. "It's my day off. We don't have to be in any kind of hurry."

Of course, she thinks I'll stay the night. It's what she'd sung to me. It's what we'd sung together. It's what my actions out back behind the show barns implied. But I can't stay over. I'll be grounded for my senior year if I do something like that. Or I'll have to come up with a really excellent lie, which is more of an Emma thing than a me thing. And even though I totally loved being in that moment with Lou, now that it's over, I'm riddled with doubt. If I stay over, things will need to be reciprocal. I'm sure Lou will be happy to teach me the things I don't know, but her friends' reactions to us all night left me feeling like the butt of Lou's latest joke. I don't like it.

Whatever. I'll figure it out later.

"Sure. The van's over here."

Lou takes shotgun and Elliot stretches out across the back seat. My phone is where I'd left it. I wonder if Piper texted me back. It seemed like she was going to come out tonight. If she had, would this night have turned out differently?

Lou's hand shoots across the console and lands on my upper thigh, blocking my phone from reach. Opening my phone would be like opening a can of worms. It can wait.

Then Lou leans forward. And as she moves, her foot scrapes back across the stack of mail on the floor, including the latest issue of *Fast Company*, the one with Janelle Monáe on the cover. "Oh man." Lou reaches down. "I love her." She looks at the cover, then starts flipping through to the article, then she flips back to the cover. "This has your name on it. But hold up." She turns to look back at Elliot. "I thought you said you lived off Red Lynx Road?"

"I do." Elliot is oblivious to where the question came from.

She looks at me. "But this has your name and an address in town? I thought you were living with Elliot. I didn't know you had your own place."

"She's living with me." Elliot, still oblivious, is working hard to keep my charade going. But it's futile and I really do hate stacks of lies. Besides, Lou is picking up other mail. Things addressed to Emma Pearson and Conrad Pearson and the Pearson Family.

"I don't live with Elliot."

He sits up in the back seat.

I think about pulling over but it seems too dramatic, so I keep talking while I drive. "I wasn't totally honest with you when we met. I actually live here, year-round."

"That's cool." Lou puts her hand back on my thigh.

"I have a year left of high school."

She takes her hand away from my leg.

"But it's okay, I'm eighteen, not a minor or anything creepy like that." I glance at her and she's shaking her head and laughing. "What, why are you laughing?"

"Because typically, I'm not the one left feeling like a putz. You totally played me."

"I . . ."

"No, admit it. You played me with your whole I'm so innocent and inexperienced and stringing me along with phone calls and innuendos. Oof, I worry for the lesbian world when you truly get out in it. You've got the lies down pat."

Elliot leans forward. "Kat is not a liar."

Lou looks back. "Oh really? Because you were right there going along with her story." She drops the mail. "Look, you're a sweet girl, and tonight was fun, but I only hang out with grown-ups. Still in high school, even if you're eighteen, doesn't count. No matter how good you felt pressed up against a barn wall."

"I knew it!" Elliot gloats from the back.

"Shut up, asshole," I growl.

She pats my thigh like I'm a child. "But hey, glad I could be of service to you. No harm, no foul. As they say. Why don't you take me back to my truck? It's been a while since I had my last beer. I'll get myself home."

In the parking lot of the Equestrian Center, I get out and walk with her to her truck. It seems like the polite thing to do.

She turns and leans in and kisses me on the cheek. "Call me in a few years."

I don't know what to say. "Thanks, I guess."

She opens her truck door.

"Wait!"

"Yeah?" Her foot rests on the running board.

"Do you . . . did you think . . ."

"Think what?"

I spit it out. "That I was vanilla?"

She grins. "Vanilla's my favorite flavor. Sweet and nuanced. But those lies. Straight-up rainbow sprinkles."

With that she gets in her truck and closes the door.

I watch her taillights disappear into the night.

chapter twenty-six
PIPER

There are so many reasons to be excited to go through the airport security line. I'm going back to North Carolina. Dilara actually emailed me a training schedule along with my work schedule. On MY horse. Dantoar. Mom got me signed up for online courses and I should be able to finish my high school degree by December. And even though both my parents insisted I start at least community college the following fall, it means I'll have from the end of December till the start of the fall community college schedule to do nothing but ride, train, and compete.

But this, this piece of laminated plastic I'm showing to the bored TSA agent feels like the biggest accomplishment of all.

I can't wait to show it to Kat.

Kat.

When I get to my gate, I look at the pictures on Elliot's feed again. When she'd finally texted me late Sunday night she hadn't said much. That she was sorry I hadn't come out. That it'd been fun. That she'd actually sung karaoke, which of course I already knew. But when I'd broached the subject of Lou, her texts had gone dry. I'd gotten a simple it was fun, and that was it.

On Monday, I'd been so focused on my practice driving, sorting out the details of actually moving to North Carolina for the year, and squealing on the phone when MaMolly called to tell me that Dantoar was ours, I hadn't even bothered trying to reach out again.

The flight attendant walks the aisle and this time I'm ready. Phone off. Seat upright. Tray table closed.

But as soon as she disappears to the back of the cabin, I pull out my phone for one last text.

On a plane. Headed back. I have so much to tell you. Want to come over and ride again?

The bubbles appear immediately.

Just a walk?

Of course, I answer. **I'll make you my famous chocolate chip pancakes after we ride. See you at 8 tomorrow morning?**

Okay.

I'm about to turn my phone back to airplane mode when the bubbles pop up. I wait, even though I can hear the clomp of the flight attendant's shoes in the aisle.

Do you like rainbow sprinkles?

Love them, I type back. **Why?**

No reason, she answers with a blush face emoji. See you in the morning.

I get my phone put away just in time.

KAT

After I text with Piper, I decide to put my mind at rest about the new photo I'd seen on her ex-girlfriend's feed. Why can't they still be friends? It's not like I don't come without my own tiny bit of recent lesbian history. The most important thing is that Piper's coming back for the rest of the summer. And she seems excited for us to hang out.

I find Dad in the kitchen like I hoped I would.

"Hey." I slip into a chair at the table.

"Smoothie?" he asks.

I nod. "Sure."

His eyebrows raise. "Really? You never go for my smoothies. What's up?"

I push the cloth napkin at my spot into a heap. Now

seems as good a time as any. "You heard Elliot came out to his parents?"

"I did hear something along those lines."

"What if there was more to the story?"

"What do you mean?"

I take a deep breath about the same time my sister trips into the kitchen. "Ungh," she grunts.

"I think your sister might need a private moment with me." My dad starts to shoo Emma away.

"No, it's okay. She can stay," I say.

Emma looks between me and our dad, then sits next to me and grabs my hand under the table.

I take a deep breath. "Me, too."

"You too what?" Dad asks.

"Coming out. To my parent."

My sister squeezes my hand.

My dad doesn't move from the blender, just looks over his shoulder with a smile. "Is there a girlfriend I need to meet?"

I pause, maybe a little disappointed I didn't get more of a reaction. Especially since I've been grappling so hard-core inside myself for the last couple of months. But what did I expect? Everyone around me seems like they were only waiting for me to find my moment.

I answer, "Not yet. Though I might have somebody in

mind. Even if she's not convinced yet."

He hands me the smoothie. "I've always said you can tell me absolutely anything. You know that. We talked about that. I love you, kid. Now about this somebody. Do your sister and I need to put in a word?"

"I'm good," I say.

He settles down next to us and nudges Emma. "We can sing her attributes, right, Emma?"

"Right." My sister grins. "But I think Kat's good. I think she's got this in the bag."

I sure hope my sister is right.

But really, it doesn't matter, because this moment, in our kitchen, it's magic.

chapter twenty-seven
PIPER

MaMolly knows what I need before I say a word. She stops, once we get off the interstate, and switches places with me. I drive us straight to Dilara's barn, not scared, not even anxious. Well, okay, maybe a little anxious. I have only had my license for forty-eight hours.

"Are you excited?" she asks.

Excited doesn't even begin to cover it. I have a horse. An amazing horse. An impeccably well-bred Hanoverian with the sweetest temperament imaginable. And I get to spend the next year riding my ass off with one of the best of the best.

"MaMolly. You've changed my whole world. I'll never be able to thank you enough."

"You never have to thank me. You're my granddaughter. This is for all of us. I can't ride like I used to. Your mother doesn't want to ride like she used to. But you do. And I can make it happen. Your parents love you so much and for as much as your mother may have balked, she came through in the end, didn't she?"

"She really did." A warm rush fills me as I think about her parting hugs when she and Dad dropped me off at the airport this morning. They even promised to make a trip down in the next few weeks to meet Dan and see us train together.

I park MaMolly's Range Rover and practically run out of the car and down the barn aisle to Dan's stall. He's there, big brown eyes and velvety muzzle poking out over the yoke of his stall in anticipation of the peppermint I'm fishing from my pocket.

I feed him the treat from the palm of my hand, then wrap my arms around his warm neck. He hooks his head over my back and pulls me toward him in a perfect horsey hug.

A voice sounds from down the aisle. It's Franz. "You're back. Good."

Then a second voice. "Nice horse you got there."

It's Lou.

"Thanks. I can't believe he's really mine."

"You looked good on him the other day. Glad I'm an eventing girl so I won't be competing against you in the big dressage ring."

It's a nice thing for her to say, I guess. "Thanks."

"Well, see you around." She walks past me with a wheelbarrow and doesn't give me a clue as to what went down with her and Kat the other night.

I open my mouth to call her back, to ask her something, anything, but MaMolly has joined me next to Dan and what would I say anyway without giving it away that I'd been creeping on their good times. Better to let things evolve the way they will.

Like this opportunity with MaMolly and Dan.

I snap a couple of quick selfies with me and my horse. My horse. I don't think I'm ever going to get tired of saying that.

"You should send one of those to Kat." MaMolly nudges me as she looks at my phone. "You look cute."

"MaMolly!"

Her smile gives nothing away, but I'm onto her now.

And my force of a grandmother just may be onto something herself.

I hit send before I can second-guess the decision.

KAT

I pull into Mrs. Malone's driveway right at 8:00 a.m. Piper stands on the front steps waiting for me with a smile, her hand behind her back. When I get close, she pulls out her hand, flashing something small and shiny at me.

"Oh my god! You got your license."

"Wicked cool, right? And it's all because I had an excellent teacher."

"So that's why you flew back home?"

"Yep. But there's more."

"More?"

"Come on, I'll tell you while we ride."

I have a hunch it has something to do with the horse selfie she sent me last night, but I wait for her to fill in the details.

She leads the way to the barn and we repeat every-thing we did before. She gives me the boots I wore, brings out the horses, hands me the brushes, then tacks them up. When we get out on the grassy path, I can't stand the sus-pense anymore.

"So? What's the more."

Her smile explodes on her face. "MaMolly bought me the horse you saw me ride. The one in the picture I sent you. I'm going to be able to compete at higher levels. Train to go further than I have before."

"Wow. That's so cool. How will you get the horse back home?"

"Well, that's the even better part. Remember how MaMolly said she was working on keeping me around longer?"

"Yes."

"She convinced my parents. Well, we did. I'm not going back. I'm staying and finishing high school online and training with Dilara. I'll be here. In Harmon."

Piper's going to be here. In Harmon. Which means maybe her ex is still her ex. My brain voice, who I now realize is not a separate entity inside my actual brain, but is actually a more empowered me simply waiting for her moment to be heard, clucks her tongue. *Just ask.* So, I do, "What about you . . . and Judith?"

She doesn't hesitate and maybe even seems happy as

she says it. "Still broken up. I saw her when I was home. It was good. I'm glad we're friends, but I'm extra glad we're not girlfriends anymore."

Extra glad. What does she mean by that. My brain voice pipes back up. *Cause maybe she's into you, dumbass.*

It's a little scary to believe that could be true, no matter how empowered I'm feeling after my short-lived tryst with Lou and coming out to my family. I'm nervous now, but it has nothing to do with the horse.

"Can we go faster?" I ask.

"Really?" She's surprised.

I nod.

"Give her a little nudge with your calves and cluck. Just follow me."

Piper takes off at a trot and I follow along, trying to imitate the way she lifts up and down out of the saddle. Fonty gets bored after a few strides and goes back to a walk. But the exhilaration breaks me out of my momentary freakout. If she's come clean with me, it's time for me to do the same. To really answer her about Lou, which I'd kind of avoided when she'd texted me about karaoke night. But it's not like she and I are together. I may have hooked up with Lou again, but it was only because I needed to prove something to myself. If I'm honest, I wish it had been with her.

"You remember asking me about Lou while you were gone?"

"Yeah." She slows so we're walking side by side again.

"Well, it was nothing. Wait, that's not true. It was something. It was enough of a something to show me that what I know about myself is true."

"What's that?" Piper asks.

"That I'm definitely, for sure, into girls. Romantically." I pause. "Physically."

I only let that word settle for a second before I add, "Oh, and I came out to my family and Elliot."

She can't even hide the smile that breaks out across her face. The dimples are too damn deep.

"You are a badass, Kat Pearson. Let's celebrate!" She spurs her horse forward before I have time to think and this time Fonty doesn't slow down.

"Piper. Stop. I'm going to fall off."

"You're not. You're awesome. Life is awesome."

She's right. Despite my nerves. This is awesome. I'm out. She's out. Our families are supportive and nobody cares. I can be me. Hopefully with her.

When she slows her horse, I catch up to her again.

I can't believe I'm doing this, but I have absolutely zero to lose. "Remember that night at the party?"

"Yeah."

"You know I overheard you talking to Judith."

Piper turns red. "Kat, I . . ." She takes a breath and

starts again. "I really didn't mean for you to hear me say those things and honestly, I don't know why I did. I'm so sorry."

We ride along for a few more strides, then turn the horses back toward the barn.

"It's okay. You weren't entirely wrong, you know. I'm not well traveled. And I guess I am kind of vanilla in ways. But I want to be more than that. I plan on being more than that."

She laughs. "You think I haven't figured that out between now and then? You're strong even if you seem soft on top. There's steel underneath that fetching exterior." She brings her horse to a stop at the fence but before she dismounts she looks at me. "I like the things you told me that night at Lou's party."

I get off Fonty. "Which things?"

"The things about how you saw us. As girlfriends."

"You didn't like when I kissed you."

"Me and Judith had been talking some and I wasn't sure if kissing you would be considered cheating. You caught me off guard, that's all. I really wanted to kiss you back, but it didn't seem like the right time."

"Oh." I reach my hand to the horse's shoulder and run my fingers over her soft coat. This confession is another item on the growing list of things that make me like Piper.

"So one day, if I get consent, you might let me kiss you for real?" This new me is kind of cool. She surprises me with her boldness.

Piper looks at the trees and says something that sounds like "frying pan."

"What'd you say?"

"Not important."

"Friends for now?" I ask.

"Friends are good," she says.

We stand for a second, neither of us saying anything, then Piper stumbles forward when her horse puts his nose into her back and nudges her in my direction.

She stops a foot away from me and words spill out. "But you know, girlfriends can be good, too. Given the appropriate amount of time and all." Her smile is shy.

I take a deep breath. "And kisses?"

"I can think of worse things."

"Just to be clear. That is an affirmative on kissing?"

She rolls her eyes. "Yes. Affirmative. Positive. Go."

"But only within the appropriate amount of time."

"Kat."

She doesn't have to say another word. I lean forward, my insecurities gone, and put my lips on hers.

This time, she kisses me back.

Acknowledgments

I've been a horse girl since I was old enough to point at a field of them out the car window and declare "bow, wow." (True story—eventually I figured out how to neigh.) My first lesson barn was owned and managed by the first lesbians I ever knew, the two sisters Ellie and Melba, and their friend, Ruth. There I learned to ride on Clyde, the Shetland pony, and Tony, the lanky Saddlebred. Though I was too young to know or understand or care about the mechanics or details of their private lives, those women inspired in me the drive to get hay on my clothes and wish for horse-scented perfume. I got my first personal horse at age twelve and I haven't stopped riding, owning, and caring for horses since then.

It's no wonder I eventually found my way to a horse girl story. Which is why it brought me such an immense amount of joy when my editor, Tara Weikum, turned out to love Piper and Kat in her own horse girl way. I cannot thank her and Sarah Homer enough for being my coconspirators on this book and working with me to shape and mold it into the happy love story I was aiming for. And thank you to my copy editors, Jessica Berg and Veronica Ambrose, for catching all the pesky details and saving me from myself.

I also need to thank the entire wonderful team at HarperCollins for such a fun cover, especially Jessie Gang, designer, and Colleen Reinhart for her incredible artwork that truly brought Kat and Piper to life.

Thanks as always to my agent, Alexandra Machinist, and to foreign rights agent Roxane Edouard for all that you do.

Many bags of carrots and apples go to frontline readers, listeners, and advice givers—my sweet wife, Ann, who though not a horse girl, is officially Horse Adjacent and supportive in all things and ways; Pat Esden as always (and hopefully forever); the Nebo gang; my Fiery Bitches; the Annapolis crew; Kat P. (for your name and advice— who knew this book would turn out to be so prophetic?); my barn family (thanks, Rhonda, for loaning me Fonty's name); the real Dilara; and my horses, past and present.

No book would be a book without its readers, so to those of you reading, I thank you most of all. I'm glad you like books about girls who love girls.